DAINTREE

Annie Seaton

Porter Sisters: 2

Annie Seaton

Porter Sisters Series

1. Kakadu Sunset

2. Daintree

3. Diamond Sky

4. Hidden Valley

5. Larapinta

6. Kakadu Dawn

ISBN 978-0-6487948-8-2.

As always, to Ian, the love of my life, who is always there for me.

A dazzling commingling of shades, colours, and intricate minutiae of outline that would puzzle even a Millais to paint or a 'Laureate' to describe; the deliciously scented arums, all in full bloom, and hanging moon flowers greeting us, as we passed, with whole greenhouses of rich perfume.

G.E. Dalrymple, Reports and Narrative of the North-East Coast Expedition, 1873.

The Daintree

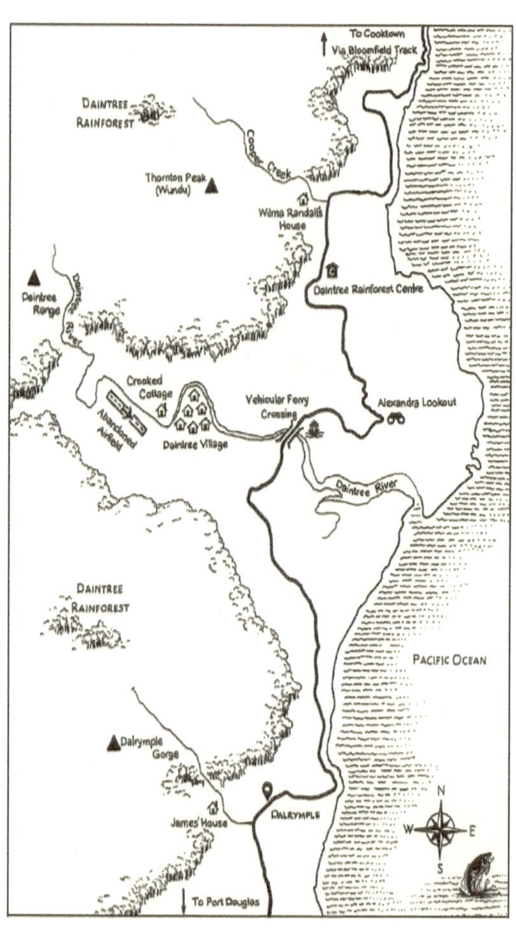

Chapter 1

Saturday morning – North Queensland – Daintree Village

'Hoy!'

Emma Porter pulled the cotton blanket over her head, snuggled deeper into her feather pillow and tried to ignore the voice calling from outside. Cocooned in soft warmth, she slipped back into a doze and tried to pick up the fragments of the dream she'd been immersed in. A sparkling, sapphire-blue swimming pool, a sun lounge, a mango cocktail in her hand and not a patient in sight. A tanned waiter with a beautiful smile offered her a hot towel with a pair of silver tongs. The muscles in his bare chest rippled as he leaned over—

'Hoy! Ya there, Doctor Em?'

With a deep sigh, Emma rolled over and opened her eyes. She'd pulled the blind down low before falling into bed in the early hours of the morning, but a sliver of sunlight still managed to peek through the gap at the edge of the window. Even though her gritty eyes tried to tell her she'd only had a few minutes sleep, the small bedside clock confirmed her fear that it was indeed morning.

Seven-thirty. But still way earlier than she'd intended getting up. It was Saturday, and today was her first chance to sleep in after pulling six straight night shifts in emergency. She'd managed to catch a few hours sleep every morning before she'd headed back into town to her clinic for open surgery each afternoon.

'Doctor Em!'

Her slim hope of staying in bed was shot to pieces with the third call from the kitchen and Bowser's excited yipping. Swinging her legs to the floor, Emma rubbed her eyes and reached for a pair of shorts and T-shirt buried on the bedside chair beneath most of the clothes, scrubs and underwear she had worn this week.

She'd have to get to the washing today. *And* the house cleaning. *And* the shopping. But that would be after she gave her poor neglected animals some attention, and took some time out for herself.

Padding barefoot down the hallway, she rubbed her hands through her tangled hair. The polished timber boards were smooth beneath her feet and the cool breeze coming through the back door carried the muddy smell from the river, but that was preferable to the musty smell pervading the house. The fresh air was welcome; the house had been closed up all week.

Emma pulled her hair back as best she could and dug into her pocket for an elastic band. Last night she'd been too tired to braid it and now the messy tangle would need a good dollop of conditioner in the shower.

'I knew you were home.' A wide welcoming grin of gappy and broken teeth met her when she entered the kitchen. George was an old bushie who'd lived in the village all his life. He'd helped Emma and her mother settle into Crooked Cottage when they'd moved to the Daintree and was almost part of the family—the uncle Emma and her sisters had never had. Now that Mum had moved down to Port Douglas, he looked out for Emma like a grizzled old watch dog.

'You're a pain in the arse. You do know that, don't you,

George?'

'And you should lock your door at night. Anyone could stroll in.'

'Don't change the subject.' Emma shook her head and smiled at him. 'I *was* planning to sleep in.'

'But I've got the kettle on for you, luv.' The smile got wider. Beneath his often crusty exterior, George was a larrikin with a heart of gold. 'You look like you could do with a cuppa.'

'Great.' She tried to inject some enthusiasm into her voice. He meant well, and she knew he was lonely, but it was an early visit. She could have done with a sleep in this weekend. 'What are you doing here? I've been on night shift all week.'

'Fed the girls for you.' His eyes crinkled at the edges.

Emma softened.

'And I collected the eggs.' George lifted up a bowl full of brown speckled eggs and Emma gave in to a grin.

How could she stay cross with the old coot; he loved keeping an eye out for her and she appreciated it. As usual, his pants were secured with a bit of fencing wire and his khaki work shirt hung open, most of the buttons missing. The old T-shirt underneath proclaimed: '*Leave the Daintree alone*.' A few months back he'd taken great pride in showing Emma and Mum the teeth marks where the German Shepherd police dog had ripped the T-shirt back in '83 when he'd been part of the demonstration against logging in the rainforest. They'd been trying to block the road being developed to Cape Tribulation. Emma hadn't even been born then.

She walked over to the window and leaned over the

sink. The stiff sash window creaked as she pushed it up to let more fresh spring air into the musty kitchen. Stretching up to her tiptoes, she leaned forward and glanced down at the riverbank at the bottom of the yard. 'Where's the punt? Didn't swim, did you?'

'Not bloody likely. I've seen what's in that water,' he said with a shiver. 'I came the long way. Have to drive up to Cooper Creek. Got a big day planned. Thought I'd call in and bring you some tomatoes on the way. I came over and checked on Bowser every day, like you asked.'

George lived across the river in the small village of Daintree. Emma's house was on the other side about half a kilometre upriver, and unless you took the vehicular ferry and then the long, winding, back road through Cooper Creek, the only other way to reach her place was by boat—she had a small punt that could be pulled across the water by hand. It was one of the reasons that she'd got Crooked Cottage and the acre of land so cheap. It was only a short walk along the path on the riverbank to the small village. It wasn't really even a village. There were only half a dozen houses and a coffee and craft shop for the tourists that was closed more often than it was open.

'Thanks, you're a gem. What are you up today?'

'A bit of this and a bit of that.' He wouldn't meet her eye. 'Look, I brought you some crickets for your frogs.' A brown paper bag appeared from deep in his back pocket and he handed it to her. I gave the frogs a squirt every day too and switched around their basking bulbs. Can't have them freezing to death while you're out working yourself to the bone.' George crossed to the wooden stand that was tucked into an alcove where the old combustion stove had once stood; her terrarium now filling the space. He ran his hand down the rough timber and turned to her with a wide grin. 'Jeez, the bloke that built this stand for you sure did a good job.'

'You did. And there's no need to suck up. I'm awake now.'

'All the tadpoles hatch okay this time?'

'Yes, this batch has been really successful.' Emma followed him over and reached up and turned the night bulb off, replacing it with the daylight basking bulb from the shelf at the bottom of the stand.

'Do you reckon if I got some tadpoles, that research mob would pay me too?'

Emma laughed and shook her head. 'You know I'm not getting paid. You could volunteer too. A few other locals are logging some breeding cycles.'

George shrugged and a soft grunt escaped his lips. 'Bet those blokes at that rainforest centre get paid.'

Emma slipped in the new bulb and patted his shoulder on her way back to the sink to make the tea. 'Of course they do. They work at the Rainforest Tourist Centre; they're National Parks and Wildlife staff.'

She pulled down two mugs from the cupboard and two tea bags and leaned back against the sink as she covered a yawn with one hand. 'God, it's been a big week. Down one doctor and waiting for the new guy to arrive.'

'Lots of sick people?'

'Yep . . .. and a few accidents too.' There had been a constant stream of patients at the hospital at night and at her clinic all day. Murphy's Law; it always happened when they were understaffed. She picked up the brown paper bag next to the sink and peeked inside. 'Thanks for these. Oh wow, look at the size of those tomatoes. *Now* I forgive you for waking me up.' The smell of the fat, red fruit wafted through the kitchen.

George smiled at her. 'Ox hearts. Only type worth growing.' His hand disappeared into his other pocket and he pulled out a small bunch of fresh basil. 'Though this would go well with the scrambled eggs and tomatoes you're going to cook us for brekkie.' He rubbed a leaf between his fingers and Emma rolled her eyes as she caught the sharp aroma. How could she stay cross at him?

She touched his shoulder as she crossed to the table and picked up the bowl of fresh eggs. 'So scrambled eggs for two, seeing the girls have performed so well this morning.'

'Sounds good to me. You cook the eggs and put those tea bags back in the cupboard. I'll make us a pot of real tea and we can have a yarn. You can tell me all about your busy week, luv.' George picked up the battered old silver teapot, peered into it and sniffed. 'Phew. The tea leaves have gone mouldy.'

'I've barely been home. It's a wonder there aren't mould flowers hanging from the ceiling.' Emma shivered. The first summer she'd lived in Crooked Cottage, she'd gone away to Brisbane for a month to finish up a course. Mum had gone back to Townsville to stay with a friend; with her mental health being so fragile, Emma hadn't been game to leave her alone. When she'd pushed open the door of the cottage on her return, mould had covered the kitchen cupboards and bench tops. It was one of the downsides of living in the Wet Tropics in the summer—the tourist brochures never showed you *that* side of things.

Emma looked up as Bowser, her little black staffy, came hurtling through the back door, his short tail going nineteen to the dozen as he yapped a welcome in his own unique way.

'Hey, little man, where have you been?'

George shook his head. 'He was out chasing snakes in the side paddock when I walked up the track.'

The small dog ran around her in dizzying circles and Emma bent down to rub his back. 'Haven't seen you much this week, have I, boy?' A cold wet nose pushed onto her hand. 'Have you been good? Did you miss me?'

'He'll end up getting bit one day.' The voice of the old bushie held a smidgeon of worry.

Emma washed her hands and then pulled the fridge open and reached for the butter. 'I wish he'd leave them alone, I'm terrified of the blasted things. Give me spiders any day.'

'Snakes are on the move early this season.' George dumped the sludge of mouldy tea leaves into the sink and gave the pot a scour out. 'You watch out when you get in and out of that boat at night.

'Don't you worry, I've got a big torch and I'm very careful.' Emma wrinkled her nose and busied herself at the stove. 'I don't mind the keelbacks. At least they keep the cane toads down. We've actually had our first snakebite for the season already. Troy brought a tourist into emergency this week.'

George reached up to the shelf above the gas stove for the tea caddy. '*Hmph.* That city slicker.'

'Who? Troy?'

'Yeah. Don't like him.'

Emma flicked him an irritated glance as she reached for the pan. 'He grew up on a cattle property near Mt Isa. He's about as far from a city slicker as you can get.'

Emma had met Troy Greaves through the Young Professionals social group a few months ago when he'd moved to Dalrymple to manage the Daintree Rainforest Centre. They had a lot of interests in common: he was well-educated, passionate about the environment and shared her interest in preserving the Daintree. He was the one who'd suggested including her frog collection hobby in the breeding research project and they'd hiked into the rainforest together to gather tadpoles from O'Keefe Creek where some of the species were declining.

'You know three frog species have completely disappeared over the last twenty years.'

'What's causing that?' she'd asked and he'd shrugged. 'Global warming is the main theory.'

As they walked to the creek, a colourful swarm of butterflies drifted by. Troy knew each by name: the blue and black Ulysses and the lime green Cairns Bird Wing. . .

As well as being a really interesting guy, he wasn't too bad on the eye. Rugged and outdoorsy, he was very different to the medical students she'd hung with at uni in Sydney.

'Still an outsider who thinks he knows everything about the forest when he's been here five minutes. One of them bloody do gooders. They should stop pandering to bloody tourists and not let them traipse through our rainforest.' George's gruff voice cut into her thoughts and Emma smothered the smile that tugged at her lips. It had been a long time since she'd daydreamed about a guy.

'He cares about *our* rainforest as much as you do. I think you'd be surprised how much you pair have in common. We all have the same goal.' Emma shook her head. 'And besides, you don't like many people as far as I can see.'

'I'm here with you, aren't I? And I like your mum.'

'That's two.'

George rubbed his fingers on his whiskers. 'When you get to my age, Em, you'll realise there's not many people out there worth liking.'

'Oh, George, that's a sad outlook. I meet lots of nice people in my job every day.' Emma smiled at him. 'And with any luck, soon I'll be meeting even more.'

'Yeah. How's that?'

'I've applied for a position with the Outreach Program, setting up some small medical clinics up the Cape.'

'Sounds right up your alley.'

'It will be—if I get it. I've got a pretty good chance I think.'

Don't tempt fate. Her dad's superstitious voice flitted through her mind and Emma tapped her knuckles on the wooden bench top. Having a scientific mind and a medical degree didn't mean you let family habits go.

George was standing by the stove and he chuckled as she knocked.

'What?' Emma picked up the eggs. They were still warm from the nest.

'How are you going to fit all that in with the hospital and your clinic?' He poured the boiling water onto the tea leaves and the smell of brewing tea filled the kitchen.

'I'll sort it out.'

George frowned. 'You could stop all that nature stuff you do.'

'What nature stuff?'

'Working with that rainforest guy, and collecting all those leaves and things you use for your remedies.'

'Maybe.' Emma smiled. She had no intention of putting aside her 'remedies' as George called them. She would reduce her hours at the hospital before she'd cut back on her clinic work. Being involved in the establishment of new medical outposts in the far north would be satisfying. Wilma Randall had already introduced Emma to several of the aboriginal elders and she believed she was well placed to liaise with the isolated communities. 'Anyway, fingers crossed.'

The egg shells made a nice crack when she whacked them on the edge of the stainless steel bowl. The yolks were a deep golden orange.

'Bright bold orange yolks, healthy, happy hens.' Emma could almost hear Dru's deep, husky voice. When they'd been growing up, her youngest sister had been the keeper of the hens. As Dru had done with her chickens on their farm in the Territory, Emma had built her chickens a run. She'd fenced off part of the yard and let her ladies roam around to their hearts' content. Most afternoons—when she was home—she let them into her small veggie garden to pick off the bugs and eat the broccoli leaves, and she reaped the benefit of orange yolks . . . and memories. She missed her sisters; seeing them infrequently was the downside of growing up and leading

your own lives.

'Here you go.' George's voice intruded on her thoughts and she looked up to see a plate of chopped tomatoes and onions held out in front of her. God love him, he'd even chopped the basil finely and sprinkled it on top.

'Thanks. You want the basil cooked, not sprinkled on top?'

'Course I do. Not meant to be eaten raw.'

Emma smothered a smile. She dropped a knob of butter into the pan, and when it sizzled and turned golden brown, she tipped in the tomatoes, basil and onion. A mouth-watering aroma filled the kitchen and she took a deep breath. 'Beaut tomatoes, thank you.'

'You're welcome.' George pulled out a chair and straddled it, watching Emma as she deftly folded the eggs.

'So what's happening out at Cooper Creek?' She flicked him a glance. 'You're on your way early.'

'Not much.' George dropped his gaze and shifted uncomfortably.

Emma frowned. 'You're not getting yourself into any trouble again, I hope?'

She'd long suspected that George applied his green thumb to more than just his vegetable garden and she knew he'd recently had a caution from the local police, when one of the coppers had come across a small plot of marijuana growing in a clearing deep in the rainforest up near Cooper Creek.

George denied all knowledge and had been most indignant that the cops had even warned him, but Emma knew better. The first time George had taken her for a walk into the ancient rainforest she'd been awed by the sheer beauty of the pristine environment, and she'd turned a blind eye to him watering plants in a small clearing while she ambled along the track beside Roaring Meg Creek.

'Nah. Just going for a wander.'

'Hmm. You know what happened last time.'

'*Pah*. A warning from a copper who looks like he should still be in school. Don't go worrying about me. I can look after myself.'

Emma dished out their scrambled eggs and George followed her as she carried their plates out to the verandah. It was shaded and the mornings were still cool enough to sit outside. The heat of the day would become more intense as the sun climbed higher in the late spring sky. As would the ever-present tropical humidity. Better to be up and get the work done around the place before it got too hot. Then she could spend the afternoon lying around without a list of chores hanging over her.

As they ate, the only sound was the scraping of cutlery over their plates but the silence was comfortable.

'Bugger.' George stood, hitching up his trousers and tightening the wire. He pointed downstream to the punt. 'Looks like you've got company on the way. I don't need another talking to from that wanker. I'm outta here.'

Emma groaned. There was a police car parked at the boat ramp across the river and Constable Craig Anderson was climbing into the punt.

She stood and followed George as he scuttled down the hall to the front door.

'Thanks for breakfast. Do you need anything while I'm

up at the creek?'

'If you're going anywhere near Wilma's, I do need some more cocky apple bark.' She frowned at George. 'But don't you go getting it yourself either. Only get it from Wilma.'

Even though he cared about the rainforest, George had no concept of trespassing and considered the Daintree open to him wherever he wanted to wander. Wilma Randall, the local aboriginal healer, lived in the rainforest at the turnoff to Cooper Creek Road. She had come into the clinic to have an infected burn treated last year and had been pleased to see that Emma was using natural therapies and that the infusion of cocky apple bark had quickly healed the wound. Emma had been more concerned about the elderly woman's cardiac health. Their friendship developed and a mutual respect grew but it was a few months before Emma could persuade Wilma to take some tests down in Port Douglas and they had diagnosed a valve problem, as well as her angina. She was supposed to have a stent inserted, but Wilma had refused. So she was on medication as a temporary measure to alleviate her symptoms.

Wilma was happy to share her knowledge of bush medicine with Emma and they had become firm friends. George sometimes accompanied Emma to the rainforest but he always refused to get out of the car when she called into Wilma's house on the way back. Despite all his protesting, he had listened when Emma explained what the plants and barks were used for on the way home.

He stared at her. 'No way. I can't stand the old witch. Anyway I don't know why you need all that hocus pocus stuff. *You're* a doctor.'

'Yes, and I also practise alternative medicine.'

'Well, she looks like an old witch.'

'Wilma is lovely. Even some of the people in Dalrymple drive out to see her for her bush remedies.'

'She threatened to set her dog on me when I took a shortcut through her land a couple of weeks back.' The creak of the rarely used front door blended with the indignation in his voice as he pulled it open.

'Ah, now we're getting closer to the truth.'

Emma shook her head as she stroked the soft fur behind Bowser's ears. 'I'll ring Wilma and let her know you're doing me a favour.'

'All right. I guess I can pick it up for you. Just this once.'

Emma watched until George disappeared into the scrub at the side of the dirt road, and then whistled to Bowser as she walked back around the side of the house to wait for Craig. She smoothed the dog's shiny coat as she looked across to the river. 'You're a naughty pup. I'm going to have to lock you in if you keep chasing snakes,' she murmured.

The water was flowing slowly this morning, the gentle eddies and whirlpools adding to its silent beauty. A red-tailed black cockatoo screeched as it flew across the water, its giant wings flapping ponderously as it headed for the dead tree in the paddock beside the cottage.

Emma lifted her hands to run her fingers through her hair and then pulled a face and dropped them to her sides. Last thing she cared about was looking good for Craig.

A couple of months ago she'd made a stupid mistake

and ended up spending the night with him. Craig had seemed lonely at the Young Professionals dinner at the club and she'd gone back to his place for a coffee. One minute they'd been deep in conversation and before she knew it, he'd pulled her into the bedroom. When she'd woken the next morning, self-recrimination had washed over her in a cold wave. It was the first one night stand she'd ever had and Emma vowed she would never make the same mistake again. She'd opened her eyes to see a wedding ring on the top of the chest of drawers and that had made it ten times worse. She'd shot out of Craig's bed and was out the door while he was still asleep. She'd left a noncommittal note and headed to work at the hospital. And kicked herself the whole way.

Craig had been following her around ever since. In his eyes, it appeared that one night of sleeping together guaranteed the beginning of a relationship. He was in for a shock; Emma didn't date married men. Emma didn't date period.

She'd tried a relationship a long time ago and it had reinforced her need for independence. No man—or his family—was going to call the shots and tell her what to do with her life. Or tell her what was wrong with her viewpoints and philosophies. Or tell her she didn't measure up to some social standard. She was in control of her own life now and it would stay that way. Especially someone like Craig.

No matter how much she tried to get the message to him, he had started to call in at the hospital when she was on shift and the more she saw of him the more he showed his true colours.

A bully and a liar.

Happily, being so busy at work with one doctor down over the past couple of weeks meant she'd seen little of him at the hospital. But it looked like he'd finally caught up with her.

Craig was obviously on duty today because he was in his police uniform. She watched as he pulled the rope and propelled the small vessel across the channel, the sun glinting off his blue-black hair. He gave the rope a final yank and the muscles flexed beneath his blue police shirt as the punt sped across the last five metres. She reached out and grabbed the small boat as it nosed into the muddy bank. The punt slewed around and the bottom scraped noisily on the concrete ramp. He jumped out and Emma looped the rope over the steel post and secured the small boat.

'Hi Craig.'

'Emma.' He took her arm and leaned forward to kiss her but she stepped back out of his grip. His eyes narrowed. 'I don't know why you have to live over here when there is perfectly good accommodation in town,' 'I don't like you taking the boat across this river by yourself.'

She didn't bother to tell him that it was none of his business where she lived or how she lived her life. She was tired and didn't want to make his visit any longer than it needed to be.

If only she hadn't already slept with him

'Haven't seen you around for a couple of weeks.'

'I've been busy. I've put in some long days at the clinic and the hospital. We're still one doctor down. How come you're working on a Saturday?'

'Need the money. There was an overtime shift up for

grabs and I took it.'

'So what are you doing here? On your break, or is this official business?' She forced a smile.

'I was going to call you, but I had to come down to the village so I thought I might as well come across. Kettle hot?'

'I've only got time for a quick cuppa. I have a busy day ahead.'

'Sounds good.'

Emma turned and strode towards the house and as Craig followed her, she was conscious of her shorts and bare legs.

'Take a seat. I'll be right back.' Emma gestured to the seat George had just vacated.

Discomfort prickled through her when he ignored her and followed her inside. He pulled out a chair at the kitchen table.

'Breakfast?' Craig lifted his head and sniffed appreciatively but his expression darkened as he spotted the two plates and mugs on the sink. 'Overnight company, Emma?'

'An early visitor.'

Emma put the kettle back on and put a teabag into a clean mug, aware of his eyes on her; she felt like pulling her shirt down to cover the backs of her bare thighs. It was way too cosy in this small kitchen. She turned back to the table and waited for the water to boil.

'So why were you going to call me?'

'I wanted to see if you were going to the seventies night at the pub tomorrow night.' Craig's eyes stayed on her at her.

Emma busied herself at the sink as the kettle boiled. 'Yes. I'll be there.'

'Are you dressing up?' he asked. She quickly made the tea and placed the mug on the table before sitting opposite him.

'Yes. I love a good dress up.'

'I'm not. I think it's a stupid idea.' His expression settled into a sneer.

Emma drew a breath and glanced over at the clock on the wall. 'We're a *social* group, Craig. The Young Professionals hold lots of different events to raise money. And getting into the spirit of things is all part of the fun.' His attitude was making her angry and she changed the subject before she lost her cool. 'Wait till you see the get-up of the tug-of-war teams at the Rainbow Day.'

'Whatever.' His tone was dismissive. 'Anyway I thought we'd go together.' He lifted his cup and blew on the hot tea as he continued to stare at her. 'You can get ready at my place and stay the night.'

Emma held up one hand. 'Craig. I'd like to make one thing very clear. When I went home with you I didn't know you were married and there won't be any more "staying the night" at your place.

'I'm not married. We're separated.'

'Look, Craig, even if you're separated, just because I stayed one night at your place doesn't mean we're in a relationship.' She closed her eyes and took a deep breath, biting back the inward groan. 'I'd had a big week, and having a few drinks on an empty stomach wasn't such a good idea.' She could kick herself for the mistake she made that night; casual sex was way out of character. She softened her words with a weak smile. 'I'm sorry if I gave you the wrong idea

I'm not in for the long haul with anyone.'

'But—'

She held one hand up. 'No.'

'I hear you've been out hiking with Troy Greaves.'

This time her voice was cold. 'I don't think what I do in my time off is your concern.'

He shrugged and the cold glint in his eye was replaced by a smile that she felt was forced. His sullen persistence was making her uncomfortable.

'Okay. But you are still going to the pub? I will see you there?' Craig's eyes were wide. They suddenly reminded her of Bowser's when she'd been ignoring him. That hangdog look that said *pat me please*.

Emma forced a conciliatory smile onto her face. 'Yes, I'll see you there. Along with everyone else.'

Craig stood slowly and tucked the chair in, and she walked down to the riverbank with him.

'So I'll see you tomorrow night then,' he repeated. He unlooped the rope from the post and gave the boat a shove. Emma was relieved when he jumped in and pulled the punt away from the bank.

She tried to shake off the bad mood that had settled around her. It had been like Pitt Street Mall in her cottage this morning. The day had to get better.

Emma cleaned up the house, demolished the mountain of washing and tried to put Craig out of her mind.

She had made her position clear to him and he could like it or lump it. He'd probably move on soon anyway; the last policeman had only been in Dalrymple for six months before transferring back to the city. If Craig stayed longer than that, she'd deal with it. She'd been in Dalrymple before he'd arrived, and she'd be here a lot longer than he would. Emma had no plans to move anywhere; she was here in the Wet Tropics to stay.

She'd fallen in love with the Daintree when she'd come north with a hiking club in her last year at James Cook University in Townsville. The lush green of the rainforest, the sapphire seas and the slow pace of life had appealed. Stunning scenery surrounded each small town and when the job at Dalrymple Hospital had been advertised, she'd known it was the right move for her and was delighted when she was offered the position. She'd quickly settled into the small community and when she'd bought Crooked Cottage it meant there was enough room for Mum to move in with her too. Establishing her clinic, making close friends and watching her mother's health slowly improve had left Emma in no doubt that she'd made the right move. Mum had bought a unit and moved to Port Douglas last summer and was happy and settled.

Just on dark, the loud buzz of a plane overhead distracted her as she took the last load of washing in from the clothes line at the side of the house. She watched curiously as a vehicle pulled up at the end of the runway in the paddock across the river. The plane taxied along the fence line and the vehicle's headlights switched to high beam illuminating the paddock. Emma put her hand to her eyes as the vehicle turned and caught her in the bright light.

By the time she had the washing off the line and in the basket, the vehicle had headed back past the village and the plane had taken off again. Strange. It was the first time she'd seen that runway used since she'd moved here. Usually freight planes used the small airport behind the sugar mill in town.

Emma picked up the basket and inhaled the clean fragrance of freshly laundered sheets. Despite the full day of housework, the hard work was worthwhile. Mum and her sisters had always teased her about being the little homemaker. Her memories of growing up were centred in the kitchen back at the family mango farm. If she hadn't been poring over the recipes in her grandmother's old tattered exercise book, she'd be at the sink, cleaning up after Mum had made her famous mango chutney. The television would be blaring in the lounge room and Ellie and Dru would be arguing over who was going to wipe up.

She closed her eyes and smiled at the memory. Dad had always teased Mum about being the messiest cook in the world and Emma had taken on the role of organising her sisters to clean up when Mum cooked the annual batch of mango chutney. For a moment the silence around her was empty but there were many memories to fill the loneliness.

Precious memories of days when life had been simple and uncomplicated. Precious memories of Mum being happy. Precious memories of Dad, larger than life, before the greed of others had cut his life short.

Back when she and Ellie and Dru had been an invincible threesome.

Bowser's yap brought Emma back to the present.

'Come on, Bowser. Teatime.' The little dog followed her inside and she soon forgot about the plane.

Chapter 2

Saturday morning- Sydney

Jeremy Langford sat in the large foyer of the specialist practice in Macquarie Street, waiting for his father. He glanced impatiently at his watch before lifting his eyes to the wall. The sooner he was out of here and on the way to the airport, the closer he'd be to his new home, and his new career—his new life. The marble-tiled wall was lined with gold-framed degrees and memberships, telling all who perused them how well qualified his father and two older brothers were. A specialist practice, catering to the cosmetic needs of the rich and famous, laid out in documentation, for everyone to admire the men of the Langford family who had deigned to treat them. *Look at us. We're special. We have the paper to prove it.* Each frame was positioned so that the lights recessed in the specially positioned chrome rail below highlighted the gilt writing on the parchment. There was his father's degree in medicine above his registration with the Australian Society of Plastic Surgeons, and the Royal Australasian College of Surgeons. His brothers were quickly catching up. Alex's degrees were on the second row and the document listing him as the current chair of the Australian Board of Plastic and Reconstructive Surgery took prime position. Brenton's achievements, although along the bottom row, were equally impressive.

The air was cold and the sterile smell of the air-conditioned office sent a shiver down Jeremy's back. He stood and crossed to the window, looking out at the people scurrying purposefully along the footpath below. The thick sandstone walls muted the sound of the traffic crawling along Macquarie Street. He wondered what the view would be like from the hospital up north. Excitement unfurled in his chest and he bounced lightly on his toes.

Jeremy had as many degrees and qualifications as Alex and Brenton, and indeed had topped his final year at Sydney University, but that alone had not satisfied his father. The expectation had always been that he would join the family specialist practice. The moment he had made it known that he had no desire to practise in the field chosen by his father and brothers, had been the day any relationship with the Langford men—and there had never been much of one—had finally withered and died. The past year had killed any chance of resurrecting it. Losing a family member had been the last nail in the coffin of his relationship with his family. He'd felt so bloody helpless that night. No matter how fast they had worked, it had seemed as though it was happening in slow motion. He should have been able to do more. He should have recognised the syndrome more quickly and seen that Brianna's body temperature was out of control.

He still couldn't think about that night without shutting down. Clinically he knew they couldn't have done any more to save Brianna. Emotionally, he couldn't accept that he'd failed.

Jeremy shrugged. Nothing else mattered if you couldn't save a life. The degrees, the intent, the artificiality of these rooms; it meant nothing.

Unlike most of the specialists on Macquarie Street, Dr.

Alan Langford opened his rooms on a Saturday morning; sometimes Jeremy thought his father preferred to be here than at home. He looked at his watch again; the traffic had been heavy on the way to the city If Dad didn't appear in the next ten minutes, he would have to go without saying goodbye. He had a plane to catch.

It had been bad enough seeing the disappointment on his mother's face this morning. She'd brushed a light kiss across his cheek, her hair stiff and the smell of hairspray mingled with her cloying perfume. He'd called a taxi to bring him from Point Piper into the city, but she hadn't been able to wait to see him off. A charity breakfast awaited Mother and her perfectly made-up face, which of course needed little enhancement with three plastic surgeons in the family. She was a walking advertisement for the Langford practice—his father probably wrote her off as a tax deduction.

'I still cannot understand why you have to leave Sydney.' Her voice had been as cold as her kiss. 'Are you aware, Jeremy, of your father's disappointment?'

'Yes.' His nod was brief. 'Of course, I am. But my mind is made up, Mother. I need a change. I can't stay in Sydney and I certainly can't work with Brenton. Surely you can understand that.

He rubbed the back of his neck as her clipped words continued.

'And poor Polly. She was almost suicidal when you broke off the engagement. I was so looking forward to another wedding.'

Jeremy bit the inside of his cheek to stem the words that threatened. There was no point. He'd agreed to be the one to break the engagement to so that Polly could save face. It didn't matter to him - just another mark against his name.

'I've met someone else, Jeremy.' The words from his fiancé had been a blessed relief. He was sure they had fallen into an engagement to suit the social calendar of the North Shore set where Polly lived with her lawyer parents. For a while their life together had been pleasant. They'd shared similar interests and had a circle of friends in common. But after the incident, when it had become clear he wouldn't join the family practice, Polly had lost interest in him and it hadn't taken her long to find a replacement. She had the looks and the family money to choose whoever she wanted. The relief that had filled him when she'd broken it off had broken into that cold place for a few hours.

But he was not going to get into another argument with his mother, not today. Not the day he left to start afresh. Nothing was going to interfere with his excitement and the anticipation of moving to another state, to fresh horizons and working in a new position.

A new life.

'Well.' She'd gathered up her Prada handbag and car keys, and turned to face him again. 'Take care of yourself, dear.'

Jeremy was surprised to see the glint of tears sheening her eyes. But of course it wasn't the fact that he was leaving. It was the disappointment at how he had let the family down. No fancy, over-the-top wedding in a marquee by Sydney Harbour for her to look forward to. No mention of the third Langford son in the society pages this summer.

Now the door to the consulting room opened quietly.

Oiled and flawless, like everything else in his family's life. Houses, possessions, and spouses, there was never any noise, no fuss, no bother.

No life. Always keeping up appearances.

Until the tragedy. A senseless death and the waste of a young life. The actions of his niece were insignificant when compared to what his parents viewed as his failure.

His father crossed the room and picked up the coffeepot warming in the small alcove behind his desk. 'Do you have time for a coffee?'

Jeremy shook his head. 'No, thank you. My flight to Cairns leaves at eleven.'

His father put the coffee pot down, turned to Jeremy and held out his hand. 'As much as this may come as a surprise to you, I do wish you well, son.'

Jeremy shook the proffered hand and was surprised at the strength his father put into the handshake. The expected sting came in the next words.

'However, I know you will be back. This is your place.' His father gave an awkward harrumph, and cleared his throat. 'If you want to specialise in another field, I am sure the practice could accommodate another specialty.'

The unfamiliar warmth in his father's voice filled Jeremy with surprise. The arguments they'd had when he'd first made his intentions known had not prepared him for this about face.

Jeremy shook his head. 'No, Dad. Thanks, but we've been over this a hundred times. It's a move to rural medicine for me. And the more isolated the better.'

His father raised his eyebrows. 'And Cairns is isolated?'

'I'm not in Cairns. I'll be based a couple of hundred miles north in Dalrymple, and from there I'll be travelling to some remote clinics.

He may as well have said he was going to the moon. His father's expression was one of disdain tinged with frustration.

'I thought it was a purely administrative position.'

'It is. I'll co-ordinate the setting up of the service and supervise the medical—' Jeremy's frustration rose to the surface as his father raised his hand '—staff in at least six isolated clinics. It's a huge responsibility and it's an opportunity that I am really looking forward to.' He didn't mention that he was going up early to help out at the local hospital for a week.

'Enough. What the hell can I do to talk you out of this, Jeremy?'

'Nothing.' He kept his voice as clipped as his father's. 'You know how much I loved those couple of months I did out at Broken Hill. I know I can do this.' His father turned away.

It was a waste of words and a waste of time. There was no point getting into an argument with his father, nothing to be achieved apart from more ill feeling.

'Wish me well, Dad. Please.'

This new move was a fresh start for him and he was excited by the opportunity, and he was damn well going to do it. The sabbatical of the last twelve months had been spent completing his MBA and researching positions combining management consulting and clinical practice. The Outreach Program was a perfect match to his qualifications and his needs.

'We'll miss you at home.'

Jeremy fought down the usual guilt that burned in his chest. He'd learned to live with it.

Almost.

'It's about time I flew the family coop.' He glanced at his watch. 'I'm sorry I've missed Alex and Brenton. Tell them I said goodbye.'

His father inclined his head in a cool nod. 'I will.'

'Goodbye, Dad.' Jeremy let the air expel from his chest as he closed the door quietly behind him. His shoulders felt lighter as he headed for the elevator.

***

Eight hours later, a blast of noise hit Jeremy as he pushed open the door of the hotel in Dalrymple. The air hung hot and heavy, saturated with the smell of beer and a sweet smell that Jeremy realised came from the smoke pumping from the sugar mill he'd passed. As he'd driven north from Cairns airport his anticipation had built as glimpses of sapphire blue water had beckoned through trees where brightly-coloured birds hung upside down, chattering as they sipped the nectar from brilliant red flowers. The landscape was green and lush, and he smiled as he crossed a river and saw the town sign announcing he had reached "Dalrymple: the Sweetest Town on the Coast."

He waited until the barman finished serving at the other end of the bar and walked up to the counter where he waited.

'Gidday, mate. What can I get you?'

'I've got a room booked here for a couple of weeks.' Jeremy reached into his pocket for his wallet. 'Langford.'

'Hi, the new doc! Welcome.' The barman held out his

hand and his grip was firm as Jeremy shook it. 'I'm Rod Barber. I work at the hospital when I'm not moonlighting here.' He rolled his eyes as the noise at the end of the bar increased.

'Fix the bill when you leave.' He reached under the counter and pulled out a key. 'Room three. Top of the stairs. If you need anything just holler. Dinner's on in the bistro from six and it's a good feed. I'll talk to you later when this mob goes home.'

Jeremy took the key and headed up the stairs to check out his lodgings. The registrar had assured him there was no shortage of rental accommodation, short or long term but he wanted to check out the town before he rented anywhere. He'd picked up a hire car when he'd flown into Cairns and booked it for a few days until he got himself settled. A four-wheel drive vehicle came with the Outreach Program so there was no point having a car up here. When he decided to leave Sydney he'd sold his silver Porsche and donated the money to a Drug Awareness program in schools. Leaving behind the trappings of his lifestyle had been cathartic, but restlessness still tugged at him mercilessly; he still couldn't settle and sleep eluded him. He was confident that this move would dispel the uncertainty that churned inside him.

He was over the whole Sydney scene.

Since that terrible night in the emergency room, the niggling worry that he'd chosen the wrong profession had become a more general dissatisfaction with the purposelessness of his life. Sure he kept up the facade. There were plenty of friends around; he socialised, followed the party circuit, was seen with the right women on his arm at the races and played team sports. He went to the hottest new bars in Surry Hills on Friday nights. But this constant striving—to have the highest paying job, the best water view, the latest model European car—was not for him.

Medicine was supposed to be a noble vocation, but the only time Jeremy had experienced deep satisfaction was during his clinical placement in the outback. There he'd found it easier to connect with patients. Even though the medical issues were the same, life was slower and there was time to talk.

One night a few weeks ago, he'd come home and made a life-changing decision. It was either move on or drown in the life he was pretending to live. With his MBA completed he'd found the Outreach position advertised the next week and he knew it was the right thing to do.

The two interviews had been conducted by videoconference and he'd waited nervously until he received the call advising him of his success.

He shook himself and dragged his mind back to the tropics. Back to his new life.

Dalrymple had surprised him as he'd driven to the hotel. It was well away from the tourist beats of Cairns and Port Douglas. Everywhere he looked there were trees and brightly coloured flowers. Even the sky seemed to be a deeper shade of blue.

Perfection.

This new position excited him and he was going to do the best damn job he could. At university he'd been surprised he'd loved his first taste of rural medicine, even though his girlfriend at the time had teased him mercilessly about being away from his favourite barista.

Emma Porter. Her face flashed into his mind; he hadn't thought about her for a while. At university they'd been voted the couple most likely to last.

Em and Jem. He could smile now but it had been hard when it had ended so suddenly.

She'd left without a word and he often wondered where she had ended up. He should have tried harder to track her down but it had hurt that she had left without telling him in their second last year.

He took a deep breath as he walked along the verandah looking for his room. Looking down at the street below, he couldn't help but compare it to Macquarie Street and the frantic pace of life in the city. A lone cyclist rode along the railway track that ran along the side of the street and crossed the highway. Tropical birds whirled overhead, and screeched as they dipped to the trees. There was one set of traffic lights at the corner and that was it for the whole town. In fact, that was all he'd seen since he'd left Cairns.

Jeremy's hopes were pinned on this, the opportunity to be involved with the Outreach Program from the ground up. The contract was for one year; that would give him plenty of time to make a decision about his future.

The call from the regional director of health last week had surprised Jeremy. 'How would you feel about coming a bit earlier and filling in at the hospital before your contract starts? For a week or so? We're short staffed. You wouldn't believe how hard it is to get doctors in these rural towns. It'll give you an opportunity to get settle in and get to know the place.'

He'd agreed and made plans to head north immediately.

As he put the key in the dark timber door of his room his phone buzzed with a text message.

'*Sorry I missed you. Kill 'em, up there, bro. Ah . . . maybe not.*'

Alex, his oldest brother, was the only one who understood his move to the north.

Jeremy pushed open the door and smiled.

Chapter 3

Sunday afternoon – the Daintree Rainforest

The sun was high by the time George got back to his battered four-wheel drive ute and drove up Cooper Creek Road into the rainforest. The road from the north side of the river where the vehicular ferry docked was winding and consisted of numerous hairpin curves. You had to have your wits about you because there were always bloody tourists stopped in the middle of the road, taking photos of cassowaries. He'd caught up with Jack, his old mate, on the way yesterday and helped him build a fence and it had been too late to go to the forest. So he'd had a few beers by the fire with Jack and camped out in his swag.

He passed through two open gates and turned off the road into a clearing, parking in a thicket of trees. No one needed to know he was in the rainforest; it was no one else's business. He lifted out the old paint tin from the back of the vehicle and slammed the door shut, reaching for a cigarette before he remembered that he didn't smoke any more thanks to Dr Em's persuasion. He dug deeper into his pocket and pulled out a wad of that nicotine gum she'd given him, chewing it for a few seconds before he spat it into the bush with a snort of disgust.

Blasted stuff was supposed to help but it tasted like chook shit.

He grinned when he passed the old woman's house. It

was all shut up and there was no sign of life. The curtains were closed and there was no smoke coming from the chimney. Good, he didn't want to go in there. No matter what nice things Doctor Em said about her. On the couple of times she'd seen him go past, the old woman had stood and stared at him as though she could tell what he was thinking. It gave him the willies. Better to stay away from her. She gave him the creeps with that long grey hair and wrinkled up face. Not that he was a spring chicken himself. Anyway, the doc would just have to wait for her cocky bark stuff. He had business of his own in the rainforest.

He left the track for a while and took a shortcut across to the creek where he knew it was shallow enough to cross before he re-joined the track further up the hill. The rough-barked bloodwood trees were heavily blossomed and the forest was filled with their sweet perfume. As he pushed deeper into the forest, the light dimmed and a hush filled the small valley. Granite boulders protruded from the steep hill on his left and the only sound was the leaf litter crunching beneath his feet. As the creek widened at the head of the valley, the babble of water across the rocks filled the silence and the pale green light was diffused by a fine mist drifting down from the peak.

As George ambled along the track towards the top of the hill, the peace was suddenly broken by the raucous shriek of cockatoos. He stopped and watched as a flock of red-crested black cockatoos swept through the towering, green canopy with a rush of wings. He cocked his head and listened as the birds disappeared into the tree tops. The peaceful silence of the rainforest surrounded him again as they settled into the high branches. He made his way towards the clearing.

Muffled voices drifted up to him. Someone was coming up the hill ahead of him; whoever it was must have disturbed the cockatoos. It was unusual to see anyone on this track so deep in the rainforest, although he'd heard that rainforest centre bloke was planning to bring tourists out this way on walking tours. If that happened he'd have to find a more secluded clearing for his plants. It would also mean carting the water a bit further from the creek until the rain arrived with the onset of the wet season.

The voices got louder and George stepped quietly off the track into the forest. He reached a wide strangler fig and pressed himself hard against the trunk on the side away from the track. Three quarters of the way up, the trunk split into two and started spiralling. The curtain of vine that hung from the knotted loops of the vine provided a screen for him. For a moment he thought about leaning around but it wasn't worth the risk. He didn't want to be seen out here. He wondered who the men were. They'd better not be after his plants.

'Jeez . . . I hate how quiet this bloody forest is.' The first man's voice was clear now as they walked up the hill towards his hiding place. 'Except for when those birds get squawking . . . did you hear the racket those cockatoos made?'

'Keep your voice down.' The man who answered sounded unimpressed. 'If you hadn't made so much bloody noise the other day and frightened them, we wouldn't have had to take another trip.'

'I couldn't help it. It hurt when that bastard cockatoo bit my finger.'

'If it's too much of a bother, I can always get someone

else.' The man's voice was cold.

'No. Don't be fuckin' stupid. I need the money.' The voices were clear as they passed George's hiding place. He frowned. Get someone else to do what? If they *were* after his plants, he'd have to move them quick smart.

'If we don't get finished today, tomorrow's our last chance. Are you around?'

'I'm not working. I can meet you out here if we have to.'

George strained to hear more as the men passed his hiding place. He took a step back and a piece of fallen bark split beneath his foot with a loud crunch.

'What was that?'

'Just an animal.'

The footsteps stopped and George held his breath.

There was no noise for a while apart from the leaves rustling and the distant babbling of the creek. Then the voices started up again.

'So who else knows what's out here?'

'More than you'd guess. You'd be surprised how big this is. Money talks, mate.'

The voices faded until he couldn't hear what they were saying anymore. He stayed hidden behind the strangler fig for a while longer. It couldn't be his half a dozen plants they were talking about. What was going on? Maybe these blokes had a crop out here too. Strange, he'd been coming out for years and he'd never seen any others. Didn't make a lot of sense. Taking a step out from behind the trees, he walked stealthily, making sure he didn't stand on any of the dry leaves. He reached the track and peered down the hill, straining his eyes in the dim light of the rainforest. They'd disappeared. He leaned forward and grunted with frustration.

They had to come out the same way they went in; it was the only track for miles. He'd hang around until they came back.

George stepped back onto the track and headed back the way he'd come. There was a good vantage point about five hundred metres along where he could hide and still see the track. His plants could wait until later. Before he's taken a step forward, a rush of air passed his ear and something hard crashed into the back of his head. He hit the ground hard and put one hand out to save himself. His arm twisted and he rolled onto his front. A firm hand pushed his face down into the path and he closed his eyes as the sharp stones cut his face.

'Ah, fuck it.' The voice was familiar. 'My bloody finger's bleeding again.

'Shut up,' the other man said in a low growl.

'Don't worry. The old turd's out to it. I hit him good and hard with that rock.'

George kept perfectly still as the men stood beside him. He kept his eyes closed.

'So what now?'

'You go back. I'm not going to risk anyone else seeing us together. I'll go and get this lot.' George didn't recognise the voice. 'You can go and suss out the old woman's shed.'

'As long as I still get my cut.'

'You will. You better not have killed the old bastard. What's he doing out this far anyway?'

'He had some dope plants out here. I warned him off,

but he must have moved them.' George held his breath.

'Pull him off the track and get moving. I'll call you later.'

George tried not to make a sound as one of them grabbed his feet and dragged him face down along the path. Pain exploded in his arm and the buzzing in his ears covered their voices as he passed out.

Chapter 4

Sunday evening-Dalrymple

Emma spent Sunday pleasurably. In between chores and reading, she caught up on sleep, lying in her hammock chair on the verandah, enjoying the light breeze coming off the river. She'd had a great Skype chat with Mum and both her sisters after lunch. Mum seemed more settled by the day. Ellie and Kane were planning their wedding in Kakadu. Even Dru had been talkative for a change; she was excited about the huge Ferris wheel project she was working on in Dubai, and she'd mentioned a new guy she'd been spending some time with. Emma would have been more than happy to have another early night at home—a night spent at the pub with the social club in fancy dress costume wasn't terribly enticing—but she'd promised to go and she knew if she didn't haul herself into town, they'd probably send out a search party. Besides, she'd grabbed a spare minute between patients last week to visit the op shop at the end of the main street and she loved the emerald green skirt she'd found.

Before she headed to the punt to cross the river to her car, she grabbed her work clothes; she planned to spend the night at the clinic to save going in early in the morning. She had morning rounds at the hospital from seven am with open surgery at her clinic after that. There'd been no sign of George yesterday afternoon, so she would collect the bark from him when she picked up her car. She checked that Bowser was secure on the front porch and then locked the gate—after George's mention of snakes, she didn't want him outside on his own.

It was a half hour drive from Daintree Village into Dalrymple even in the best conditions, so, Emma often spent the night on the fold-up bed in the back of her clinic when it was too late to drive back home, or if the river was up. It was easier than pulling herself back across on the punt in the middle of the night.

When she reached the other side, she walked up to George's house and pounded on his door. 'You there, George?' She waited but he didn't appear, so she walked down around to his shed. A neighbour called over the fence. 'He's been away all weekend, love.'

'Thanks.' She waved and opened her car door.

George often camped overnight in the bush and she could wait for her bark. She smiled as she started the car. If he'd remembered to get it. She'd go out to Wilma's place during the week. She wanted to check on her anyway.

The trip from the village into town was uneventful. There were few cars on the highway. The traffic from Cairns and Port Douglas up to the Daintree and Cape Tribulation always eased off at sunset when the tourists made their way back to the various resorts scattered along the coastline.

The 'Welcome to Dalrymple' sign loomed ahead and Emma drove slowly across the bridge on the north side of town, thinking of her sister Ellie as she always did when she saw the crocodile warning. She still shivered every time she imagined what Ellie had gone through. She turned to more positive thoughts. With any luck, she would know the outcome of the Outreach Program interview this week.

Fingers crossed, she thought. Even though she was making a difference in the hospital and at her clinic, Emma knew she could contribute a lot to the new project. She knew the local aboriginal community both in the hospital and in her clinic. She'd even visited a couple of the areas where the future clinics were proposed with Wilma. She'd done her best to convey her local knowledge to the interview panel last month. The successful applicant should have been announced by now; it was taking ages.

Emma parked the car at the back of her clinic, unlocked the back door and put her overnight bag before flicking on the outside security lights and pulling the door shut again. Then she flicked her braid over her shoulder, shoved the keys in her handbag and adjusted the narrow headband wrapped around her forehead as she crossed the road to the pub on the corner. The long skirt of her costume was already sticking to her legs—this seventies garb was hot. The humidity was high and it was only early November.

Emma lifted the crushed velvet skirt that brushed the tops of her flat leather sandals and pushed open the door to the foyer of the Federal Hotel. The graceful old building sprawled on the corner on the northern edge of town overlooking the single track railway line where the sugar cane trains chuffed past on their way to the sugar mill west of town. The familiar mix of sweat, spilt beer and stale cigarette smoke—absorbed for years by the timber and the threadbare carpet in the days before smoking was banned in Aussie pubs—embraced her like an old friend. The sour smell mixed with the sweet aroma of sugar cane coming from the skin and clothes of the cane harvesters. When each day's quota of bins had been filled and sent off to the local sugar mill, the pub filled quickly as the workers headed to the pub for a cold beer. Didn't matter that it was Sunday night. At the end of the harvest season, the cane was harvested seven days a week as they rushed to beat the rain of the upcoming wet season, and the pub was full and rowdy every night.

Emma crossed the foyer and went through the archway into the main bar. In an old-fashioned town like Dalrymple, Sunday was still treated as a day of rest by the business community. Most of the shops in the long, straight main street stayed closed, apart from the big Woolies south of town, and the bakery only opened for a couple of hours from nine, tempting the locals with the smell of fresh bread on their way home from church.

Emma looked around. She was early—as usual—and it looked like she was first to arrive unless the others were already out in the beer garden out the back. Fingers crossed that Troy had the night off; he'd been a big part of the social group since he'd arrived in town, especially since most of their fundraising was for the preservation of the rainforest. Emma made a mental note to check if he was off work next weekend. He'd mentioned hiking to the top of Thornton Peak with her. He was keen to collect some Thornton Peak Tree Frogs for the breeding program at the centre. It was another species in danger of extinction, he'd told her. Maybe they could go this weekend? Working the hospital and her clinic meant her days off didn't coincide with his free time often, but she was going to make an effort. She needed to collect some more tadpoles and it would be great to hike with Troy. The last time they'd gone into the rainforest, he'd talked about the unique nature of the world heritage site as they'd wandered through the quiet gullies. He was passionate about the Daintree and she was surprised by how much she'd learned from him in the short time he'd been here.

'What'll it be, Doctor Em?' Rod held up a beer glass.

Emma shook her head. 'Just a lime and soda, thanks, Rod. Early start tomorrow.'

'It's been a long week.' Rod turned to the display fridge behind the bar and pulled out a tray of sliced lime.

'It sure has.'

She looked up as laughter erupted at the far end of the bar and smiled at a couple of the guys she'd seen this week. One of them had come in for stitches in his leg—he'd narrowly missed an artery with his cane machete—and the other had brought in a child with an earache. Obviously all was well now.

'The clinic's been busy too.'

'Good to hear. Looks like the oldies have accepted you.'

'Finally. Half of them are so old-fashioned they still don't believe a woman can be a real doctor.'

'Jock Newby still on your case?' Ice tinkled as Rod scooped it into the glass before topping it up with soda from the post-mix tap. When the local pharmacist discovered she'd studied complementary medicine—it didn't matter that it was a Masters degree from a recognised university —he took every opportunity he could to have his say to whoever would listen. *'A doctor should know better,'* he said.

She was polite—although she'd had to bite her tongue on more than one occasion—but she kept practicing complementary pharmacy; it was the perfect addition to her medical background. She'd studied externally and although the residential school in Brisbane had filled some of the gaps in her practical skills and allowed her to register as a complementary and alternative practitioner, the local knowledge she'd gained from Wilma over the past year had been invaluable.

'Everything's fine. And getting busier by the day. Once the new doctor arrives, things will be great.' 'Not long to wait then,' Rod said with a grin. 'That's the new doc over there.'

Emma turned and her gaze swept the room before it settled on a man sitting alone in the corner. She hadn't noticed him when she'd come in. Her breath caught in her throat and she blinked before turning her attention back to Rod.

'*That's* the new doctor? The guy in the light blue shirt? Are you sure?'

'Yup. Said he was, anyway. Seems like a nice enough bloke.' Rod headed off down the bar to replenish the beers at the other end.

No. It can't be. The last time she'd seen Jeremy Langford had been on the footpath in Surry Hills when his mates had picked him up for a football trip to Coffs Harbour. He'd kissed her goodbye, ignoring the horn tooting and the smart calls from his mates

It was the last day Emma had spent in Sydney.

That call from Dru had changed her life in a moment. Emma had dropped everything and gone straight to the airport. When she had told the airline staff of her family tragedy, they had had her on a flight to Darwin within an hour. She'd been back at home in Kakadu before dark that same day. And she hadn't seen Jeremy since. She'd called him and written to him but he'd never spoken to her again. His silence had left her feeling sad and confused, but that had been lost in the grief of burying Dad.

Emma shook her head. She couldn't believe that Jeremy Langford was sitting over there in the front bar of the Federal Hotel in Dalrymple.

Jeremy. *Jem*. The first, and if she was truly honest, only love of her life.

Here in Dalrymple. In *her* town. And coming to work at *her* hospital.

He hadn't changed one bit—if anything he was even more handsome than he had been five years ago. Neatly cut sandy hair brushed his tanned forehead. High cheekbones and full lips that had resulted in an offer of modelling work when they'd been at uni.

Emma and the rest of their group had gone to lectures looking like typical students. Even when they'd been on their hospital visits, their white coats had covered jeans and T-shirts. Not so Jeremy. He'd always looked as though he had stepped from the pages of *GQ* magazine. He'd copped a ribbing from the other guys when he'd first appeared in the David Jones catalogue, modelling Calvin Klein boxers but they'd soon got used to it.

She'd often wondered whether if it was a touch of arrogance or just a genuine cluelessness about the advantages that his privileged background had conferred on him. Even the modelling work had been a lark to him. It sure beat serving at Maccas like Emma had done to supplement her scholarship. Her parents hadn't been in a position to help much, the farm was rarely in the black. All her friends knew was that she came from the Northern Territory and she'd played it up as an exotic background.

She looked down at her drink sitting on the bar as memories flooded back. Could she just slip out the back? No, she should go over and welcome him. She took a deep breath. It was going to take a while to get used to Jeremy being here.

They say your first sexual experience always stays with you—and her memories of Jem were the ones that Emma sometimes pulled out and dusted off when she was feeling a bit blue. Lifting her head, she allowed her gaze to travel down from his broad shoulders to his slim hips to the shiny black shoes she could just see under the table.

The first time she'd seen Jeremy in the queue at the cafeteria at Sydney uni she'd done the same thing. Gaped right along with every other woman in the cafeteria. Oozing sex appeal, he carried himself with a grace that belied his prowess on the rugby field.

Nuh. He hadn't changed at all. He was as sexy as ever, polished and perfect even in this dingy pub in Northern Queensland. Beneath the looks, he'd always been a decent guy. They'd shared their studies, their days and their dreams and she'd missed him in her life. It had taken her ages to get over him.

Jeremy Langford in Dalrymple. This was a turn up for the books.

His attention was focused on the iPad propped up on the table in front of him. His pale-blue collared shirt was crisp and the ironed-in creases on the short sleeves had a sharp edge. Still fastidious; that aspect of his character had annoyed her so much when he'd picked up after her in her tiny flat. It had been a novelty to him. He'd always had someone to look after him in the Langford's posh house at Point Piper. Well, now she could meet him on equal terms. She was a doctor with her own clinic and she had achieved all of that by herself with bloody hard work. Emma picked up her drink, took a deep breath and slowly crossed the room.

Keep it casual.

'Hello, Jeremy.'

Watching his face was like watching the frames of a movies flick by in slow motion. Shock . . .surprise . . and finally—if she still could read him properly—confusion. Jeremy lowered the iPad to the table as his forehead wrinkled in a frown. He looked at her crushed velvet skirt and then up to the headband on her forehead.

'Emma?' He pushed the chair back and rose gracefully to his feet. For a moment there was confusion as he first held out his hand, then dropped it and held his arms open. 'My God. Emma Porter, it really is you!'

Emma put her drink carefully on the table and leaned into Jeremy as his arms closed firmly around her, horrified by the rush of memory that coursed through her when his shirt pressed against her cheek. It was as though the last five years disappeared in a breath. The smell of his freshly laundered shirt mixed with the same woodsy cologne he had always favoured surrounded her in a comforting cocoon, and for a brief moment, she closed her eyes and enjoyed the memory.

No.

Tempted to draw in another deep breath, she closed her

mouth and focused on breathing slowly She'd hyperventilate at this rate.

'Yes it's me,' she finally managed as she stepped back.

'It's so good to see you, Em.' Jeremy's next words were like a dash of cold water. 'It must be five years since you dropped out of med school.'

Anger began a slow burn in her stomach. She should have known he'd make that assumption.

Assumptions.

Even if Dad hadn't died and she'd stayed at medical school in Sydney, they wouldn't have lasted. The punters would have lost their 'Em and Jem' bet. Emma Porter from Kakadu just didn't measure up to the requirements of the Langford family.

'Emma?'

She realised she was staring at him and she pulled her hands out of his.

'Yes. It is. Five years.' Memories crowded into her head and she made a conscious effort to keep the conversation light. Tilting her head back, Emma held his blue-eyed gaze, ignoring the sharp little frissons jumping around in her stomach like fireworks. 'How are you, Jeremy? You look very well.' She forced a nonchalant grin to cross her face. 'And as pretty as ever. Still modelling on the side?'

A light flush stained his high cheekbones but he smiled at her. 'I'm very well, thank you.' The smile widened, showing his perfect white teeth. 'And no, I gave away the modelling. The fan mail was clogging my letterbox.' Jeremy shook his head as he looked down at her almost as though she was a figment of his imagination. He had always looked older than the other students and when they'd first met he'd seemed mature beyond his eighteen years. As they'd become friends, Emma had learned that the arrogance he wore like a cloak actually covered a lack of confidence, though there was no way he would ever admit it. In the five years before she'd left, she'd watched his confidence grow. Slowly their friendship had blossomed into love and within two years he was her boyfriend.

And her first lover.

'And what about you?' he asked. 'Do you live up here or are you travelling through?' He obviously hadn't heard her conversation with Rod; the noise from the other end of the bar would have drowned out their words.

She tightened her lips as he waited for her to answer. His expression was curious. A little older, and if she looked closely a little thinner; small lines were etched beside his eyes and his full lips.

She stared back at him as he took in the hippie clothes she wore. His eyes finally rested on the peace sign that nestled on the cheesecloth top between her breasts.

Dropped out. His words left a bitter taste; the two word assumption confirmed that she would never have been good enough for his family—and if the truth be known, not good enough for him in the long term. Well, he was in for a surprise tomorrow. She would play this to the hilt.

'Yes, I do. Live here, that is. I've a small piece of land in a little village just north of here. Daintree Village. Just enough to try to keep myself self-sufficient. I've been here for a few years now. Beautiful place to "drop out." I've got a cute little dog, chooks, frogs and a fabulous veggie garden.'

'I thought you'd gone back to the Northern Territory. I was . . . surprised when you left.'

Emma shook her head. 'I did go home for a while. Long story.'

Jeremy turned and gestured towards the table. 'Join me? We can catch up. I'd love to hear all about it.'

'I've already told you what happened.'

'What? When?' A frown creased his perfect brow.

'In the letter I sent you. I have to run. I'm meeting my friends out the back. Maybe later.

She leaned closer, grateful that someone had turned on the old jukebox at the other end of the room. The room had filled with more mill workers and it was getting noisy.

'Where can I find you in town?' Again he was staring at her clothes.

Emma flicked her braid over her shoulder and lifted her chin high. 'I have a little alternative therapy clinic across the road. Alternative Alchemy. Anyway, it was great to see you again. She held up two fingers to him in a peace sign. Jeremy had never been able to understand her interest in alternative therapies when they had been studying.

'Peace, man.'

The look on his face was comical. 'Catch you around town, for sure.'

Emma walked through the archway that led to the outside beer garden and laughter bubbled up in her chest. She didn't look back. The tables were almost full and she joined the group from the hospital at the table across from the outside bar. A good crowd had turned up and most were in theme. All of the regular Young Professionals were there—

she looked around—with the exception of Craig and Troy, it appeared.

Emma stood beside Jenny Lennox, one of the doctors from the hospital. 'Hey Jenny. Love your dress.'

'Wow, look at you, Emma. You could have stepped straight from the seventies. Great skirt.' She moved her chair across so Emma could get to the chair on her other side. 'Unfortunately, I can't stay long. I'm taking over in emergency at nine.'

'You drew the short straw.'

By the time Emma had caught up on the hospital news from the weekend her irritation at Jeremy had mostly disappeared, and she was glad she came out to socialise. She was relieved that Craig wasn't there and hopeful that Troy might still show up. She took a deep breath; one thing she had learned since Dad had gone was how to control her feelings. She'd had to be strong for her mother.

Death soon put life into perspective. And the sadness and occasional tragedy that were a constant part of a doctor's working life had taught her to cope.

Okay, so Jeremy's sudden appearance had thrown her into a temporary spin, but she would deal with it. She had to. They'd be working side by side at the hospital.

Her close friends, Jeff and Cissy Gray, arrived and the beer garden became a hubbub of noise. Jeff was the local vet and Cissy worked part-time in the office at the hospital.

'Hey guys, love the costumes.' Jeff was wearing a pair of bright orange flared trousers with a yellow paisley shirt tucked in to the high waistband. Cissy was wearing a pair of white satin culottes and a long blonde wig.

'Channelling, Abba, Cis?' Emma smiled as she looked down at the platform shoes peeking beneath the culottes.

'Yep, sure am.'

As she greeted them, Emma wondered if Jeremy had lasted in the bar as music blared from the jukebox in the front of the pub.

'Why did we have to dress up anyway?' Jeff grumbled. 'It's bloody hot out here.'

'Your Afro is slipping.' Cissy pointed to her husband's wig and Emma giggled as Jeff frowned and pulled off the wig.' Good crowd here for a Sunday night. I nearly didn't come.'

'Just as well you did,' Cissy said.

'I know, Rainbow Day is getting coming up fast and we've still got some organising to do.'

'Is the meeting still on Wednesday night?' Cissy put the wig on the floor beside her bag. Rainbow Day was an annual fundraiser in the town for the preservation of the Dalrymple Gorge.

'It is.' Emma fanned herself. Knowing Jeremy was in the hotel was wreaking havoc with her mood and the heat was getting to her. Perhaps she wasn't at good at controlling her emotions as she thought.

'I need to let everyone know.' Emma picked up her glass and a spoon to get everyone's attention but Jeff shook his head.

'Wait a while,' he suggested. 'There's still a few to come. And the more we get to the meeting, the more help we'll have on the day.'

'And the more money we'll raise,' Cissy chimed in.

'Hold that thought,' Emma said with a smile. 'I'll wander around and see who's remembered.'

The bistro staff kept the food coming and Emma moved around the group, garnering support for Wednesday night's meeting. She looked up when Cissy clapped her hands.

'We need a judge.' Cissy stood at the end of the table and beckoned over to Rod. It appeared that the crowd had lessened in the front bar. He was collecting glasses in the beer garden.

Rod put his hands on his hips and surveyed the group. 'First up. All of you slackers not in costume. Five dollar fine.'

Cissy picked up an empty glass and walked around collecting the fines from the few not in costume.

'Clear cut winner.' Rod rubbed his hands together. 'Jeff, did you really wear those flares in the seventies?

Jeff stood and posed. 'I did, but not this pair. I've gained a lot of muscle since then.' He rubbed his hand on his paunch to good-natured heckling. 'So where's my prize?'

'A dinner voucher at the club.' Emma grinned at Jeff as she sat back at the table pleased that she'd made the effort to come. Her mood had lifted in the company of her friends.

Eventually, everyone began to drift home citing the working week ahead. It was almost closing time and there was still no sign of Troy.

'Well, I'm going to pull the pin too.' Emma reached for her bag and slipped on the sandals she'd kicked off beneath the table.

Cissy stood. 'Us too. Come on, Jeffrey boy, we've both got an early start tomorrow.'

Emma was reaching for her bag when the door opened

and Troy walked in. He waved across the room and mimed getting a drink. Maybe she'd stay just a little bit longer. She put her bag back on the floor with a smile.

Cissy leaned over and gave her a quick hug. 'He's a good looker, that Troy. You going to stay a while now?'

'Yes. I want to talk to him about my frogs.

'Sure you do.' Cissy winked and nudged her with her elbow. 'See you at work.'

'You will.' Emma put a hand to her mouth. 'God, I'm not with it tonight. We haven't decided on a venue for the meeting yet.'

'I'm pretty sure everyone will know it's either here or at the sports club. Let's say the club and I'll send an email around.'

'Thanks, Cis. You're a sweetheart.'

As she watched Jeff open the door for his wife, a pair of warm hands rested on her shoulders and she turned around with a wide smile.

'Hello, sweetheart.'

Ugh. Craig.

His voice was slurred and she reached up and pushed his hands away as he leaned forward to brush his lips over her cheek. But before Emma could dodge him, she saw Troy emerge from the bar with a drink in each hand. His cold stare was fixed on Craig as he walked across to the table.

Chapter 5

Emma leaned back away from Craig's hands, and hit him with a glacial stare. 'What do you think you're doing?' she whispered.

'Just saying hello to my lady.' Craig's words were slurred and his breath was beery. His eyes narrowed as he looked up and saw Troy approaching. 'That'd be bloody right,' he muttered as he stepped back. 'I need another drink.'

'Hi Emma.' Troy put a soft drink in front of her and looked from her, and across to Craig who was lurching towards the bar, and raised his eyebrows. 'I asked Rod what you were drinking.'

'Thanks.' Emma looked down at her drink. A slight headache was niggling at her forehead.

'Craig's not a happy camper. Looks like he's got a few on board.' Troy acknowledged the glare that he was directing their way. Craig frowned at him before turning his attention to Kylie, the local vet nurse who was leaning on the bar beside him.

Just great. Could the night get any worse? Emma rubbed at her temples and the tight band eased.

'I'm pleased you're still here. I got held up at work. Thought I might have missed you.'

'I was about to leave. I've got an early start tomorrow. 'So they dressed like that in the seventies in National Parks?'

Troy looked down at his work clothes with a rueful grin. 'We did. And still the same logo too. Would you believe I had a great costume all picked out. Afro wig and all.'

Emma laughed. 'The costume comp has already been

judged. Jeff took the prize.'

Troy lowered his voice and leaned closer, his breath brushing her cheek. 'You look gorgeous tonight.'

'Thank you. I love dressing up.'

As Emma picked up her drink, Craig caught her eye again. He winked at her and made an obscene gesture with his hands, obviously meant to refer to her and Troy.

Troy moved his chair closer to hers and lowered his voice. 'Be careful with Craig. I've heard he's got a real nasty streak.'

'It's fine. I can handle myself.' Barely, she thought as she turned her back to the bar where Craig was standing.

'How are the frogs doing?' Troy put his glass down and smiled at her.

'Really good. All hatched and thriving.'

'I'll have to come over and look at your set-up.'

'It's nothing scientific.' Emma said with a smile. 'One of my neighbours built the stand for the terrarium.'

'I was going to suggest another hike. Further up Thornton Peak if you have time.'

'I'd love to.' Troy reached over and squeezed her hand and didn't let it go. 'Next weekend? I'll double-check the schedule. I don't think we've got any functions on at the centre. We could take a picnic.'

'I'd love that.'

Troy smiled and his brown eyes crinkled at the edges. His face was tanned and his sandy hair brushed his collar.

Just after nine-thirty, Rod called from the bar. 'Fifteen minutes, folks. Last drinks.' The announcement was met with a few groans. The crowd from the front bar had spilled into the beer garden and it was getting rowdy where Craig was propping up the bar. Kylie had gone home and he had joined a group of mill workers. His voice was argumentative and Emma saw Rod flick a warning glance at him.

'It was good to finally catch up. I'm going to head off now.' Emma leaned over to Troy when there was a lull in the noise.

'You're not going all the way back out to the village tonight, are you?'

Emma shook her head. 'No, I'm bunking at the clinic. I brought my work clothes with me.'

'I'll walk you across the road.'

'It's not that far.'

'In that case, I insist.'

Troy stood and waited while Emma reached down for her bag. 'All right then. Thank you. I'd like that.' She looked up as Rod called out from behind the bar. 'Phone call for you, Troy, it's the security guard at the rainforest centre.' He pointed to the phone on the wall.

'Too noisy in here.' Troy shook his head with a grimace. 'My mobile's in the car out the back. I'll go and call them. Won't be long.'

Emma shook her head. 'No, it's okay. You go. I'll see you soon.'

'That would be good. I'll call you this week.' A lazy smile lifted his lips and he reached for her hand and lifted it to his lips before he headed out to the back car park.

Emma stood and cursed beneath her breath as she tripped over the long skirt that tangled around her sandals.

'Damn.' As she righted herself, a hand grasped her arm

above her elbow.

'Looks like your new boyfriend's dumped you. Let me walk you out.' A pair of bloodshot eyes held hers as Craig held her arm in a firm grip. She'd noticed how quickly he'd been knocking back his beer. Self-disgust curled in her stomach. The sooner she got over that mistake the better.

'Thank you.' She forced a pleasant smile onto her face; he looked like he was going to insist. 'But I'm fine. I'm parked just out the front.' There was no way she was going to tell him she was staying in town tonight.

'I said I'll walk you to your car.' His voice was loud and Emma pulled away. Everyone was immersed in conversation, but she wasn't going to let him push her around.

'I said, I'm fine. Leave me be.' Emma lowered her voice and then turned her back on Craig, grabbed the front of her skirt with one hand and stepped quickly towards the front bar.

She looked around, not really expecting Jeremy to still be there. He wasn't sitting at the table where he'd been when she'd arrived. Rod was stacking glasses behind the bar as she hurried to the front door.

'Emma!' Craig was right behind her and grabbed at her arm.

She turned and spoke quietly. 'Piss off, Craig. Go back inside.'

He didn't reply but gripped her arm so tightly her skin burned.

'Did you hear me?' This time she raised her voice a little and Rod glanced over to them. He put the glasses down and watched with a frown.

'Go back inside!'

Craig ignored her and began pulling her towards the door. He was the same height as she was, but his grip was strong. She narrowed her eyes defiantly as his beery breath brushed her face.

'No need to be jealous, sweets. Kylie's got nothing on you. No decent boobs there.' He let go of one hand and tried to grope her breast.

'Take your hands off me, Craig. Now.' Emma gritted her teeth and tried to pull away but he held firm.

'Or what? You'll call the cops?' His laugh boomed around the empty room. Emma looked over his shoulder. Rod had lifted the flap at the end of the bar and was heading towards them. Before he could reach them, a familiar voice came from behind Emma.

'I believe the lady asked you to let her go.'

Craig's head flew up as Jeremy stepped towards them, took his arm and pulled him away from Emma.

'Mind your own business, mate,' Craig slurred. He swayed unsteadily. 'This is between me and my lady.'

'Wait outside, Emma. I'll deal with this.' Jeremy's voice was quiet.

Rod stepped up beside him and took Craig's other arm. 'And I'll help him. I don't care if you are the local cop, Craig. I'm in charge of this hotel and you're being a dickhead. I'll get someone to drive you home. You're in no fit state to drive.' He turned back to Emma. 'Are you going to be okay?'

Emma felt her cheeks redden. She was mortified. 'I'm fine. Thank you. I'll just go.'

Craig's slurred voice followed her as she turned away.

'Yeah. Fuck off, then. You weren't much of a screw

anyway.' His loud voice followed her as she hurried along the footpath.

***

The guy wrenched away from their hold and wove an unsteady path back to the bar.

'You fuck off too, mister.'

'I'll sort him. You go and check Emma's okay,' Rod said. He followed the guy and Jeremy stepped to the door. A glimpse of Emma's bright green skirt caught his eye as she disappeared around the corner across the road. He looked to the left and right but it appeared the cane trains didn't run this late at night. He'd listened to them come and go all afternoon as he'd settled into his room.

Lucky he'd come down to get the charger for his iPad from the rental car when he did, because the situation could have turned nasty. Jeremy had treated more than enough patients in emergency to recognise a drug-fuelled rage. That guy—policeman or not—had more than alcohol in him. He'd put money on it.

He'd seen the look on Emma's face when she'd turned away and he wanted to check she was okay. The guy was obviously a dropkick, but to speak to Emma—or to any woman— like that was disgusting. Jeremy ran across the road and turned the corner. There was no sign of her but a security light flicked on at the side of a small building with a sign at the front entrance saying ALAL. The front was lit up but he didn't stop long enough to read the rest of the sign. As he opened the gate, another security light came on at the back of the building. Emma was almost at the end of the side path that ran along the high fence line.

'Emma. Wait up.'

She stopped and turned slowly as he called. Her eyes were wide with fear.

He felt the urge to comfort her, but then he remembered this was not the Emma of his past, the woman he'd once thought he would spend the rest of his life with. This woman who was now living an alternate lifestyle, dabbling in alternate healing and—if that guy was anything to judge by—making very poor relationship choices, was not the same woman he'd been in love with. The Emma who had fled from him without an explanation.

God forbid, he hoped she wasn't into the drug scene too. Surely not.

'What?' Twin spots of colour sat high on her cheekbones but she didn't look away.

'I just wanted to check you were okay.'

'I'm fine, thank you. Totally embarrassed . . . but fine.'

'He didn't hurt you?' Jeremy took her arm gently as he caught up to her. She began to walk towards the back of the building.

'No. He didn't. I'll be fine now. I'm sorry you had to see that. Thanks for checking on me.' As she spoke, she tripped on her long skirt and Jeremy caught her arm before she fell onto the gravel path. 'God. This fucking skirt. Can this day get any worse?'

Jeremy stepped back as she looked up at him. Her hazel eyes were shimmering with unshed tears.

'I presume meeting up with me again contributed to this bad day?'

'Oh, you were just the icing on the cake.' Emma sighed,

and she was the first to drop her gaze. 'Look. I'm fine. Craig wouldn't have hurt me. He's the local policeman, for goodness sake. And just for the record, I am not his lady. Or anything else.'

The red flush on her cheeks darkened as she obviously realised that he might interpret that as a declaration of her availability. 'And I don't want to be.' She closed her eyes, embarrassed. 'Anybody's.'

He kept his voice gentle. 'Calm down, Emma. It was quite obvious that he was out of control. I've seen enough of that in emergency to know he was irrational. It wasn't your fault.'

'Thank you.' She let out a big sigh. 'Look, really I'm okay. . . but thanks for stepping in.'

'I'll walk you to your car and see you on your way. Where are you parked?'

'Down the back.' She gestured to the dark yard ahead of them. The security light further on had clicked off again. 'But I'm sleeping at the clinic tonight. I have an early start tomorrow.

'Okay. I'll see you inside and when you've locked the door, I'll go and check that everything's okay back at the pub. Doesn't hurt to take a bit of care, even if he is a cop. I'm staying upstairs so I was going back there anyway.'

'Thank you.' She dropped her head and took off ahead of him. Jeremy followed slowly, sensing that she didn't want to talk. Her cheeks were still flushed. But he wasn't going to leave until she was safe inside.

As he rounded the corner of the building, the security light came back on and Emma yelled out. 'Oh my God.

Jeremy, quick.'

Chapter 6

Emma dropped to her knees. George was lying on the path, the gravel around his head splashed liberally with dark red blood. He was cradling his right arm protectively with his left arm across his chest. She put her fingers to his neck, feeling for a pulse, was relieved to feel a strong and steady beat. His shirt was wet with blood. Now that she could see his chest rising and falling, Emma expelled the breath that she'd been holding. Focusing on sounding calm, she leaned down close to his head. 'George? George, can you hear me?'

She almost missed the muttered affirmative as Jeremy crouched beside her.

'What happened, mate?' Jeremy's voice was firm.

'I fell out of a tree.' His voice was faint. 'Who's he?' George tried to lift his head but Emma held him down gently.

'It's okay. Doctor Langford is the new doctor at the hospital.' Emma looked up at Jeremy and saw that he'd removed his shirt and was folding it into a wedge. Now he crouched back down and slid it beneath George's head.

Her mouth dried as she looked down at his bare chest. Not the time to stare at bare skin.

'Where's the blood coming from, George?' Jeremy's voice was calm as he felt around the back of George's head. 'Ah. There it is. You've got a decent gash at the bottom of your scalp.'

'I have dressing packs inside.' She focused on George as Jeremy ran his hands over him.

George tried to sit up again and this time Jeremy's hands brushed against hers as she gently pushed George back.

'Lie still till we see how badly hurt you are. Where was this tree? How did you get here?'

'Drove here. But I got a bit dizzy when I got out of the car.' He turned to Emma. 'I don't want him touching me. I want you, Doctor Em.'

Even though the light was dim, Emma saw the sceptical look Jeremy threw her way. She pushed herself to her feet but before she could speak, Jeremy's clipped voice stopped her in her tracks.

'Perhaps you'd like to slip inside and get us a dressing, Emma.' His blue eyes held hers in the dim light and she took a deep breath.

'Yeah, do something, Doc. My arm's hurting.' George's querulous voice got her moving. She fumbled for her keys and pushed open the door, flicking the second outside light on as she ran down the back hall. Quickly, she washed her hands and grabbed a dressing pack from the examination room, pulling on gloves as she hurried back outside.

George was arguing with Jeremy when she crouched down beside him. 'I ain't going to no hospital. Doctor Em can stitch me up. Here.' He shot a glance at Emma. 'You've done it plenty of times before, haven't you love?'

The waves of disapproval coming from Jeremy were palpable. Emma ripped open the gauze dressing, pushed aside the sacrificed shirt, and applied pressure to the back of George's head until the bleeding slowed.

She turned to Jeremy. 'You go and wash your hands and get some gloves on.' Pressing with gentle firmness against the old fellow's scalp, she inclined her head towards the hallway behind them. 'Grab a sling from the exam room while you're in there.'

Jeremy moved swiftly through the door and down the hall.

Emma looked down at George and bit back a gasp. In addition to the wound on his scalp, the now-bright light showed he had two black eyes and lacerations across each of his cheeks. She narrowed her eyes.

'Sorry, George. You are going to have to go across to the hospital. We'll take my car. As well as that head of yours needing stitches, you need an X-ray. I don't like the way your arm is sitting. Once we get you to the hospital, you'll need a jab of local anaesthetic and they'll clean that wound up properly.'

'Haven't you got something here to fix me up?' George shot Emma a hopeful look as she supported his head. 'And I didn't get that cocky apple bark you asked me for.'

'That doesn't matter. Let's worry about getting you sorted.' Jeremy's shadow fell across them. 'Cocky apple bark?' He looked at her with eyebrows raised. Of course, he came back in time to hear that. Emma ignored him; she didn't care what he thought. 'You keep the pressure up and I'll bandage his head.'

Jeremy refused to be dropped off at the pub on the short trip to the hospital. He sat in the back of Emma's car supporting George.

'There's no need for you to come in. There'll be a doctor on duty.'

'We'll see George in safely and then I'll make sure you get home okay again.'

George must have picked up something in his voice. 'Again? What's happened?'

'It's all right. Don't get yourself all bothered.' Emma glanced in the rear vision mirror and caught Jeremy's eye. 'Doctor Langford is from the city. He just doesn't know how safe it is up here in a small country town like Dalrymple.'

George turned his attention to Jeremy. 'So why's a city doctor bloke need to come up here? We're quite happy with Doctor Emma.'

Emma smothered a smile. 'You know we're short staffed at the hospital, George.'

A muttered humph carried across to the front of the car as she turned into Emergency.

Jeremy paused when they reached the door. Emma looked up at him and frowned. His mouth was tight and a tic pulsed in his cheek. He hesitated for a moment before he pushed open the door.

As she watched, he took a deep breath and opened the door with his free hand. Jenny Lennox was the doctor on duty and she smiled at George as they walked him in, each supporting him on one side.

'Haven't seen you in here for a while, George.' Her eyes widened as she turned to Jeremy and copped an eyeful of a bare, tanned chest.

Jeremy nodded at her and looked down ruefully at his bare chest. Then he held up his gloved hand. 'Hi, I'm Jeremy Langford. This wasn't quite how I was expecting to be introduced to the staff but my shirt was needed elsewhere. I used it for a pillow for George's head outside Emma's ... Emma's place.'

Jenny's eyes widened further when she looked up at Emma and saw her hippie costume. 'Ah, you've been at the pub. Good night?' She kept talking as she helped them lift George onto the bed in a cubicle at the far end of the emergency room.

'Fine. Good,' Emma said briskly.

'Not that I mind the sight of a male chest, but come on over and I'll give you some scrubs. Jenny laughed as she led Jeremy across the room, leaving Emma with George. 'We don't want to give the other patients the wrong idea.' Already a mother nursing a small child was throwing an interested glance their way.

'I'll see you in the morning.' Emma leaned close to George and lowered her voice. 'And then you can tell me what really happened.'

'What?' George's mouth pursed into a straight line. 'You callin' me a liar?'

'Yep. If you fell out of a tree, I'll . . .'

'You'll what?' The obstinate tone was back.

'I'll think of something.

Emma pulled the gloves off and dropped them in the yellow clinical waste bin. This skirt was going in the bin too when she got home. She'd only paid five dollars for it.

'I wanna go home.'

'Well, you can't. I'll come and see you in the morning.' Emma bit her lip as she straightened.

'We'll get you sorted soon and in a comfy bed for the night.' Jenny walked across to George who wore a face like thunder. 'See you in the morning, Emma.'

Jenny bestowed a high wattage smile on Jeremy. Even

though he was now clad in navy blue scrubs, Emma knew his bare chest would be the talk of the hospital for the next week. It didn't take much to get the gossip machine going in a small town like Dalrymple. Once Jenny told the story, the staff would be lining up to check him out. Emma let out her breath in a small huff. Typical, he hadn't even started work and he was already the hospital's pin-up boy.

'You want to walk back to the pub or would you like a lift?' She kept her eyes fixed on his face, avoiding the tanned chest that peeked out through the opening in the front of the gown. It looked like he'd been on holiday for a while if the depth of his tan was any indication. Probably on a tropical island somewhere.

'I'll come back with you and grab my shirt. When you're in safely, I'll walk back across. It's not far.' He looked down at the pale blue gown. 'Even in scrubs.'

'Right.' Emma had to hurry to keep up with him, holding the skirt up from her ankles. He took off out the door almost at a run.

They made the short drive back to her clinic in silence. Emma was worried about George. He'd got himself involved in something shady, which wasn't unusual, but it was the first time he'd been hurt. She could tell by looking at George that he'd copped a hiding from someone. She'd get to the bottom of the tree story tomorrow and if she had to involve the police, so be it.

Jeremy must have read her mind because he turned to face her as she turned the car off. 'Is George . . . shall we say . . . accident-prone?'

Emma shrugged and pulled the keys from the ignition.

'Strange to have injuries on the back of his head and his face from falling out of a tree.' Jeremy's face was in shadow and she couldn't see his expression.

'Maybe he rolled over when he fell.' She opened the door and climbed out of the car.

'So how did he get the gash on the back of his head and two black eyes? And the lacerations on his cheeks?'

'I don't know. I wasn't there.' Emma was tired and cranky and couldn't be bothered being polite. 'Thanks for looking out for me. As you can see, everything's okay. I'll see you round.'

Jeremy waited beside her as Emma put the key in the lock and stepped inside. 'Well . . . good night. I'm pleased we've caught up with each other again.'

Emma ignored the shiver that ran down her spine. The evening was cool; it was nothing to do with the familiar cadence of his deep voice.

'I look forward to catching up on that long story of yours.'

'Good night,' she said without looking at him. She closed the door softly and leaned back against it. Jeremy's footsteps faded as the loose stones on the path crunched beneath his shoes.

Oh, lord. The next few days were going to be very interesting.

DAINTREE

Chapter 7

Monday – Dalrymple

Jeremy woke just after sunrise to the sound of a beeping truck backing through the driveway of the pub. Then a loud bang sounded at the back of the building as the skip bin was emptied and he gave up the idea of going back to sleep. Rolling over onto his back, he put his arms behind his head, looking around the room. It was old but the timber above the picture rail was polished and held a rich gleam. The old chandelier that hung above the bed was a myriad of tiny crystals, and the floral curtains and plain green bedcovers were dated but homey. This room had life, and it had a history, and he was sure it would hold some stories.

His surroundings and the events since he'd arrived less than twenty-four hours ago had somehow made him feel alive. The heat was enervating and his blood thrummed through his veins and the vague, cloudy feeling that often dogged him when he first woke up was gone. Tropical North Queensland was bright and colourful, tropical flowers everywhere and pungent aromas filled the air. For a small country town, he'd sure seen some action in such a short time. And met some characters like the old guy he'd helped Emma with last night. Everyone from the barman to the housemaid in the hotel had made him feel welcome.

Except for Emma.

What letter was she talking about? He'd never got a letter from her after she'd left. And what the hell had she done with her life? From top of the fourth year in med school at Sydney uni, she'd gone and become a bloody hippie running some alternative therapy centre. What a waste it was. She would have made a wonderful doctor with her warmth and empathy, not to mention her intelligence. Jeremy had always wondered whether the pressure of university had been too much for Emma in the end and she'd burned out. He reached over to the bedside table and grabbed his phone. It was only five-thirty—way too early to go down and expect to find breakfast. His appetite was back full force and he grinned as he rolled out of bed. He doubted if there was twenty-four-hour room service at the Federal Hotel.

And he liked that. The slower pace of life was sitting comfortably with him already.

Five minutes later, Jeremy pulled on his running shoes and let himself out the back door of the old building. Even though there was no one around, it wasn't locked. Taking a deep breath, he inhaled the warm, tropical air. The smell of damp grass was fresh and overlaid by the ever-present sweet smell from the sugar mill that was already puffing white plumes of smoke onto the still morning air. When he'd run in Sydney, the traffic had been heavy in the early morning, and even on the harbour, a pall of smog was often visible. Here, the air was pure, and mist hovered over the high mountains to the west of town. He set off at a slow pace, deciding to run through the main street and check out the rest of the small town, past Emma's clinic. Small timber shops with large glass windows lined the side footpath and most of them had a tub of brightly coloured flowers against the front posts. A street sweeper cruised past and Jeremy waved back to the guy driving the large vehicle when he called out a greeting. The town was old but it was well looked after. The grass growing on the median strip was freshly mown and edged with more flowers. At the northern end of the street, he could see a large park surrounded by trees and, further in the distance, a bridge crossed the river.

He waited for the traffic to pass and glanced to the other corner to ALAL. For a moment he thought of going across and reading the sign on the window but decided against it. Emma could fill him in when they caught up.

The town was quiet, apart from the occasional semi-trailer breaking the silence as the driver hit the air brakes at the fifty-kilometre zone where the highway turned into the main street. The shops were all closed, but there was some activity at a bakery across the road. Keeping an eye out for trucks, he jogged across the highway, bent and tied his loose shoelace. He wasn't used to this humidity, and already perspiration was soaking the back of his singlet despite the early hour. As Jeremy straightened, the sound of feet thudding on the concrete footpath behind him caught his attention. He turned to see Emma jogging towards him, but her head was down and she didn't notice him until she was almost on top of him. She looked up and came to a stop.

Her expression closed as she looked back at him, and there was not a glimmer of welcome in her expression. Almost as though he was something unpleasant that she'd stepped in.

'Morning.' He kept his voice wary—she obviously wasn't happy to see him. 'You still run too, then?'

She reached up and removed the small earphones from her ears. 'Sorry. What did you say?'

'I said you still run?'

'When I can.' There was a glimpse of the Emma of old when she gave him a small smile as she caught her breath. 'I usually head north across the bridge at the creek but I came this way to pick up an apple turnover from the bakery for George on my way back.'

'I imagine he'll like that.'

His first glimpse of her without those loose hippie clothes showed a fit and toned body. Her dark hair was pulled back into a high, swishing ponytail and her cheeks were slightly pink from the exertion. There were a couple of fine lines around her eyes that hadn't been there five years ago but her skin was glowing, and she looked vital and full of life. Their birthdays were only a few days apart so he knew she was just short of her twenty-eighth birthday, but Emma looked no older than the eighteen she'd been when he'd first met her. Unlike him, she hadn't broken a sweat. The familiar lemon fragrance that she'd always favoured drifted across to him.

No matter what he'd said or done last night, everything had seemed to get her offside; he wasn't about to start another day doing the same. He looked over Emma's shoulder into the bakery and nodded. 'Can I shout you a coffee? The pub doesn't open up till seven for breakfast and there's no coffee machine in the room.'

'Welcome to Dalrymple.' But he sensed her smile was forced. 'Sorry, but no thanks. I have to be somewhere else.' Emma strode past him into the bakery.

Jeremy stood on the footpath debating whether to keep heading south or turn around. The highway to the south narrowed. By the time he decided to turn back and run towards the park he had noticed opposite the pub, Emma walked back out holding a small brown paper bag.

She placed it on the small table outside the door, put her headphones back in and gave him a quick nod before she picked up the pastry packet and loped off down the street. He stood and watched her run and the past five years disappeared in a flash.

***

Three hours later, Jeremy stood in front of the old timber wardrobe, knotting his navy-blue tie in front of the cracked oval mirror. The breakfast in the pub's dining room had been hearty and he already regretted the second cup of coffee. But it would keep him on his toes as he ventured into the hospital. He picked up his car keys and then put them down again; it was hardly worth the drive.

Flipping his suit jacket over one shoulder and picking up his briefcase, he locked the door behind him as sweet anticipation flooded through him. If all went well today, Dalrymple would be his base for at least the next year.

A new beginning. It was time to get his life in order.

Chapter 8

'You can't keep me here. I can do what I want.'

As she headed up to the first floor of the hospital, Emma could hear George complaining all the way from the stairs. She'd called into the ground floor ward and checked on her other two patients first, knowing that he would be chafing to get out of the hospital, and that she'd have to spend extra time soothing him. As much as she loved the old fellow, he could be hard work. She would have some talking to do to him to entice him to stay.

As usual, he didn't let her down. 'I'm ready to go home, now.' His wrinkled face lit up when Emma stopped in the doorway. She shot the night duty nurse a sympathetic smile.

'Right now.'

'Long night, Judy?' Emma walked over to the bed, the brown paper bag hidden behind her back.

'A very long night, Doctor Porter. Mr Clarke here has been talking about discharging himself, but he hasn't been down for his X-ray yet.'

Judy handed the observation chart to Emma, and she removed her hand from behind her back and juggled the pastry bag with the chart.

'You go and do whatever you have to. I'll see that Mr Clarke stays here at least until we get his arm sorted.'

'I'm going home.' George folded his arms and glared at them both.

The paper on the bakery bag crinkled as she flipped over the first sheet of his observation chart.

'What's in there?' Interest flared in George's expression and he sat up a bit straighter.

'In where?' She grinned at him.

'In the bag with the baker's name on it.'

'Oh this?' Emma held it up. 'I brought you an apple turnover for breakfast, but if you insist on going home, I'll take it downstairs for my morning tea.'

'All right. I guess I can stay.'

That was easier than she'd expected. Emma put the pastry on the table next to the bed and scanned down his obs. It all looked good. George's face had been washed and the wounds on his cheeks had been attended to. His arm was strapped to the front of his chest over the hospital gown. The bruises around his eyes were a deep purple.

'We'll leave it here and I'll get Rod to take you down to X-ray.' She'd seen him on her way in. Emma didn't know how he juggled the two jobs. But then, people said the same thing about her. She narrowed her eyes as she looked at George. 'And then when you come back you can tell me who hurt you.' As much as she didn't want to see Craig, as soon as she'd found out who'd hurt George, she would be down at the police station reporting it. With a bit of luck, the sergeant would be on duty instead.

George looked down as Emma kept her eyes on him. 'Will you wait with me?'

Her heart went out to him. As far as she knew he'd never married and had no one apart from a couple of neighbours in the village who looked out for him. It was the least she could do to repay the care he had shown to her and Mum since she'd bought Crooked Cottage.

She waited with George until he was taken down downstairs to X-ray although she was keen to get away from the hospital before she ran into Jeremy. Last night, she'd been looking forward to him discovering she was a doctor at the hospital and not a dropout, but she now realised that had been immature. Today all she felt was irritation that he was here to complicate her life. It would mean digging up the past, and she'd prefer to just get on with her life and not revisit those hard times.

She glanced at her watch; it was just before nine. With a bit of luck, Jeremy would still be in the nursing supervisor's office. The day registrar didn't come on duty till midday, so Greg, the senior nurse, would show Jeremy around.

She decided to stay out of sight till George got back and then go over to the clinic after that. Jeremy would be sure to hear that she was a doctor on staff and he'd have time to digest that bit of news before they met again.

What she had done with her life was no one's business but her own. It was her life, her town and she suspected he wouldn't stay here too long. If things went as she hoped and she got the job, she'd spend much of that time visiting the outlying settlements up on Cape York.

If she got the job. She also knew Jeremy's opinion on alternative therapies, so any hope she'd held of the new doctor moonlighting at her clinic had disappeared. They'd had many a fierce argument on the subject at uni and his mind had been closed. But it would be satisfying to show him some of the successes she'd had practising holistic medicine. And at least she'd be less busy now that there were three doctors at the hospital again.

'And this is the last ward. As you can see, we are a small hospital. We have less than thirty beds in the main building, but we do have an eight-bed residential aged care unit on the grounds.'

Emma drew a quick breath as Greg's voice carried up the corridor. He must have decided to take Jeremy on the whole hospital tour straight up. She hurried over to the door, her rubber-soled shoes making no sound on the faded lino. Pushing open the door she let herself out onto the wide verandah that overlooked the car park.

The verandah was deserted and Emma walked to the far end and sat on a plastic chair, waiting for them to go back downstairs. She would rather explain to Jeremy in private what she'd really been up to after she left Sydney.

'The alcohol and drug unit attached to the hospital keeps us busy. Even in a small town up here, the ice epidemic has taken hold.' Greg said. 'Although the funding gets less and less every year, we seem to have more clients to look after.'

'I know. The drug problem is widespread. Kids seem to think it's no worse than alcohol and there are nowhere near enough resources to fight it.

Emma craned forward trying to hear. She nodded as Jeremy's voice drifted out to the verandah.

'It's hard to know where to start. The police service can't cope. The best we can do is try to educate the kids about the dangers of all these so-called 'party' drugs.'

She'd never heard him speak with such passion about a cause before. She'd been the one who took on all the causes back at uni. 'So, what do you think of the place? Not too small for you, I hope?'

'I don't imagine I'll be spending much time here.'

'That's true,' Greg said.

Emma frowned. *Why not?* Maybe he didn't like what he'd seen already and was going to leave. One could only hope. He wouldn't fit into this community; it was light years away from what he was used to. Maybe he'd realised the tropics weren't all tourist resorts and cocktails. This was a hardworking town where people needed good medical facilities.

Their voices came closer and she stifled a groan as Greg's intention to show Jeremy the whole place became clear.

'The new nursing home and the respite centre are located on the hospital grounds. You can see the buildings from out here.' The door creaked as it pushed open a few metres along from her.

Emma jumped to her feet and turned to face them as Greg stepped onto the verandah, followed by a very dapper looking Jeremy.

'Ah, Emma, I was hoping we'd run into you. What are you doing out here?'

'I'm waiting for George Clarke to come back from X-ray.'

'Doctor Langford, I'd like to introduce you to Emma Porter. She'll be able to tell you a lot more about how that place works on a day to day basis.' Greg turned to Jeremy. 'Doctor Porter's one of the best, she practises holistic medicine and we've all learned a lot from her in the couple of years she's been with us.'

'Actually, it's over three years,' she said, holding Jeremy's gaze steadily.

He held out his hand and took hers in a firm clasp. He turned to Greg. 'I already had the pleasure of meeting Emma last night.' His hand was warm and his expression was unreadable. 'But she was Doctor *Emma* when we attended to George.'

Emma's hand shook as she removed it from Jeremy's

clasp.

Greg grinned. 'Most of the clinic patients call her Doctor Emma. Emma's holistic approach has been hugely successful, especially in our aged care facility. Treating the whole person, not just the symptoms of their disease has seen some rapid improvements. They all love her down there too.'

Emma folded her arms and smiled at Greg. 'It's been a team effort.'

'Yes, but you're the driving force.'

Jeremy's eyes held hers, full of questions and she looked past him back to Greg.

'You have no idea of the pleasure it gives me to meet you as *Doctor* Porter.' Greg probably wouldn't pick up his meaning, but she understood what he was saying. Greg looked at them curiously and Emma shook her head slightly before Jeremy could say any more. She didn't want their previous acquaintance to become grist for the hospital's gossip mills. She lifted her head and smiled back at him.

'It's a pleasure to have you on staff too. It's been hectic here since the locum moved on.'

'Jeremy's not working here. They still haven't filled the vacancy, so you're going to be busy for another month or so.' Greg opened the door and held it open but Emma turned to Jeremy with a frown.

'I'm confused. Why are you here then?'

'I'm helping out here for a week or so before I take up my contracted position. I've been appointed to establish an Outreach service up into Cape York.' Jeremy's quiet voice poured cold water on her dreams. 'I'll be based here at the hospital, but I expect to be on the road a lot of the time. It's only twenty-five hours a week so if there is a need here I'm happy to fill in when it suits.

'Outreach? You? Oh.' She had to say something. 'I didn't think that position had been filled yet.'

He spread his hands. 'Yep, I'm here and I'm looking forward to getting to work.'

'Good. Well, I won't take up any more of your time. You have plenty to do, I'm sure.' Emma headed for the door. 'I have to go check on George.' She tried to disguise the disappointment in her voice with a cough. There was no way he was going to find out that she'd wanted the Outreach job. That'd be right. Just waltz in with the silver spoon in your mouth and take what other people had worked their butts off for.

Jeremy and Greg followed her into the hospital corridor.

'How is George this morning? Did you find out what happened to him?' Jeremy asked.

So he was going to be persistent. It was hard to keep her voice civil.

'Not yet. I'm waiting for him to come back up from X-ray. He seems to have a bit more movement in his arm this morning. I don't think it's fractured. We all know George well, here. He's accident-prone and often very reluctant to share what actually happened to him - isn't that right, Greg?' If he thought she was trying to make him feel like the outsider, though.

'That he is. George is one of our more interesting . . . and regular patients.' Greg turned back to the door after directing a curious glance at Emma. 'Come with me, Jeremy and I'll show you where your office is.'

Jeremy nodded. 'It was a pleasure to see you again, Emma. Perhaps we can meet this afternoon and you can show me the ropes, so to speak.'

'I'm busy at my clinic this afternoon.'

Jeremy's mouth was set in a straight line and he held her gaze steadily as Greg walked towards the office at the end of the corridor. 'Another day then.' He nodded curtly.

Good, he was getting the picture.

Emma groaned and walked back out to the verandah as soon as they disappeared into the office. She slumped into the chair and let out a big sigh. Disappointment warred with anger; she'd been so hopeful of getting that position. Okay, so she didn't have years of experience under her belt, but neither did Jeremy. And he didn't know the community up here like she did. What else could he offer?

Surely she should have been notified she hadn't been successful before the new person took up the job? It must be because he'd arrived early. There'd have to be a call—or a letter—this week. She'd be interested to receive feedback about her application.

Jeremy of all people.

Nothing was fair. She should have learned by now that life wasn't fair.

By the time George came up to the ward, Emma had her emotions back under control. The happy look on his face cheered her up a little.

'So I guessing by that smile that it's not broken after all?' she said as Rod helped him from the wheelchair.

'Nope. I'm a tough old bugger.'

'An old bugger who has an awful lot of accidents.'

'So I guess you can run me home now, hey?'

'Mr Clarke had a bit of a dizzy spell down in X-ray, Doctor Porter.' Rod glanced at her as George clambered up onto the bed, his bad arm against his chest. The hospital gown flapped around his bare scrawny legs as he slid down into the bed. Emma bent over and pulled the top sheet up. Rod gave George a quick salute and left the room.

'Did you now? Hmm.' She frowned and peered into his eyes. Maybe there was some lingering concussion—the wound on his head was quite deep.

Once he was settled into the bed and the pillows had been plumped up to his satisfaction, Emma pulled up the chair next to him and passed over the paper bag. She hid a smile as he bit into the pastry and puffs of icing sugar settled on his wrinkled cheeks. 'So tell me what really happened.'

George stopped chewing and his eyes narrowed. 'I told ya. I fell out of a tree.'

'And I'm going to slip on my fairy wings and fly out the window.' Emma tapped her fingers on her arm. 'Tell me the truth, George.'

He dropped to his chin to his chest and looked at the apple turnover. 'You don't wanna know. And I don't want you to go rushing off to that wanker down at the police station telling stories. You'll end up getting me into trouble again.'

'If someone's tried to hurt you, it has to be reported.'

He wouldn't meet her eyes and he shook his head. 'No, it doesn't. It was my own silly fault and I don't want you getting involved. I just had to move a couple of things and I wasn't careful. I probably got—' He broke off and Emma waited without speaking. 'Look, I didn't see who hit me. I heard footsteps and the next thing I knew I woke up with my mug stuck in the dirt.'

Emma stood by the side of the bed and put her hands on her hips. 'So what things were you moving?' She had a fair idea.

This time George squirmed in the bed and he jutted his chin out. 'Just some things that belong to me.'

'Do you think you stepped into someone else's territory? Maybe where they had their *things*, ah . . . shall we say growing?'

'Maybe that was it.' This time his smile was crafty.

'Okay. I guess I can't make you tell me, but you can promise to stay out of trouble from now on?'

'All right. I promise. I just don't want to have the police involved. It's okay, love. I'll be more careful next time. Spit to death and hope to die '

Emma grinned; she hadn't heard that phrase since the primary school playground. She reached over and touched his hair lightly. 'I worry about you George.'

His mouth stretched in a wide grin and he lifted up the empty paper bag. 'Wouldn't happen to have another one of these, would you?'

'Don't change the subject.' His quick admission that he'd been up to something was out of character for the argumentative old sod. She had no intention of letting it go. One way or another she'd find out who the coward was who'd taken to an elderly man and left him unconscious deep in the rainforest.

'I might have a look around when I go out to Wilma's to

get the bark.' She dropped her head and lifted her stethoscope, watching him from beneath her lids.

She was taken aback by the fear that crossed his face but when she lifted her head to meet his eye, the expression had disappeared.

'No!'

'Why not?'

George ignored her question. He scrunched up the paper bag and put it down on the bed tray. 'There's no need. I'll go out again and get that bark stuff for you in a few days. The witch wasn't home.'

'George!'

'Sorry, sorry. The old woman wasn't home and I didn't go on her land like you said. I know she's your friend so I'll go back out and get your stuff and check on her. You're too busy.'

'You're going to get yourself better before you go anywhere. I've got a day off tomorrow and I'm going out to see Wilma. If she's not there, I'll go out and get it myself.'

'No! I don't want you going out there.' George's scrawny fingers circled her wrist.

'Why on earth not? Look George, if there's such a problem out there, you'd better tell me. It's unusual for Wilma not to be home.'

'Well, just go to her place, but don't go wandering around in the bush.' His eyes narrowed. 'There's a lot of snakes about, like at your place. It's not safe. It would be better if you didn't go out there at all. You know how you hate them. And I heard the old woman's got a houseful of 'em. The fellas at the pub reckon she keeps some strange pets.'

Emma sighed.

'Hmm. I've never seen any snakes out there. I think it's a bit of pub gossip.' She stood and took the bag from the tray and lobbed it into the bin beside the bed. 'I'll go and look at the X-ray and we'll see how long you have to stay. Probably just tonight if your arm's not broken.'

'The lady down there already said it ain't broke. She told me, so I can go home now.'

Emma shook her head as she tipped his head back gently and looked at his eyes again. 'Not with that dizzy head. One more night and I'll take you back tomorrow.'

'No.'

'You'll get three good meals here.'

'The food here is crap.'

And I'll bring you another pastry.' She stared him down and finally he dropped his head.

'All right. So long as you promise to take me back home tomorrow.'

'I'll call in tomorrow afternoon. Be ready. Okay?'

'I'll be ready,' he grumbled.

Emma gave him a wave and headed for the door. Snakes be damned. That was just an excuse. George wasn't hiding something. The sooner she went out to the forest to check on Wilma, the happier she would be. It was odd for her to go away and not let Emma know.

And besides, it would give her something to focus on instead of her disappointment about the Outreach job going to Jeremy.

DAINTREE

Chapter 9

Jeremy leaned back in the chair in his office—actually it was more of a cubby-hole behind the nurses' station— and stretched his arms, fighting the yawn that threatened. The starting date for the contract had been put back a week and the director had asked him if he was willing to fill in at the hospital for two weeks. If he'd known that he would have delayed his arrival. He had no choice. The hospital was understaffed and he'd already received a few heartfelt thanks from the nursing staff as he visited patients. For a rural hospital, the day had been busy and after he'd read through the emails he'd received and organised to meet with the regional director, he'd helped out in the wards. Nothing like the frenetic pace of St Vincent's. A fresh start was good but the fear of being called to the emergency ward constantly filled his thoughts. It had been hard enough being in there with George. He'd been up and down the stairs to the wards a couple of dozen times and taken a few trips over to the aged care building, but so far he'd managed to avoid the emergency ward.

There had been one bad moment when the duty doctor had asked him to collect a file from emergency on his way past. He'd stood outside for a few minutes and pretended to check his phone. Flashing blue and red lights from the ambulance bay flickered through the door as he hovered in the hall.

'Are you all right, Dr Langford?'

He'd swung around at the soft voice. Greg was standing there with a takeaway coffee in his hand looking at him curiously. He looked into the car park. There was not an ambulance in sight.

'Yes. Yes, I'm fine. Just getting used to this heat.' He nodded briskly and fled back up to the wards before sending one of the nurses back down for the file. Guilt kicked in; what if there was a fully-fledged emergency? Or worse, a drug overdose? What would he do? He felt like he was shirking work. Emergency was always the busiest part of any hospital.

'We really appreciated you pitching in this week, Dr Langford.'

He looked up. Jenny Lennox was standing in the doorway with her bag over her arm.

'Please call me Jeremy,' he said. 'No need to be formal now.'

'So you've had a good day?'

'I have.' Jeremy smiled. 'Very different to what I'm used to in Sydney but I've enjoyed every minute.' And he had. Most of it, anyway. The staff were pleasant and inclusive, the patients friendly and the hospital had been a hive of activity all day. He'd coped well apart from that damned ambulance he'd imagined.

'So where are you living?'

'I've got a room at the pub at the moment, but I'm looking for a place of my own as soon as I can.'

'To buy or rent?'

Jeremy knew she was digging to see how long he intended to stay. It was so different to the city hospitals where there was rarely time for a personal conversation.

'Not sure yet. What are the prices like around here?' He stood and followed her up the hall.

'Depends where you want to live. Houses in town are as cheap as chips, but there are some pretty swish places out towards Wonga Beach.' Jenny pulled out her keys and unlocked the door at the end of the corridor. Jeremy held it open for her as she walked through.

'Are you up here by yourself?' she probed. 'Or do you have a family to follow you up?' Jeremy didn't mind her curiosity. He'd found today that people were genuinely interested. Everyone had welcomed him warmly—except for Emma. It was a wonder he didn't have frostbite from the chilly reception he'd got there.

'No, just me.'

'I tell you what. On Friday nights, a small group of us meet for dinner at the sports club.' They walked across the car park together. 'Some of the local teachers, the vet, the new paralegal at the solicitor and the real estate agent will be there, and most of us from the hospital turn up. We call ourselves the "Young Professionals".'

'Sounds like fun.'

'We know it's a silly name but the guy that started the group way back called it that and the name's stuck. It's a bit of a hoot and we all have a good time. It's a good way to get to know the locals—a lot of us originally came from elsewhere—and a great chance to unwind at the end of the working week. And with the skills in the group, we put a lot of time into fundraising for the area.' Jenny stopped beside a small red Ford and the lights flashed as she unlocked the doors. 'And you could have a chat about houses and rentals too. But you have to be under forty to join the group. That's the *young* part.'

Jeremy laughed. 'Don't worry. I more than qualify there. I'll look forward to it.' He waited until she was in the car and then waved as she pulled out of the car park before he made his way towards the road.

A cane train was chugging slowly along beside the pub and Jeremy waited for it to pass before he crossed the road. The sweet smell of sugarcane blended with a strong peppery fragrance drifting down from a huge tree covered in large, orange flowers. As he waited, a slight breeze picked up and the petals fell to the ground, adding to the rich colourful carpet that covered the lush green grass.

He took a deep breath. Dalrymple was full of vibrant colour everywhere he looked; it gave his senses a kick-start. There was no busy surge of traffic and the pace of life was slower than he was used to in the city. Here you could take a deep breath and feel fresh clean air fill your lungs. If he had done that outside St Vincent's he would have inhaled petrol fumes from the cars roaring along Victoria Street, and the lingering smell of overfilled rubbish bins.

Contentment filled him, along with the certainty that he'd made the right decision. After one day in his new workplace, he was less stressed than he had been in a long time, even though he had no family close by and was a long way from all that was familiar. Actually, no family watching and criticising his every professional and personal move was one of the positives of getting away from Sydney.

No one here knew about his past, and he intended to keep it that way. Unless you counted Emma, but she had been long gone before the tragedy.

He lifted his gaze from the petal-covered lawn as the

last carriage of the train passed, and then looked over at the building on the corner across the road.

ALAL. Alternative Alchemy. It seemed that her passion for holistic medicine had directed her career path and she was well respected. He should have known better than to assume Emma hadn't completed her medical degree. He wondered why she'd left Sydney and where she'd finished her studies. He should have tried harder to find her when she'd left Sydney.

When he'd come back from the football trip, he'd been concerned to find her flat locked up. She wasn't in lectures and none of their friends had seen her. Jeremy's increasingly frantic calls went straight to her voicemail. He racked his brains trying to think of any contacts she had mentioned but he began to realise how little he knew about Emma's family. On the third day when she didn't show at uni and still didn't answer her phone, he'd decided to go to the police. He'd parked his car in the back of the lane at Surry Hills, checking the flat one last time. Walking around the side of the building relief flooded him when the front door opened.

But it wasn't Emma. A woman with a clipboard locked the door behind her. Jeremy hurried over.

'Excuse me.'

The woman turned with a smile. 'Yes?'

'I'm looking for Emma Porter. She lives in this flat.'

'Emma's moved out.'

'Moved out?'

'Yes. I'm the property manager for this block. I'm about to show some new tenants through.' Disbelief had slammed through him.

'Where to?'

'I'm sorry, she didn't say.''

'Do you know if she's okay?'

The woman hesitated and then smiled. He obviously looked trustworthy. 'Yes, I believe so. All she told me was that she had to go home.'

'Home?'

She didn't have a forwarding address. After a few days, anger and disappointment had kicked in. He'd listened to his mother, who suggested that the stress of study and Sydney life had become too much for Emma. She insisted that a girl of her background wasn't right for him anyway and that it was all for the best. He'd begun to believe that himself; the strength to disagree with his parents and his awareness of their prejudices had come only come with maturity.

Jeremy had tried to forget Emma but it had taken a long time before the hurt eased. Before she'd left they'd been inseparable. They'd shared common interests, both academically and in their love of sport. Emma had made him happy. She was always bright, no matter how hard she worked or how tired she was. And she worked *hard*. She was a good person and got on with everyone. He'd believed that he'd loved her.

Hell, he'd even bought a ring and had the proposal all prepared for the end of the semester. Foolishly, he'd mapped out their whole future in his head. Buy a small place and move in together. Get married when they graduated. The trust fund his grandfather had left would have seen them through university. It would have been enough to see a dozen students through.

He'd buried the hurt by convincing himself that their relationship had been less than he'd dreamed about. He'd been naive to think he knew it was more. He still had the engagement ring he'd bought for her; he kept it to remind himself to be less impulsive. He'd missed her, but he slowly realised there was life without Emma. It was hard but he'd immersed himself in his studies and surprised himself when he'd topped the year.

The door squeaked as he pushed open the door of the pub. The manager waved to him as he crossed to the stairs, and an elderly couple smiled as he passed their table.

Emma had changed.

He'd changed.

He'd made the right move coming up here, and he would make a go of it. They'd both grown up and were mature enough to start afresh as friends. He would do his best to instigate that; it didn't matter why she'd left.

Chapter 10

Thursday -Dalrymple

George's dizzy spells worsened, and much to his disgust, Emma kept him in Dalrymple Hospital for the rest of the week.

'You promised.' He shot Emma a baleful look as she checked his chart on Thursday morning.

'We're just keeping an eye on you for another couple of days,' she replied.

'Can't have you falling over again, can we, mate?' Jeremy stepped into the ward and Emma nodded.

She hung the chart back on the end of the bed. She'd come in early hoping to avoid running into Jeremy. There'd been no sign of him and he still wasn't up on the roster. She'd made it through the last two days without seeing him and had managed to put aside her disappointment at not getting the job. She'd been so busy at the clinic there'd been no time to go out to Wilma's, and although she tried to call a few times there was no answer. Last night had been taken up with the committee meeting finalising organisation for Rainbow Day. Emma had been gratified by the enthusiasm of the club members to take on jobs. She had very little to do this year, apart from doing the official thank you at the end of the day.

'Doctor Porter.' He nodded briefly and turned to George 'So they tell me you're on the mend, George? You've got a couple of good shiners there.'

Emma held the light to George's bruised eyes. She was concerned by his slow recovery. His face was pale and he winced every time he tried to move his sprained arm.

'Yes. I should be home.' He jutted his unshaven chin out as she stepped away 'I'm sick of this bloody place.'

Emma stifled a grin. 'And you can go home as soon as you can stand up without getting vertigo.' She kept her voice brisk.

'Oh la de da. Got the big words out now the other doctor's here.' George dropped his head but looked at her from the corner of his eye. Emma resisted pulling a face. She knew he was just cross about not being able to go home and trying to talk her into it.

'I'll see you this afternoon.'

'Can you get me a TV if I have to stay here. . . please?'

'I'll organise it on the way out.' Emma turned towards the door. Jeremy followed her and they stepped into the wide hallway together. He walked beside her as she headed for the stairs.

'Is there something I can help you with, Doctor?' She fought down the heat that rose up to her neck and reddened her cheeks when they reached the corridor and he put his hand on her shoulder in a friendly gesture.

'Slow down, Emma. Looks like you're so busy I need to make an appointment for us to catch up.'

'Do you think so?' Her voice was cool.

'Yes. We were friends once.' His fingers were warm against her work shirt. 'And I'd like to be friends again.

Regret filled Emma immediately at her decidedly unfriendly response. After all, Jeremy hadn't been the reason she'd left Sydney. Her father's death had been the catalyst for her sudden departure. But she would never forget his mother's words that had opened her eyes to the fact that she would never fit into his life. 'I'm sorry. That was rude of me. I'm a bit tired. And yes, you're right, I have been busy.'

He took his hand away and they walked to the nurses' station. 'So how long have you been in Dalrymple?'

'As soon as I graduated from James Cook uni. I'm surprised it's so hard to get doctors up in the Far North. They all seem to get to Cairns and stop.'

'Do you have other staff at your clinic?'

Emma swallowed a chuckle. 'I have a part-time admin assistant called Lily.' She shrugged. 'She's got a good heart, although her work ethic leaves a bit to be desired. She spends a lot of the day organising her social life.' A laugh bubbled up as she looked at him. 'But I get to work in my own place and I'll get her trained up when I have a spare minute.'

'You always had an interest in holistic medicine . . . and alternative therapies.'

Emma ignored the opening to talk about their past. 'The clinic works well. I have more time to treat the whole patient. I have longer appointments and it gets busier each week.'

'And it's just you and Lily? How do you cope with the workload?'

'We get by.' She moved away from him and changed the subject. 'Jenny tells me you're going to the YP dinner on Friday night. We can catch up there. Best I can do this week.'

'Sounds like a plan. I'll look forward to it.'

'I'll leave you to it. See you tomorrow night.' By then she would be more used to Jeremy being around. She'd asked Lily to keep the appointments clear tomorrow so she could go out to the rainforest to check up on Wilma and replenish her stocks. She was hoping to see Troy tomorrow night too. He'd rung from the centre, postponing their weekend hike due to work, but asked her to save him a seat at the club.

***

For the tenth time in as many minutes, Emma thumped her pillow and turned it over to the cool side. Flashbacks of her time in Sydney with Jeremy had been interspersed with what little sleep she'd managed. It was still before midnight when she padded barefooted to the kitchen for a glass of water. The thought of catching up with him tomorrow night filled her with trepidation. Why did he have to turn in her life again?

She told herself he wouldn't last up here. She'd seen so many doctors turn over since she'd been here. Jeremy wouldn't be any different; and as for the Outreach job, there was no way she could imagine him out in isolated clinics. He was a city boy through and through.

Whether he stayed or left, there was no way she was going to let Jeremy ruin her new life. Since the mystery of her father's death had been solved last winter and Mum had moved down to Port Douglas, Emma's life had finally settled.

'I've lived here too long, Em. It's time you had some space.' On the morning Mum moved out, she had hugged her and then pushed the hair back from Emma's face. 'You've always been the organiser and the carer. Even when you were a little girl, playing doctors with your dolls. Cooking scones and cakes for us.' Mum's eyes had brightened. 'I'm blessed with my three girls; Ellie, my little farmer, you, the nurturer and Dru . . . well, Dru will find her place one day.'

Living in her cottage and filling her days at the clinic and the hospital had given Emma a peace that neither she nor her sisters had known for a few years. The Outreach job would have made her happiness complete. Emma sat up and thumped the pillow and turned it over.

Why had she wanted it so badly? Was it the promotion that had enticed her or the acknowledgment that she was good enough?

She turned and buried her face in the pillow, letting the cool cotton soothe her heated skin. Let him have the job then. No doubt he'd charm everybody here like he'd charmed her back at university. Head to head in the university library studying together, he would lift his hand and tuck her hair behind her ear before lowering his head with a cheeky smile. She'd loved the picnics they'd had together over at North Head; they'd lain on a rug in the winter sunshine looking out over beautiful Sydney Harbour. His brother's little girl, Brianna had loved to come with them and one of her enduring memories was of Jeremy pushing her on the swing.

'Higher, higher, Uncle Jem,' she'd yell out.

They'd had their disagreements, though. When she got a higher mark than he did, he would go into a sulk and stay away from her flat for a day or two. And she'd learned that even if it was okay for him to bag out on his family, he was sensitive about his advantageous background. That was why she never told him what his mother had said to her just before she'd left. It still had the power to hurt. Her words had stayed with her for years and she was savvy enough to know that the self-doubt that plagued her then had been fed by that conversation. Mrs Langford had pulled her aside at Jeremy's birthday dinner and given her the third degree.

'What school did you attend, Emma?'

'Jabiru.'

'Is that a new Jewish private school?' The eyebrows had almost met the perfectly coiffed blonde hair. 'I haven't heard of it.'

Emma had smothered a laugh. 'No. It's a public school in the Northern Territory.'

'And what does your father do?' The plum in her voice would have been at home in a BBC period drama.

Emma refused to look away, knowing she was found wanting because she hadn't attended Abbotsleigh or Ascham. 'We have a farm.'

'Sheep?' Perhaps a wool cheque would have been acceptable to the Langford family. Some of the girls in the medical course had come from massive properties in western New South Wales, but they'd boarded at the 'acceptable' schools for at least their senior years, and were all very comfortably ensconced in Sydney society by the time university began.

'Mangoes.'

The eyebrows rose higher. 'Mangoes?'

'Yes . . . and oh, Dad sometimes works part-time at the pub in town too.' Might as well let her have it with both barrels. Stuck-up bitch. She could see where Jeremy's occasional arrogance came from.

'How nice.' The words had been ice-cold. Mrs Langford's pale blue eyes, so much like Jeremy's, had held hers steadily. She didn't need to say it; Emma knew she had been judged, found wanting and dismissed. As Mrs Langford told her, Polly was much more suitable for their family.

A few weeks after Dad's funeral Jeremy still hadn't contacted her. Emma had called Sydney one Sunday afternoon. His mother had answered the phone and when she had asked to speak to Jeremy, Mrs Langford's response had added to her certainty that Jeremy had moved on.

'Oh, I'm so sorry, Emma. He and Polly have gone away for the weekend to the south coast.'

Her voice was dull as she replied. 'Please tell him I called.'

That call had been a turning point for her and she and Dru had moved to Townsville at the start of the next semester. Mum had moved with them and stayed with their aunt.

But it was time to put those memories away.

Even though the hot nights of summer were a few weeks away, her room was stuffy and sleep eluded her; her thirst taking her to the kitchen for the third time at 4.00 am. She turned the light on, reached for a glass and headed to the stone water filter next to the sink.

As she stood at her kitchen window looking out into the dark, a bright light flashed past the window, lighting up the backyard and reflecting off the river. She narrowed her eyes, surprised to see a vehicle moving slowly along the other side of the water. The car turned into a paddock and its lights went off, plunging the landscape into darkness once more. As she watched, Bowser shot out from beneath the kitchen table and began scratching at the door. Emma crossed to the door and as soon as she opened it, the little black dog pushed past her and ran across the yard to the edge of the river, barking madly. Not wanting to draw attention to herself from whoever was parked across there—she was half-naked in her T-shirt and undies—Emma left the porch light off as she let herself outside.

She slipped on a pair of rubber thongs and walked carefully to the riverbank, where Bowser was running up and down, his loud yaps carrying across the water. Reaching down, she grabbed his collar and hissed at him.

He fought against her grip as she dragged him back to the house. 'You're so naughty. Shush,' she chastised him quietly.

There was a flash of movement to her left and a loud rustle in the grass and as she jumped back, Bowser began to bark furiously. By now Emma's eyes had adjusted to the dark, and the dark tail of a snake whipped into her vision as it headed back towards the water. Its head was raised and was moving from side to side as the long reptile moved quickly across the path between her and the house. The path she'd just walked down in a pair of thongs.

A shudder ripped through Emma and fear turned her legs to a quivering mass of jelly.

A dark brown snake.

'Bloody hell. A taipan,' she whispered. Her throat closed and she held her breath. Moving slowly, inch by inch, she leaned forwards and tightened her grip on Bowser's collar. 'Just as well neither of us stood on it, you silly pup.'

Emma stood there, measuring the distance to the back door as she tried to catch her breath. Another quick movement made her jump, but it was a small rodent running across the path near the clothesline.

The snake froze. Emma jerked at Bowser's collar as he whimpered and strained to get away from her hold.

'Be quiet.' The last thing she wanted was for the snake to change direction towards them. As she watched in the dim moonlight, the taipan raised its head and hurled itself at the rat, issuing several quick bites in succession.

Emma backed away slowly, but as she turned to flee to the house, she was suddenly bathed in bright light from the headlights of the vehicle across the river. Putting her free hand up to cover her eyes, she stopped and glanced back to make sure the snake was gone, and then took off again, dragging Bowser along behind her as he yapped in protest, his short legs dragging along the path. She flung the back door open and threw him inside ahead of her before slamming it shut behind her. Kicking off her thongs, Emma crossed to the sink and stood at the side of the window away from the bright light that shone on the house.

Her hands were shaking and she tried to grip the side of the bench but her palms were damp with perspiration. Raising one hand, she wiped the perspiration from her forehead. Her heart was thudding and she remembered George's warning about snakes being on the move early this spring. Light swept across the kitchen walls and then the house darkened as the vehicle across the river turned and moved slowly back towards the village. It was hard to see anything in the dark, but it looked like a white ute of some sort. It had been up near the old airfield. She watched as it turned away from the houses and headed along the Dalrymple road.

Emma went back to bed but there was no way she'd get

to sleep now. She wondered what someone was doing out there in the middle of the night. It was a quiet village, and she knew all of the remaining residents. Three of the houses were empty and the occupants now resided in the aged care facility at the hospital.

She finally gave up on sleep just after six and headed for the shower. She might as well have an early start out to Wilma's.

Her car was parked across the river in George's shed. Emma pulled on a sturdy pair of boots and then reached down and tucked Bowser under one arm.

'You can stay over at the village today, pup.' She didn't want to risk either of them running into that taipan again.

Chapter 11

Friday -The Daintree Rainforest

The Daintree River vehicular ferry was just heading to the dock for its first trip across the river when Emma's small sedan rounded the last bend on the southern side of the river. With George in hospital she'd ended up bringing Bowser with her; there was too much risk of him escaping from George's backyard with him not there.

'If Wilma's not home, you'll have to wait in the car.' Bowser whimpered and then curled up on the back seat, tucking his little head beneath his paws.

There was only one other vehicle ahead of Emma's in the queue and once she'd driven onto the ferry, she parked and climbed out of her car, leaning on the rail of the old barge as other vehicles drove on behind her. The sky lightened as the sun cleared the tops of the trees in the east and a shard of sunlight hit the smooth surface of the river. Morning in the Daintree was always spectacular, whatever the season. The tide was low and dozens of birds covered the mud flats as night transitioned into day. Three small crocodiles lay at the edge of the river ignoring the grey herons that pecked around them in the shallow water.

The rattle of the chain cable preceded the movement of the ferry and it glided away from the southern edge towards the middle of the river. The ferry was the sole access to Cape Tribulation and although this part of the Daintree River was wider than the narrow neck of water up at the village near

Emma's house, it was still only a five-minute trip across. She took in a deep breath of the fresh, clean air. No wonder this was such a popular tourist destination: a tropical climate, ancient vegetation, beautiful surroundings and a vast array of wildlife and birds. God, she was waxing poetic this morning. She grinned to herself as she remembered Troy's words at a talk at the Rainforest Tourist Centre when he'd taken over the management.

'"The Daintree is one of the oldest rainforests in the world and a place of exquisite beauty. It is home to some amazing natural phenomena like Hope's Cycad, a relic from the age of the dinosaurs and probably the first plant on the planet to incorporate an animal into its reproduction process. It's also home to several endangered animal species include the musky-rat kangaroo, spotted-tail quoll and the southern cassowary. As a member of the National Parks and Wildlife service, and as a someone who has come to love this special place, I am committed to ensuring this forest not only survives but thrives. We have a commitment to environmental sustainability and have many projects that will ensure that.'

His words had stayed in her mind because it echoed what Wilma had taught her over the past couple of years. Wilma's descriptions were more down to earth but she appreciated Troy's knowledge. She glanced down at her watch; she'd swing into the centre and surprise him on the way home. Maybe he could make time for a coffee. As long as she got back early enough to collect George from the hospital on the way through. She was disappointed that Troy wasn't able to make their weekend date, although to be honest, the week had been so topsy turvy she'd barely given him a thought since Sunday.

'You look like a tourist there today, Doctor Porter.' Clive, the ferryman, interrupted her thoughts as he leaned on the railing beside her. 'Day off?'

'Sort of. I'm going up to see Wilma. I'm hoping she's at home. Has she been across the ferry this week?'

Clive shook his head. 'Haven't seen her down this way for a few weeks.'

'She should be at home then.'

He headed to the front of the barge and Emma looked up as the morning lightened.

The sky deepened into a brilliant pink as the sun rose higher in the sky. It was going to be a hot day. With any luck, Wilma would have a supply of the cocky apple bark Emma needed, and she wouldn't have to go deep into the forest herself and could spend more time with Wilma. She suppressed a shiver; that taipan had really spooked her and she wasn't too keen on going into the bush today. She was happy to help Wilma out by paying cash for the bush medicines the elderly woman collected from the rainforest. As far as Emma knew Wilma relied on an old-age pension, supplemented by her treatment of the local Aboriginal community up near the cape. From what Emma could glean, many of her patients paid with homegrown vegetables and produce; Wilma seemed to live a frugal life.

She was also interested in the sandpaper fig treatment that Wilma had told her about. One of the elderly patients at the hospital had a nasty fungal infection and Emma was keen to try the leaf part of the treatment. She'd shivered when Wilma had described the next step of covering the treated area with a green ants' nest. Apparently, the stings and the formic acid from the ants made for a very effective cure. She wouldn't be implementing that side of the process on Mrs Abernethy. She grinned as Jeremy popped into her thoughts. That would certainly destroy any credibility she had gained with him. Greg had given her a good rap and she appreciated it.

Wilma had taught her about many of the plants already. When Troy had heard about her interest in bush medicine he'd had given her the new information booklet from the rainforest centre. A survey in the 1960s had listed at least 124 different species of plants in the Daintree that had been identified by Aboriginal people as having healing properties: sedatives, ointments for sores, remedies for stomach and gut complaints. Emma was fascinated to read that only one percent of rainforest plants had been scientifically studied. When Emma showed the booklet to Wilma she'd smiled approvingly. "That Troy fella's been speaking to my mob."

The ferry nudged against the ramp on the northern bank, and Emma climbed back into her car with a quick wave to Clive. She negotiated the road slowly; at this time of the morning the wildlife were on the move back into the forest, and the last thing she wanted was to hit a cassowary. Through the deep valleys, she negotiated the winding bends in the dimly-lit rainforest until the road widened and Thornton Peak loomed ahead. As always the top of the lush green mountain had a crown of clouds. The low timber bridges rumbled beneath the wheels as she crossed the occasional creeks. The arching glossy fronds of the King Ferns sprouted from the ground along the edges of the dimly-lit streams. Troy had told her they were one of the most ancient ferns in the world. They grew along most of the creeks in the rainforest needing the constant moisture to support the huge fronds.

She passed a roadwork crew as she made her way up to the Cooper Creek turnoff. Two tourist buses whizzed past, out early for the sunrise tours of the Daintree rainforest. By the time she turned onto the short track to Wilma's small property, the sun was high and the leaves were dappled with flecks of sunlight.

Emma frowned. The gate was closed and padlocked. It was the first time she'd ever seen it closed, let alone padlocked.

'You stay there.' She brushed her hand over Bowser's head and he opened one eye from where he was curled up on the back seat. Emma unwound each window a few centimetres before she opened the door. 'I won't be long.'

He tucked his head back on his paws, seemingly unconcerned that she was leaving him to snooze in the car. Checking the ground carefully before she put her feet down, she climbed out of the car and locked the door. She'd come back for Bowser once she saw if Wilma was at home, but it wasn't looking promising.

She climbed over the metal gate and followed the short track down the hill. The small yard was deserted and Wilma's car wasn't parked outside where it usually was. No smoke puffed from the chimney. Looked like she was away after all; maybe she'd gone north to Cooktown. She stood and looked from the house to the deep rainforest behind it that skirted the base of the mountain.

The rainforest was eerily quiet apart from Emma's

footsteps on the narrow path. Goose bumps rose on her arms as the damp air settled on her skin. There was not a breath of wind and the utter silence spooked her a little. Her leg muscles tightened as though she was poised to run at the first sound. She glanced back at her car parked at the top of the hill.

'Don't be stupid,' she muttered crossly. She shook her head to dispel the unsettled feeling and turned back to the car to get Bowser and her backpack. She couldn't take the dog into the bush because it was a protected World Heritage site, and it was too long to leave him in the car so she'd have to tie him up at the back of Wilma's house while she went into the rainforest.

It took an hour to walk into the grove where the cocky apple bark trees grew at the base of the mountain. The first time Wilma had brought her into this part of the rainforest— previously George had only taken her along the well-trodden creek tracks— it had been like entering a whole new world. She was humbled by Wilma's willingness to trust her and teach her aboriginal bush medicine. It had been Bill Jarragah, Dad's aboriginal offsider at their farm who had first taught Emma and her sisters about bush medicine and that had led to her decision to pursue medicine as a career.

Wilma had taken her to the grove and pointed upwards. 'I am of the Eastern *Kuku Yalanji* people and *Wundu* has a great spiritual significance to my people.'

'*Wundu*?' Emma had frowned as she looked up through the towering canopy to the misty mountain top.

'You call it Thornton's Peak.' Wilma's voice was soft. 'The track we have followed is part of a network of walking tracks that my people have walked for many years. There are two major tracks, one along the coast and one further inland which connect to all of the tracks connecting places of cultural importance and places where we can collect food and medicine.'

That day stayed in Emma's mind and had been the beginning of a respectful friendship with the elderly aboriginal healer.

Emma's sense of unease dissipated like the mist that cleared at the top of the peak as she walked along the same track. Birdlife called and small creatures rustled in the undergrowth as she passed by. She kept a close eye on the mossy track but there was not a snake to be seen. Finally, she came to the place where the cocky apple trees grew. She stepped off the track and carefully pushed aside the hanging fern that shielded the large grove. Craning her neck, she peered up at the majestic mountain, hundreds of metres above her. The ever-present clouds rose over the peak and Emma shivered as the wind picked up and a large puff of grey cloud blotted out the sun.

The cocky apple trees were grouped in a circle as though they'd been cultivated that way. The climbing fern formed a pretty curtain but the foliage had thickened in the few months since she was last here with Wilma, and Emma frowned as she pushed away the tangled wiry stems. A flash of light caught her eyes as she stepped into the clearing. A large cluster of white orchids tinged with purple nestled in a fork of the first tree. She was filled with calm as she looked around, and the disappointments of the previous days lifted along with the unease that had filled her as she'd started out.

The cloud had moved on and dappled sunlight played on the leaves of the trees as the soft breeze picked up again. The small white flowers drifted to the ground forming a pretty white carpet on the soft green grass. A small stream edged by a flat grassy bank gurgled along the base of the mountain and Emma sighed with pleasure. For a moment she wondered if she could bring Troy down here. It was a hidden grove and she had a sense from Wilma that it had a sacred meaning to her. Perhaps not. It wasn't Emma's place to show.

She slipped her backpack from her shoulders and pulled out a bottle of water. Once she'd slaked her thirst, she reached for the knife and leaned down to put the bag at the base of the tree. She frowned. There were two pieces of white plastic pipe lying in the long grass. She reached down and picked one up, looking at it curiously. It looked like a piece of the plastic pipe that led from her cottage to the rainwater tank. The only difference was that this pipe had small holes drilled in straight lines down one side.

Maybe they were part of an irrigation system? She stuffed them into her bag; whatever their purpose, they were unsightly litter in the pristine rainforest.

Emma walked to one of the smaller trees—about twice her height but well developed— and put her backpack on the ground beneath it. The spiral buds were sparse but some of them had opened. The delicate flowers were large, white and fleshy with numerous long pink and white stamens. The bark was corky beneath her fingers as she slipped the knife between the layers. She made a cut and slowly peeled the bark from the trunk in a long narrow sheet. Finally, it reached the first fork in the branches. A strange burbling noise was coming intermittently from above.

She looked up and immediately jumped back in fright as a large bird poked its head out of the fork of the tree just above her fingers and gave a raucous squawk. She dropped the knife and the bark and put her hand on her chest, sucking in her breath.

There was a hollow in the tree beneath the fork and the bird had obviously nested in it. Keeping completely still, Emma observed the bird and it looked back at her. Wilma had told her that the tree was named cocky apple because the cockatoos ate the quince-like fruit, This one was a breed she'd never seen before, a huge, dark-grey cockatoo with a mid-pink patch covering its face from its mouth to beneath its eyes. It had a distinctive crest of narrow, curved feathers like an Indian headdress, and a huge curved bill. As she watched, it stretched up and bit off a narrow stick from the end of the branch above its head. Emma held her breath as the cockatoo transferred the stick to its feet and began to beat it against the tree where her fingers had been only moments before. Loud resonant drumming filled the air. A smile crossed Emma's face. It was almost as though he was showing off, especially for her. He tipped his head to the side and made a strange sound as he beat the stick against the hollow branch.

Slowly, trying not to spook him, she inched her hand around to her back and pulled her phone from the pocket of her cargo pants. Even more carefully, she lifted it and switched the phone to video mode. As she stared back at the bird, holding the camera high, the colour of the patch on his cheek darkened and he stopped beating. Instead, he put the stick back into his mouth and bit clean through it with one bite. He continued to crunch through the stick and as it broke into smaller pieces he picked them up with his feet and dropped them one by one into the hole in the tree, without taking his eyes from her.

With a final ear-piercing squawk, the beautiful bird spread his wings and took off gracefully, soaring out of sight into the treetops. Another flash of colour came from above as another bird swooped down from the top of the tree and followed him.

'Oh wow,' she whispered as the cockatoos disappeared into the lush foliage on the side of Thornton Peak. Emma realised she had witnessed something very special. She was excited to have captured it on her phone—maybe Troy could help her identify the species.

She rolled up the long piece of bark and tied it to her backpack with the string she carried with her. The rainforest was quiet as she made her way back to Wilma's place. When she opened the gate to the cottage, there was no happy yapping to greet her. Bowser was not there.

'Oh, no.' Panic built inside her as she looked around for her little black dog. If he'd escaped and tried to follow her, she'd have no chance of finding him.

'Bowser.' Emma let out a shrill whistle but there was no answering bark as she hurried across the yard. She found his lead on the ground next to the post she'd tied him to. As she looked at the house, a curtain moved in the window by the back door.

'Over here.'

She put her hand to her chest again. The door opened a crack and Wilma peered around the door. 'Emma. Don't worry. Bowser's here. Inside with me.'

'Oh, thank goodness.' She put down the lead.

'Ssh. Hurry up, come inside. Quickly.'

Emma frowned as she crossed to the door and bent to slip her boots off. 'What's the matter?'

'Don't be silly, leave your boots on. Don't worry about them. Come inside.'

Emma followed Wilma into the house and put her backpack down on the scarred timber floor. The old woman's house was an original settler's cottage that was in need of refurbishment. . . or demolition. 'What's the matter?'

'Please tell me you haven't been down to the grove.' Wilma stood in front of her, hair tangled and clutching her hands to her frail chest as she saw the piece of bark on the backpack 'You've been to the base of *Wundu*? To the trees?'

'Why? What's the matter?'

'Oh, Emma, I've been so frightened.'

Chapter 12

Friday – Dalrymple Hospital

Jeremy came out of the meeting with the regional director of the Tropical Public Health Service with a spring in his step. The Outreach Program was full of exciting possibilities and would give him scope for expanding his administrative career in rural medicine as the clinics were established in remote locations. Previously the residents of those areas would have gone without medical assistance or had to travel long distances to Cooktown or across Cape York to Weipa.

'It's unusual to see a medical and business qualification combined. We were very pleased to receive your application. The director had held his hand out to Jeremy. 'With your experience in the city and in the outback, I am sure you will take on the added initiatives very well. It will be all administration, though. Are you happy with that?' His look was probing.

'I am. My future is in medical administration.'

As the director walked out of the office in the hospital with Jeremy, he mentioned the four-wheel-drive vehicle that was due to be delivered, for him to drive to some of the more remote locations where it was proposed to set up clinics.

'You can leave it here at the hospital if parking is an issue. How long till you move to your own place?'

'I'll start looking this week, now that everything has been finalised.' Jeremy paused as the director stood by his car and reached for his keys.

'Thank you for meeting with me today. It's a great

initiative that I'm excited to be a part of.'

'And we are very pleased to have you onboard, Dr Langford.

'There was no one in the local area that you considered?'

A frown crossed the man's smooth face. 'There was one other applicant . . .' he paused and pulled out his keys and clicked the central locking for the car.

'But?' Jeremy waited for the director to continue.

'Let's just say that up here in the north procedures can be a little unorthodox at times. It was my personal decision that the job went to a man. It can be hard going out there. But please keep this to yourself. I'd hate to be up on a sexual discrimination charge.' He paused and raised his hand.

'A word of warning. Always take care when you're out in the bush. It's still frontier country and there are some unsavoury characters involved in all sorts of things out there.'

'So being a male went in my favour?'

The director cleared his throat.' It didn't hurt. But you were the best candidate for the job.'

Jeremy held his hand out. 'Okay then. Thanks for the warning. I'm sure I can handle whatever is out there. And thank you again for travelling up to meet with me.'

The director returned his handshake with a firm grip. 'You'll do very well. I hope you stay. We could do with more of the old guard up here in the north.' With those words, the director raised a hand and his sleek sedan moved off slowly, its wheels crunching on the gravel of the hospital car park.

Jeremy turned back to the building thoughtfully.

Old guard? The last time he'd heard that phrase was in

the old boys' school network in Sydney. That was one of the reasons for leaving the city behind him. He wanted his qualifications and experience to get him the job, not his connections.

He hoped he'd misunderstood the man's meaning but a feeling of discomfort niggled at him.

***

George was sitting up in his bed in the ward upstairs and looked hopefully across to the doorway as Jeremy walked in.

'Bugger, it's you. Thought you was Doctor Em.' Jeremy had seen enough of the old man this week not to be offended by the gruff reception.

'Sorry, you'll have to put up with me instead today, George.' He flicked through the chart and shot him a conciliatory smile. Emma was well-loved up here, and he could understand why. He'd watched her interacting with patients in the wards and the aged care facility through the week. Once she'd glanced at their charts, she would spend a long time with each patient and he'd listened as she'd asked about their sleeping and eating, and talked about lifestyle changes. He was interested to see her put into practice the holistic medicine that she'd talked about at uni.

This week he'd heard about massage therapy, acupuncture, exercise classes and even a pastoral care visitor that had all been introduced to the facility under Emma's guidance.

'Treat the person. Not the illness.' He could still see her standing up in a tutorial and getting the tutor offside but she'd fought for what she believed in.

He turned back to George as the older man cleared his

throat.

'The chart all looks good. No more dizzy turns?' He leaned over and checked his eyes.

'No, and me arm's as right as rain. So when's Doctor Em coming to get me?'

'Sister said it was her day off but she's gone up north to see a patient.' Jeremy, too, was disappointed when he'd heard he wouldn't be running into Emma today. 'So I guess she may be in later this afternoon.'

George sat up straight and gripped his arm. Jeremy looked down at the spotted, wrinkled hand grasping the cuff of his long-sleeved shirt.

'Where to? She hasn't gone up into the rainforest, has she?'

'I'm sorry, I don't know.' Concern spiked through Jeremy as George shook his head from side to side. The elderly man tightened his grip on Jeremy's arm.

'I told her not to go there, but that damn woman has a mind of her own.'

'That she has,' Jeremy muttered under his breath. 'And always did.' He pulled away gently and picked up the jug on the table tray, pouring water into the plastic cup. 'Why don't you calm down and take a deep breath, and when you've had a drink, tell me what you're worried about.'

George downed the water in one gulp and then wiped his mouth with the back of his hand. 'There's things happening out there that aren't safe for no woman to be wandering around in.'

'Things like what?' Jeremy frowned as he took the empty cup, concerned to see the old man's hand shaking.

That was twice in an hour someone had referred to danger out there in the rainforest.

George looked at him intently, as though he was measuring him up. 'There's some things out in the rainforest that are worth a lot of money to the right people and they'll do anything to keep it quiet. I haven't told Emma because she'd be out there like a shot trying to put a stop to it. She thinks it's to do with my little crop but it's not.' He dropped his chin to his chest and lowered his voice to a mutter. Jeremy had to lean forward to hear the words. 'She shouldn't have gone out there. I just hope they're not out today if she's gone wandering getting that bloody bark.'

'What things are you talking about? Who would be out there?'

'I'm talking about the birds.' George shook his head. 'The bastards.'

Jeremy wrinkled his brow.' You've lost me, mate. What birds?'

'The cockatoos. They're worth a bloody fortune to collectors.'

'You mean they're being smuggled out of the rainforest?' He'd watched a program on the ABC investigating the multimillion-dollar business of wildlife smuggling not so long ago.

George looked at him as though he was stupid. 'Of course that's what I mean.'

'And that's why you were king hit the other day. You didn't really fall out of a tree, did you?'

'No, I've already told Emma that but she thinks it's about the plants.' George was getting more agitated and beginning to repeat himself.

He regarded George for another minute before trying to reassure him. 'I'm sure she'll be here soon. Don't worry. If she doesn't turn up, I'll go looking for her myself. Okay?'

'Sorry, doc, but a city slicker like you wouldn't have the faintest idea of where to go. Or what to do when you got there. If you go looking, I'll come with you.'

***

'I must have been asleep when you tied the little man up outside. I wasn't expecting you to be out here so early.' Wilma moved about the kitchen, her eyes darting to the window every few seconds. Her long white plait was almost to her knees and she was wearing a dress that looked as though it had been made from a hessian bag.

Concern filled Emma as Wilma pulled out a chair. Usually, her skin was glowing and her eyes bright, but today her eyes were dull. Emma knew she was in her seventies but it was the first time Wilma had looked her age.

Emma sat at the table sipping tea from an old chipped mug. The smell of baking pervaded the small kitchen and she nodded when Wilma offered to make a sandwich. 'Yes, please.'

'How did you bake the bread? I didn't see any smoke from your chimney earlier.' She gestured to the combustion stove sitting cold and dark in the corner of the room.

'I don't want them to know I'm here so I resorted to the electric oven.' Wilma shook her head.

'Them? Who are you talking about? Why didn't you call me if you were worried about something? It's not good for your heart condition to get yourself so het up.' Emma reached over and took Wilma's hands in hers. Her dark skin was cold to the touch, and the veins were standing out on the backs of her hands. If anything she was even thinner than when she'd last seen her. 'You sit there and I'll make us both a sandwich.'

She pushed her chair back and opened the bread tin on the bench and inhaled the smell of fresh-baked bread. 'Yum.'

'There's some corned beef on the bottom shelf of the fridge.' Wilma went to get up.

'You stay there. I'll get it. Any pickles?' Emma tried to distract Wilma from the worry that gripped her.

The sandwiches made, she put them on a plate in the middle of the table and watched with concern when Wilma shook her head. 'I'll eat later.'

Emma sat down again and regarded Wilma.

'So what's going on? What are you scared of? You look ill.'

'I'm all right. I've got my medication. ' She gestured to the box in the middle of the table.

'But are you taking it?'

'When I need to.'

Emma frowned. 'You must take it all the time. I've already told you that.'

Wilma stared over Emma's shoulder, her mouth set in a tight line.

'I thought you'd gone away. You haven't answered your phone either,' Emma said.

'The line's been down since the storm a couple of weeks ago. It was fixed this morning just before you arrived.'

'So what's been happening?'

'My snakes are gone. I got up one day last week and they were gone.'

Emma shivered. 'I didn't know you had snakes. Are you sure they just didn't get out?' She felt like lifting her feet up from the floor.

'No, they were in glass cases, and the cases were smashed. I thought I heard something through the night but I didn't get up to check.'

'Who do you think took them?'

'The only person I ever see out here is George Clarke. He wanders past regularly.'

'It wouldn't be George.'

'No, you're probably right. He's only interested in his dope plants. He came snooping around one day and I threatened to set my dog on him.'

Emma smiled. 'I didn't know you had a dog.'

'I don't.'

The atmosphere lightened and Wilma smiled.

'Have you told anyone about your snakes being taken? Called the police?' Emma reached for a sandwich.

The old woman pursed her lips. 'What good would that do? They're gone. Besides I don't have a permit to keep wildlife.' Her eyes flashed. 'As an indigenous person, I don't believe I should have to have one. This is our land and if I want to be able to care for it and the creatures that live here, I shouldn't need a piece of paper to help them when they've been injured.'

'Calm down, Wilma.' Emma put her hand on the older woman's arm. 'How many?

'Two of my taipans and my three lovely diamond

pythons. I've had the old mother python for years. She was run over on the road out there when it was still a bush track.' Her eyes shimmered with tears.

'Taipans? You had taipans? My God, Wilma, do you know how dangerous they are?'

'I'm careful. I know how to handle them, don't you worry.' She muttered under her breath. 'With a bit of luck, they'll bite whoever stole them. But at least they didn't get the others.'

'Others? You've got more?'

'Yes. Thank God, they didn't think to come into the house.'

'You have more snakes in your house?' Emma squeaked. 'Here in *this* house?

A secretive smile crossed the old woman's face. 'In the spare bedroom.'

Emma lifted her legs and crossed them on the chair beneath her. Wilma patted her arm. 'It's all right. They can't escape. They're my beauties. Come and I'll show you. I'm treating the prettiest orange-naped snake.'

'No, thank you.' Emma glanced at her watch. It was heading for mid-afternoon and she realised if she called into the Tourist Centre, it could only be a quick visit. 'I'm going to have to go. I promised George I'd collect him. Look, why don't you come back with me? I've got a spare bed at my place.'

Wilma shook her head. 'No. I'm not leaving my home. There's no one to look after my animals.'

'We'll organise someone. Just until we sort out whatever's happened here. And I'll let the police know someone broke in here.'

'Waste of time. They won't be interested.' Wilma's voice was full of steely determination. 'And I'm not going to run away like a scared old woman.' She reached down behind the floral curtain across the cupboard beneath the sink. Emma drew in her breath as Wilma swung around. In her hands was a double-barrelled shotgun.

'See, I can look after myself.'

***

Despite her best efforts, Emma couldn't convince Wilma to come back across the river with her. She was a determined woman. One thing she had agreed to do was unload the shotgun and put the shells back under the sink.

'Promise me you won't load it again. Please.'

'I'm not promising anything. I'll protect what's mine.'

'And please take your medication.' Emma touched the box of heart tablets on the table.

Wilma stood at the door as Emma crossed the yard to the locked gate.

'Thanks, Emma. You're a good woman.'

Emma lifted up Bowser and clutched him to her chest as she climbed the gate to the yard. 'Over we go, Bowser.' She turned around to wave but the door was already shut and the curtains pulled over the window. By the time she reached the next gate, it was almost four o'clock.

'Damn, too late to call in and see Troy,' she muttered under her breath. Where had this week gone? George would be giving them a hard time back at the hospital.

The dirt was loose beneath her boots as she went down the end of the dirt track to the road and she slipped, grabbing for a tree as she almost fell. She dropped Bowser's lead and he took off ahead of her as he spotted her car. The low purr of an engine came up the hill and she yelled.

'Stay. Sit.' For a change, he obeyed and sat by the car as she scrambled down the last bit of the track. Emma grabbed his collar and waited as the vehicle approached.

She was surprised to see the police logo on the side of the white Pajero. Her surprise was tempered by wariness as the car came to a stop behind hers and the door opened and Craig climbed out.

'Emma? What are you doing out here? Are you having car trouble?'

'No. I'm fine thanks, Craig. I was just visiting a patient.' Technically it was the truth.

He leaned down to pat Bowser before he stood and smiled at her. In his pressed police uniform it was hard to associate him with the drunk at the pub on Sunday night. Biting her lip, she wondered whether to share what Wilma had said with him. If there were criminals coming onto Wilma's property and stealing her property, the police ought to know. And she thought of the plastic pipes that were sitting in the bottom of her backpack. She paused; the memory of Craig's aggression still rankled.

And then Wilma's worried face came back to her, and of more concern, the loaded shotgun.

'So what are *you* doing on this track?'

'I saw your car from the main road and I came to see who it was.' Craig's eyes were level with hers. 'I'm on my way to the backpacker's hostel at Cape Trib. A couple of blokes causing a bit of trouble.'

Emma frowned. She hadn't realised that you could see where she was parked from the road.

'So who's your patient?' Craig looked around and wiped his hands on the sides of his legs. She could have sworn he was nervous about something.

'It's Wilma Randall.' She decided to trust him. 'Look, can I ask you to be discrete? I'm not making a formal report or anything.' Emma chewed on her lip, considering her words carefully. 'She's had a bit of trouble in there, but she didn't want to say anything. Can I just ask you to keep a bit of an eye out without letting her know I said anything?'

'What sort of trouble?' Craig reached into his pocket and pulled out a small notebook.

'Just some people hanging around.' Emma shook her head. 'She's a tough old bird but it seemed to rattle her.'

'Seem to be a few strangers hanging around at the moment. That's why I'm up here. Listen. Sergeant Smith's on duty at the station till six. If you have time on the way back, call in and have a word with him. I might be a while up here.'

'Well thanks, anyway. I'd better get going.'

Craig's face crinkled in a smile and he put the notebook back in his pocket. He took a deep breath and brushed a stray lock of hair back from his forehead. 'Look, I really owe you an apology. For Sunday night. I was way out of line at the pub. And I'm really sorry.'

Emma lifted her head in surprise and stared at him looking for sincerity. This was a very different Craig to the abusive drunk of the other night. 'Your behaviour was very . . . rude. To say the least. And uncalled for.'

'It was. Look. I've got a lot on my mind at the moment.

We're short-staffed . . . and my wife's moving up here.' He had the grace to look sheepish.

'I hope you've learned a lesson. Apology accepted. Just don't come near me if you're drinking.'

'I won't. If I'm back this way before dark I'll go for a bit of a wander up there—' he gestured with his head to the track leading up to Wilma's place '—but I'd better get up to Cape Trib now. Don't want them complaining that the police are slack.'

Emma lifted Bowser and put him back into the car. 'Thanks. Appreciate it.' She looked curiously at his left hand. 'What did you do to your finger?'

He glanced down at his bandaged finger and grimaced. 'Slammed it in the sliding door at the back of the station.'

'Does it need looking at?'

'No. I'll live. Just a good bruise.'

Emma climbed into the car and waved at him as she put the car into gear and backed onto the road. She was uneasy as she headed back to town. Craig's apology seemed genuine, but she still felt uneasy about him. His behaviour on Sunday had not been appropriate for someone upholding the law. Hopefully, it was just a one-off. His wife was moving to town. Maybe he'd settle down once they were back together.

With a shrug, she flicked the headlights on.

Not my problem. Outside of a professional capacity, she'd stay well clear of him in the future. And she would make time to call into the station before she saw George. She'd be much more comfortable talking to the sergeant.

DAINTREE

Chapter 13

Emma parked the car outside the small police station located in the block behind the sports club. The sun had dropped behind the mountains in the west and a cool breeze had sprung up. She took a deep breath. Even though the sky was clear there was moisture in the air, and she hoped for a shower to cool things down. The gate creaked as she pushed it open and headed for the old brick building. The light was on but she couldn't see anyone in the front office.

She waited at the counter for a moment and then pressed the buzzer. A door slammed inside the building and eventually Sergeant Smith ambled through the door.

'Doctor Porter.' The sergeant wiped the back of his hand over his mouth. She held his gaze steadily and resisted a shiver. Sergeant Smith was a most unfortunate looking man. A puffy red face, piggy-slitted eyes, and his sense of self-importance all contributed to the impression of a cartoon policeman. To top it off there was a wet food stain on the front of his shirt.

'Sorry to keep you waiting. I was having my dinner. What can I do for you?'

'I bumped into Craig Anderson out on the Cape Trib road and he suggested I come into the station.'

'What's the problem?'

'A couple of things actually.' Emma swallowed and mentally apologised to George. 'First off, I treated an assault victim at the hospital the other night and second, a patient of mine out in the forest is being harassed.'

'And you're reporting it on their behalf.' His eyes narrowed. 'Can't they come in themselves?'

'No. Both of them are ill and George Clarke is still in hospital.' Emma crossed her fingers behind her back. She wasn't going to say that neither of them wanted the incidents to be reported. She wasn't going to sit back and wait for something else to happen. She would never forgive herself.

'Hmm. George Clarke always seems to be in trouble himself. Are you sure he was assaulted?'

'Yes, I am.'

'Okay.' He pulled a small black notebook from his back pocket and flipped it open.

'Full name?'

'Who?' Emma frowned.

'Yours,' he said impatiently.

'Emma Joan Porter.'

'Address?'

'Look Sergeant, is this all necessary? I don't have much time. I've got patients waiting for me at the hospital.'

His piggy eyes narrowed but his voice was full of self-importance. 'Well, doc. Do you what to make an official report or do you just want to tell me something?'

Emma tried not to grit her teeth. 'I simply want to make you aware of a situation I'm concerned about. Both occurring on the same property a couple of days apart.'

'Okay. Where are you talking about?'

'Out Coopers Creek way. In the rainforest near Wilma Randall's.'

The Sergeant snapped his notebook shut.' So George got himself beat up. What happened to the old black woman?'

His voice was disrespectful and Emma glared at him. He turned around and looked at the television that she could see in the other room.

'Someone has been interfering with her property, and trashed her shed.'

'Okay, love. Leave it with me. Is there anything else?'

'No.' Emma's voice was clipped and she turned to the door. 'Thank you for your time.'

She walked back to the car and got her temper back under control as she drove around to the hospital. Wilma had been right. Going to the police had been a complete waste of time.

As Emma approached the upstairs ward, she could hear someone's television blaring down the corridor. It covered the sound of her footsteps, and when she arrived in the doorway, she discovered that it also covered the sound of the conversation that George and Dr Langford were having. George was waving his one good hand around as he made his point.

'I'm surprised that you let her leave Sydney. What did you do? Not treat her well or something?

Jeremy was leaning forward in the plastic guest chair beside the bed. Emma narrowed her eyes and walked over to the bed and they both looked up at her.

'Who is this 'her' you are so concerned about, George?

'You. Jeremy here told me you already know each other. Where have you been?' George scowled at her.

Emma pulled the other chair over and sat down. 'He's obviously better then.' She directed her comment to Jeremy as she threw a glacial look his way

George fixed his attention on the television and Jeremy leaned across and lowered his voice.

'Don't be too hard on him. He's been worried about you and I've been practising a bit of your holistic medicine.'

'Like what? Telling him about our past history?'

'Calm down. What's the big secret anyway? George is your friend and he's concerned about you. Now he knows that I'll be looking out for you too.'

'And why does anyone need to be looking out for me?' Emma was seething. It felt like she'd lost control of her life this week.

'Calm down. He was worried about you.' Jeremy reached over and took her hand and she stared down at his fingers for a moment before she pulled her hand away.

'Why's he worried? Because I'm a bit late?'

The smell of Jeremy's aftershave wafted over as he leaned in even closer. 'He heard—'

'Well, blow me down.' George's voice interrupted Jeremy. 'Put a lid on it, you lot.'

Emma looked up at the television as George turned the volume up. Her mouth dropped open as the newswoman's voice described the chaos on the screen.

'And in news just to hand ...'

People were running across a large room, and some were already standing on the rows of chairs lining the large space. The camera panned across to a man lifting two small children onto the counter. Emma leaned forward as she saw the flight board lit up behind them.

'That's Cairns airport,' she exclaimed.

'Ssh,' George hissed and turned the volume up as the

commentary continued.

'It is believed the snakes escaped from a suitcase as it was loaded onto the luggage conveyor belt at the check-in counter. One of the snakes, a large diamond python, has been detained by airport security, but it is believed that there are at least two more in the vicinity of the departure lounge.'

The camera switched to a reporter holding a microphone in the face of a man dressed in a suit. 'Don McKinnon is head of security at Cairns Airport. Mr McKinnon, can you please tell us of the current state of affairs.'

'We are waiting for the arrival of a snake handler to assist in the recapture. Meanwhile, all departures have been delayed while the terminal is cleared.'

The reporter held the microphone closer to the man. 'Why is such a drastic action necessary?'

The head of security loosened his collar with one finger. 'This is an extremely dangerous situation. We believe at least one of the snakes is a taipan.'

'Do you have any idea how they got into the terminal?'

The man's face closed and his stare was unwavering. 'From the luggage carousel. An investigation is underway. At the moment we are unsure whether there is more than one snake but there have been unconfirmed sightings in the terminal. We will not put passengers at risk.'

The scene cut back to the studio and the face of the newswoman now filled the screen.

'*Oxyuranus scutellatus* is a local species, known commonly as the coastal taipan. The coastal taipan is considered to be the fourth deadliest land snake in the world. While their diet normally consists of small mammals, their venom is highly toxic. It is a highly aggressive reptile and will actively defend itself when cornered. The venom of one taipan is strong enough to kill up to twelve thousand guinea pigs.'

Emma gasped and put her hand to her throat as she struggled to catch her breath. 'Oh, my God.' The memory of her close encounter with the taipan in the yard last night crossed her mind.

Jeremy's face creased with concern. 'Emma, what's wrong? You're as white as a sheet.'

'I've got to call Wilma.'

George picked up the remote and turned the television off. 'He said you went up there to see her today.' He jerked his head towards Jeremy. 'I thought I told you not to go out there.'

Emma glared at him and pursed her lips. 'And since when have you been my boss?'

George shook his head. 'I told you it's not safe. If you go again, make sure you tell me. I'll come with you.'

'Would either of you like to tell me what's going on?' Jeremy stood and pushed the chair back against the wall. 'For a start, George, you're getting too agitated . . . and . . . Em, ah, Doctor Porter . . . you look like you're about to pass out at any minute. Why do you need to call Wilma?'

Emma gestured to the now quiet television. 'I think I know where those snakes came from. But how the heck did they get to Cairns airport?'

She turned to George. 'You are going to tell me exactly how you are involved in all this.'

Chapter 14

George sat up in the bed with his arms folded across his chest. He'd refused to wear the sling any longer.

'Okay. Those guys that hit me. I think it was because they thought I saw what they were doing.'

Emma reached for the remote and switched the television off. 'What exactly were they doing?'

He shook his head. 'I didn't see them or their stash, and all I heard after he hit me was that they didn't want me to find their 'cargo'. I thought it was a funny thing to call a stash and I was too crook to go looking for it when I came to.'

'George, you've got to stop breaking the law before you really get hurt.'

'What do you call this? It hasn't been a walk in the park, let me tell you that.'

'You were right about the snakes at Wilma's house.'

George's expression was smug. 'You'll listen to me next time then.'

'Wilma said her snakes have been stolen.' She folded her arms and looked down. 'Do you think it's too much of a coincidence that all of her snakes go missing—including a taipan—and then there's a news report about snakes escaping from the luggage hold at the airport?'

'And you think there's a connection between this and the guys who attacked George?' Jeremy's voice was thoughtful.

'There has to be. And that's not all. When I was at the base of Thornton Peak today—'

'Jesus, did you go down there by yourself?' George

butted in.

Emma ignored him. 'I saw some plastic pipes near where the cockatoos' nest.'

Jeremy frowned. 'Too coincidental. I saw a program recently and it showed how they smuggle birds out to South East Asia. They use PVC pipes with air holes in them and then they X-ray the birds after they are sedated.'

'Why do they X-ray them?' George asked.

'It makes them sterile and the collectors can't breed them. There's huge penalties for smuggling Australian wildlife. It's a multibillion-dollar business.'

Indignation filled Emma. 'And not only that, it has the potential to devastate our native fauna.' She pulled out her phone. 'Look at what I saw today.'

George and Jeremy watched the performance of the cockatoo in silence.

'Amazing. First time I've ever seen that and I've lived here all my life. You were bloody lucky to see that, Doctor Em.' George's eyes were wide. The bruising had faded to yellow through the week.

'So who do we report this to?' Emma spoke her thoughts aloud.

'No one yet. You don't know who you can trust.' George was adamant. 'I've got my suspicions. Just promise you won't say anything to anyone just yet.'

'We'll talk about it tomorrow when I take you home.'

George held his arm up. 'I'm ready to go now.'

'It's too late to sort your discharge tonight and I'm going to the club for dinner; I'll be back for you first thing in the morning. I'll take you back to the village straight after

I've seen my other patients.' Emma stood by his bed with Jeremy.

'You'd better, because I'll hitch home if you break your promise.' He threw her a filthy look.

'I'll be here. I promise.' Emma touched his arm briefly before she turned away. Jeremy walked out to the corridor behind her. As soon as they were out of George's sight and earshot, he turned to look down at her.

'So what's going on? Do you think George knows something about it? He wouldn't be more involved than he's letting on, would he?'

Emma looked at him for a moment before she replied. The soft light from the corridor shadowed his face.

'Wilma was frightened. I tried to get her to come back into town but she wouldn't come with me.'

'What are you going to do? Call the police?'

'I've already been to the station and it was a waste of time.' She lowered her voice. 'I mentioned George's assault too. Wilma didn't want them involved but now there's a chance of getting them back . . .' Emma bit her lip; she really was unsure of what to do. Wilma had been adamant. 'I should let her know. She's still got a collection of snakes—' Emma gave into the shiver that ran down her back '—and if these people go looking again, I'm scared that she'll get herself into trouble.'

Jeremy's voice was low. 'Do you want me to go back out there with you tonight?'

Emma flashed him a grateful smile. 'Thanks for offering but it's too late to go back out there now. I'll give her a call.'

Jeremy waited with her at the nurses' station as she

pulled up the contacts list on her phone.

'Wilma? It's Emma.' She let out a sigh of relief as the phone picked up on the first ring. Conscious of Jeremy watching her, she turned away as she explained what she'd just seen on the television news.   'I've also mentioned it to Sergeant Smith. Informally. Just so they can keep an eye on your place.

'I don't really want anyone out here.' Wilma sounded as though she was struggling for breath. 'I don't trust them.'

'All right. But I'm coming back out again this weekend to check on you. You don't sound well.'

'I'm all right. Just angry.'

She reassured Wilma. 'Just make sure you keep your door locked. And if you are ill, you make sure you call me straight away, okay?'

'I will.'

Emma shook her head as the call was cut off, and let out a deep sigh.

'Is everything okay?

'Not really. But there's not a lot I can do tonight, is there?'

Emma froze as Jeremy reached over and touched her shoulder.

'She's not another one of your causes, is it, Em? If Wilma is a patient, you need to keep perspective.'

She stepped back as anger unfurled in her chest. 'And what exactly do you mean by that?'

He lifted his hands up. 'I don't mean anything by it. I just know how you used to take on board more than you could handle at uni.'

Her voice was deathly quiet as the anger burned bright and hot. 'More than I could handle?'

'You know what I mean. The demonstrations, the marches, "Save the whales". Remember?'

'Oh, I remember. And I guess you do too.' Her voice was quiet as she turned on him. 'Do you know how bloody selfish you sound? It looks like you're still the same. You didn't care about anything that mattered then, and you obviously still don't. Why the hell are you even here? Why couldn't you just have stayed down in Sydney?'

The tightening of his lips into a straight line should have warned her.

'So that's why you took off without a word? Because I didn't care about anything that mattered?' His eyes bored into hers. 'Not even you?'

'That's about it. As your mother so kindly told me you were much more suited to Polly. Your *new* girlfriend.'

'What? Jeremy's eyebrows lowered in a frown.

The door to the office opened and Jenny walked in.

'Thank you, Doctor Langford. That was very helpful.' Emma kept her voice calm as she reached across to the desk and picked up her car keys. 'Bye, Jenny.'

She closed the door behind her without looking back.

Chapter 15

Friday night – Dalrymple Sports Club

'Settled in? Or is it too soon to ask?' Jeff Gray, the local vet had taken the seat beside Jeremy and introduced himself. A huge T-bone steak covered in chips and gravy looked as though it was about to slide off his plate. Jeremy smiled before he answered, aware of Emma sitting across the table from them.

'It's going well. I feel like I'm home already.' Jeremy was still reeling from Emma's parting shot. He intended taking it up with her as soon as he got the opportunity. She was already sitting at the table when he finished ordering his meal and collected a beer from the bar. He lifted it to his mouth, appreciating the cool liquid as it slid down his throat.

'My wife Cissy tells me you're staying at the pub.' Jeff commented as he picked up his knife and fork.

'Cissy who works in the office at the hospital?'

Jeff nodded as she cut into his steak.' That's right. You'll soon work out all the connections. Dalrymple's a small town.'

'I will. And yes I'm bunking at the pub for a while.''

'Food's great there. I wouldn't be in a hurry to move out and batch for myself if I was you.'

'To be honest, I haven't had a chance to even think about looking at rentals.' Jeremy put his glass down and glanced over to Emma. She was deep in conversation with one of the nurses he recognised from the hospital. She laughed as he watched, and bitterness rose as he wondered why she had walked away from their conversation. He wanted to know more: what had happened to her father, and what she meant by the comment about Polly.

'When you're ready, give me a call, and I'll show you around. I know this town well.' Jeff said.

'Thanks, I'll do that. Much appreciated.'

Jeff concentrated on his meal and Jeremy looked around at the activity in the small club. He yearned for the contentment that the people around them seem to have in their lives. Laughter filled the noisy room and the atmosphere was alive. Dress ranged from the cane cutters in shorts and navy blue shirts at the far end of the bar, to the group of young girls at the table beside them, dressed to the nines in strappy dresses and high heels, as they sipped on cocktails decorated with paper umbrellas.

The bistro in the back of the small sports club was humming with the noise of Friday night patrons. An elderly woman in a white bowling uniform—hat and all—was sitting next to the door selling raffle tickets for a meat raffle, and two men in Salvation Army uniforms were moving from table to table collecting money in a wooden box. It was a completely different world to the trendy Sydney watering hole in the Rocks where he'd wound down on a Friday night when he wasn't on call at St Vincent's. When the buzzers had vibrated on the table to say meals were ready, Jeremy bit back a grin, thinking of what his mother's reaction would be if someone asked her to pick up her own meal and cutlery. He doubted if she'd ever set foot in a club like this in her life. Three long tables at been pushed together for the large group of people who made up the 'young professionals' group. A much larger crowd than he'd expected; as well as Jeff he'd already been introduced to the new solicitor and the bank manager. People were still streaming in and coming to the table after they ordered their meals.

He glanced across at Emma. She was wearing a dress and had left her hair loose and her lips were shiny with gloss. She looked preoccupied, glancing around the club for someone.

She suddenly pushed her chair back and stood. 'Troy.' Jeremy looked toward the door as she waved to a man who was at the door buying raffle tickets. 'We're over here.'

The tall, solidly built man in a khaki shirt waved back and then headed for the counter just as the policeman who'd been bothering Emma on Sunday strolled through the door. Looked like every young professional in town had turned up tonight.

Emma sat back down and looked across at Jeremy. He took the opportunity to speak to her while he could. 'I want to finish our conversation later.'

'Fine.'

Jeff turned his attention back to Jeremy before he could ask Emma when they could talk. The guy in the khaki shirt crossed to the table.

'Hi, I'm Troy Greaves.'

'Jeremy Langford.' He rose and shook Troy's hand.

'You can take over the crown as the newbie in town,' Troy said with a smile.

Jeremy sat down as Troy took the vacant seat across from him, on Emma's left. A niggle of surprise ran through him when Troy brushed his lips across her cheek. He shouldn't be surprised. Why should he assume that Emma was single?

Troy raised his beer. 'So, Jeremy, welcome to Dalrymple.'

'Thanks. How long have you been here?'

'Transferred up here a few months ago,' Troy said. 'I'm managing the Daintree Rainforest Centre for National Parks and Wildlife. Love being in the wilderness.'

'It's a great spot.'

Troy looked curiously from Emma to Jeremy. He'd obviously sensed the mood between them when he'd crossed to the table.

Cissy's interruption put paid to any further conversation. 'Jeremy, I hear you were quite a hit at the hospital last weekend. Arrived shirtless. They've already got you on the list for the fundraising calendar.'

'Completely unintentional, I can assure you. It was a medical emergency.' He grinned back at Cissy.

'What about you, Troy?' Cissy leaned forward past Emma. 'Are you in for the tug-of-war fundraiser too? We need another man for the RFS team.'

Troy shot Emma a lazy smile and Jeremy's eyes narrowed as a soft pink flush tinged her cheeks.

'But I'm not in the RFS. Does that break the rules?'

'We'll join you up. We need all the men we can get. The hospital team will probably get Jeremy so our team needs someone to match him.' Cissy's eyes lit up wickedly. 'We could make it a shirtless tug-of-war this year and take photos and sell them. Or maybe make a calendar? What do you think, Em?'

Jeremy watched as Emma glanced from him to Troy and back again. 'Anything that helps us raise money on Rainbow Day is welcome.'

'What's this Rainbow Day?' Jeremy asked. 'I've heard it mentioned a few times this week.'

'Rainbow Day raises money for Dalrymple Gorge preservation.' Emma explained. 'We work with Parks and Wildlife staff—' she turned a high wattage smile on Troy and a strange feeling settled in Jeremy's chest '—it's like a fair. 'Everyone gets involved. It starts off as a market day, and we catch all the tourists and grey nomads driving through town on Saturday morning. Stalls, jumping castles, face painting and heaps of activities. The money goes towards paths and bridges so the public can see the Gorge without damaging the environment or disturbing the habitats of the native animals.'

Jeremy took a deep breath as she bestowed the sweetest smile he'd seen on her face since he'd hit town. It hit him like a sucker punch and the funny feeling moved down into his stomach.

'You will go in the tug-of-war, won't you? You're one of the few men on the hospital staff at the moment. Well, okay, technically not the hospital, but you're with the regional health service. We won't split hairs.' She leaned back in her chair and kept her eyes on him. Jeremy knew she was flirting with him to get him to join but he didn't care. While she looked at him like that, he'd go in any event she asked him to. He remembered the team sports they had been in together at uni. They'd played volleyball in a social club and competitive hockey; he was sure she was remembering too.

'You'd better show me where to sign up.'

Emma propped her chin in her hands as she looked away from him to Troy.

'Why rainbow?' Jeremy asked.

Emma shrugged and looked to the others for help. 'I can't remember. Can anyone else?'

No one came up with an answer and Emma laughed. 'We'll have to go back through the minutes if you really want to know.

Jeremy waved his hand as she held his gaze. 'Don't worry about it. I'm sure it'll be a great day and I'd love to help out.'

'The hospital has held the tug-of-war trophy for the past three years so the pressure will be on' Cissy said with a smile as she looked from Emma to Troy.

Troy moved closer to Emma and she turned to him. It was almost as though he was putting out a challenge to Jeremy.

'And the success is more to do with Emma's organising since she arrived than any team talent,' Cissy added. 'It was all her idea and this is the third year it's run. Gets bigger and better each year.'

'When is it?' Jeremy asked.

'Next weekend, so you've got one week to train.' Cissy lifted her arm and pretended to flex her muscles.

Everyone laughed and Jeremy looked down as his buzzer vibrated on the table. When he came back with his meal, Troy and Emma had their heads close in a private conversation.

***

'So where was this exactly?' Troy had turned his full

attention to Emma; they kept their voices low as the conversation at the table washed around them. She'd given the matter of the smuggling a lot of thought when she'd left the hospital and slipped over to the clinic to get changed for dinner. Troy would be the best person to ask about her suspicion that someone was taking wildlife from the rainforest. She told him about the plastic tubes she'd found in the grove and the fact that someone had stolen the woman's snakes.

'About twelve kilometres south of Cape Tribulation. There's an old road that turns into a track that goes to the foot of Thornton Peak.'

Troy nodded and rubbed his hand over his jaw. 'I know it. We've already proposed it as one of the tracks for the new eco-walking tours from the centre. I've been out there a couple of times. So what were you doing way out there?'

'I was collecting some bark I use to make a lotion.'

Troy's brow wrinkled into a frown. 'Not from the rainforest?'

'No, a friend has a few acres that run to a grove adjacent to the national park. Don't worry, Troy. I know the rules.'

He stared at her. 'You do know what the plastic tubes are used for, don't you?'

'They're used to carry birds.'

Troy looked around before picking up their empty glasses. 'Come with me and I'll get us another drink. We'll go outside where it's private.'

Emma was aware of Jeremy's interest as she followed Troy from the bar to the wide doors that opened onto the deck overlooking the Dalrymple River. Jeremy and Troy's preening had her confused. It was almost like the mating ritual of the local riflebird, trying to catch the female's attention. Why would Jeremy even care; he hadn't wanted her in Sydney so what cause did he have to be jealous now?

Troy leaned on the railing with his back to the river. The moon was full and the moonlight reflected off the large white boulders along the edge of the slow-moving water. The lazy burbling of the creek that ran along the north side of town carried across to them.

'Can I ask you to keep something confidential, Emma?' Troy lifted her chin with his fingers and she wondered what he was about to ask.

She nodded slowly. His eyes were a deep brown and surrounded by dark eyelashes. 'Of course.'

'You've been really helpful sharing what you've seen. What I'm about to tell you is extremely sensitive and if it gets out, it could mean the end of months and months of work.'

Emma nodded again. 'Of course you can trust me.'

Troy leaned in closer and the fragrance of his aftershave wafted across; an unusual woodsy and citrus mix. For a moment, she thought he was going to kiss her and her stomach clenched in anticipation but he moved back a little as he spoke.

'I think you're right about those tubes. I know there's wildlife smuggling going on in the Daintree and it's why I asked to be transferred up here.'

'While I work at the rainforest centre I can keep an eye on what's going on and share anything important with the higher-ups at National Parks and Wildlife. Sadly, there's not enough government funding to conserve these areas to the level it needs. It's so easy for our wildlife to be smuggled out of the forest. And out of the country.'

His face was shadowed but the strong planes of his face contrasted against the light along the edge of the verandah. Emma was impressed by Troy's passion.

Emma frowned. 'It's really happening up here?'

Troy nodded. 'A lot of our wildlife goes out of Australia every year. Not just in the Daintree. All over the place. It's a huge business with links to organised crime. I'll pass on what you told me to the Parks and Wildlife guys in Cairns.'

'What will happen?'

'Just go about your business as usual, but it would be wise to stay out of the rainforest for a couple of weeks.' Troy turned and looked at the creek as it gurgled over the rocks below them, just a few metres from the back of the club. He sighed. 'Don't trust anyone. You'd be very surprised to know who's involved in this town.'

'Who?'

'I can't tell you. I don't have any proof. If even a whisper of this got out, or if someone suspected that you knew about it, it would put your life in danger. I don't want to put you in that position.'

'Seriously?'

Troy ran a hand through his short-cropped hair and the bronze-coloured ring on the middle finger of his left hand flashed in the light.

'Believe me, Emma. Don't mention it to a soul, not even your closest friends.'

'I've already been to the police station and talked to Sergeant Smith about George's assault but I didn't mention anything else. I just said that Wilma was having some issues out on her place.'

'Who's George?'

'Oh, sorry. You probably don't know him. A friend of mine was assaulted out in the rainforest last weekend. Near where I saw the plastic pipes.'

But Emma didn't mention that Jeremy, George and Wilma all knew that about the suspected smuggling.

'That's okay. I've already had a word to the sergeant myself.'

Emma didn't understand what he meant. 'But why would *I* be in danger?' she asked.

'These guys will do anything to get the wildlife. If you get in their way or see what they're doing, they'd have no hesitation in—' Troy reached down, took her hand and squeezed it. 'Look, it makes some bad people a lot of money. Up here, it's snakes and birds, and their eggs. And it's a two-way street.'

'What do you mean?'

'Wildlife out, drugs in. It's easy for them to fly the wildlife out via South East Asia on small planes. The big players bring drugs in, and ship the wildlife on the return flights.

'I saw a plane the other night,' Emma said slowly.

'You did?' Troy narrowed his eyes. 'Where?'

'A small plane landed across the river from my place.'

'Where do you live? Near this river?' Troy gestured to the water below them.

'No, my place is upstream, across from the Daintree Village. The old airfield is about half a kilometre west of the village.

Troy turned to face her and his eyes lit up with excitement. 'The national parks guys said they suspected a plane was coming in but they were looking further north. Their information source has disappeared. I'll let them know.'

Emma swallowed and widened her eyes. 'Disappeared?'

'I told you it was a dangerous business. What did you see?'

'It was dark. All I saw was a white ute and a couple of figures.'

'Did you mention that to the police?'

'No.' Emma bit her lip. 'I didn't know it was suspicious.'

'Tell me more about your friend who lost her snakes. Do you know if she has a permit?'

'She's aboriginal. Does she need one?'

'No,' he said slowly. 'Does she have anything else there?

Emma hesitated. She didn't want to get Wilma into trouble. 'She's a harmless old lady who keeps pets for company.'

'Emma, don't be naive. For all you know she could be collecting them for smuggling.'

She pursed her lips. 'No chance of that. Wilma has an affinity with the land. She's proud of being an Eastern *Kuku Yalanji* woman and she would never do anything to hurt the environment.'

'Okay, I'll trust you on that. Back to what you actually saw. So you only saw some tubes on the ground? No sign of any birds or eggs?'

'Oh yes, I saw the most amazing bird. He put on a performance for me.'

Troy regarded her intently. 'A performance? What sort of bird?'

Emma described how the cockatoo had drummed on the tree.

His eyes narrowed. 'Did it have dark pink patches on its cheeks?'

'I can show you. She lifted her phone and played the video for the second time that night.

Troy watched in silence and Emma took the opportunity to study his face in the moonlight. His features were strong and his lips were full. The video finished and she turned the phone off.

'That was amazing.' Troy was almost dancing around with suppressed excitement. 'That's a palm cockatoo. They've never been seen this far south.' He turned away and murmured, 'Bugger.'

Emma waited as he stared over the water, deep in thought. Finally, she asked, 'What's wrong?'

'If there are palm cockatoos breeding there, we need to keep the tourists away to give the colony a chance to build up. We'll have to find another track for the rainforest walk. Shouldn't be too hard.'

He glanced down at his watch and then inside. 'I've got to go, Emma.' He put his finger to his lips. 'And please remember what I said. Not a word. Not to anyone else. I'll go and see the Sarge again and tell him to keep really quiet on any investigating they might do.'

Emma nodded and then followed him back inside and

went back to the table as Troy headed for the door. It was as though he'd forgotten all about her. The brief dismissal rankled a bit.

'Everything okay?' Jeremy watched curiously as Troy pushed open the door.

'Yes. Troy had to go back to work.'

'Do you want to go somewhere for a coffee? I'd like to finish our conversation'

Emma laughed. 'You're not in Sydney anymore, Jeremy. The only place you'll get coffee at nine o'clock on a Friday night in this town is from that urn over there.' But he was right. It was time to put the past to rest.

'Neither of us are working tomorrow. I'll come into town. I have to pick George up anyway.'

'Before you go, can I ask you something personal?' Jeremy leaned close and she jumped as his arm brushed against hers. 'Are you and Troy a couple?'

She lifted her face to him, a strange emotion running through her. One she couldn't put a name to.

'No, we're not.'

DAINTREE

Chapter 16

Saturday morning- Daintree Village

For the second weekend running, Emma had an early visitor to her house. Her night had been disturbed by dreams of snakes and birds, and as soon as she woke she headed for a hot shower. She slipped on a light cheesecloth dress and left her hair loose to dry. Bowser was scratching at the back door and Emma rolled her eyes.

'At this rate, I'm going to need a new back door.' The timber was chipped where he'd been scratching away, but there was no way she was going to let him out during the night. She opened the door and he shot out. Leaving the door ajar, she crossed to the sink and yawned as she filled the kettle, and switched the gas hob on.

As she waited for the water to boil, Bowser started yapping outside. She hurried across to the door. 'No more snakes, please.' She'd had enough reptiles this week to do her for a lifetime.

But it wasn't another snake. Jeremy was pulling the punt up to the post, and as she watched he looped the rope over to it. She wasn't sure if she was pleased to see him or not. Brushing her fingers through her damp hair, she crossed the yard and stood by the back gate.

'Interesting place to live.' He turned a high wattage smile to her. 'But then you never did things by halves. And I mean that in a nice way so please don't go getting cross at me again.'

'What are you doing here, Jeremy? I thought we were

going to meet in town. How did you know where to find me?'

She'd got used to seeing him at the hospital over the past week but she was still assailed by conflicting emotions every time she saw him. Once they got the past out of the way, it would be easier.

Or so she hoped.

She followed Jeremy's movement as he turned and waved. George was standing over on the other side of the river. He waved back and climbed into this ute and soon it was chugging up the slight hill to the village.

'Ah. So George told you how to find me.'

Jeremy's grin was wide. 'In exchange for discharging him.'

'I suppose it saves me a trip into town,' she conceded, folding her arms. 'So here you are.'

'Are you going to invite me in?'

She shrugged and led him inside as Bowser jumped around his legs asking for a pat.

Traitor.

Jeremy reached down and scratched the dog's ears. 'Nice little cottage.'

Emma watched Jeremy look around. His arms were loose by his side and his stance was relaxed.

'I wouldn't mind something like this myself.' He turned to face her. 'I'm looking for a place at the moment.'

'You wouldn't last a week here. A dicky water pump. A gas stove and hot water that are both very temperamental.' Emma folded her arms and observed him. 'It's not *your* style at all. You need to be looking out Wonga Beach way.

Jeremy's smile faded. 'And what would you know about

my style, Emma?'

She tilted her head to the side and looked at his immaculate clothes, running her gaze down from his perfectly pressed T-shirt, his designer label jeans and his perfectly polished boots.

'I saw where you grew up.' She managed to keep the bitterness from her voice. She'd come to believe that Jeremy must have been pleased to see her go; her leaving had been an easy out for him and she was sure that was why he'd never answered her letter. She'd put it on paper—email and text were too casual for what she wanted to tell him. She'd poured her heart out to him, spoken of the grief of losing her father, and even though she knew that they wouldn't be a couple anymore—she wished him happiness with Polly— she'd promised to let him know her contact details when she got settled in Townsville. It would have been nice to remain friends.

He'd never replied so she had known exactly where she stood, and it had broken her heart. His mother had been telling the truth. Polly was on the scene and Emma leaving town was a convenient out for Jeremy. Not even one word of sympathy about her father's death. No wishing her luck at the new university. At that time, she'd decided he was as cold as his mother, and that the Jeremy from the days and nights in her little flat in Surry Hills must have been a dream she had created in her heart.

Their relationship would never have lasted. His mother had been right; Emma's world was a long way from Jeremy's. And that's why she couldn't understand what he was doing up here in a little town like Dalrymple, so far from where he belonged.

The room hummed with tension.

'I grew up how and where I did because of the family I was born into. It doesn't necessarily mean that I belonged there. Or that I was happy there.'

Emma stared at him. 'Look at yourself, Jeremy.'

His eyebrows lowered and his forehead wrinkled in a frown. 'You think the way I look tells you what sort of person I am? I thought you of all people knew me better than that, Em.'

'Of course it does. You're good-looking, you wear the best clothes, confidence oozes out of you. I was never good enough for you or your family.' She couldn't help the catch in her voice. How had their conversation got so serious this quickly?

'Maybe I wasn't good enough for *you*. Your causes seemed to be taking up most of your time before *you* left *me*.' He leaned back against the doorframe and folded his arms as he stared back. It was hard to read the expression on his face. 'You don't know me now and you obviously never did. I loved you and you walked away.'

'You were happy to see me go! It saved you the trouble.' Her voice rose and she stabbed her finger in the air towards him. The tension ramped up and Bowser slid beneath the table.

'How the hell can you say I was glad to see you go? You broke my bloody heart.' He took another step towards her. Emma could swear she could feel the warmth radiating off his skin.

'Don't lie to me. There's nothing to be gained.' Emma's

voice roughened and she rubbed at her eyes, angry that he could bring her to this state. From a casual visit to a full-blown argument in less than three minutes; that had to be a record. But she shook her head. They'd argued in Sydney but at least they'd always been honest with each other. Now his words were slicing her heart open all over again.

'I'm not lying. One day you were there and we were happy, and then I came back from that football trip and you were gone. Without a word. Not one fucking word.' Jeremy ran his hand through his hair. 'I left dozens of messages on your phone before I realised you weren't going to answer me.'

Emma lowered her head. She didn't trust herself to look at him.

'I lost my phone on the plane. There was so much happening, I didn't ever bother chasing it up.' Her voice was low and as full of emotion as his.

'What was I to think? And what do you mean there was so much happening?' Emma lifted her head as Jeremy grasped her hands with his. 'That stuff about Polly, that's absolute bullshit. We only got together a couple of years ago, and it wasn't real anyway. Not like you and me. If you were struggling with uni I could have helped. Or was it just Sydney? Or was it me?' He pulled away and ran his hand through his short hair in frustration. 'Christ, Emma, I had no idea you were having trouble.'

'Trouble? You thought it was about university?'

'What else was I to think?'

'I wrote to you.'

'An email?'

'No, a real letter. You know. On paper. In an envelope and with a stamp. When you didn't answer, I knew where I stood.'

His eyes narrowed. 'You sent it to my home address?'

'Of course. Where else would I have sent it?'

Jeremy took another step closer. This time, his sleeve brushed her arm and she caught the smell of his aftershave. Despite the heat of the room, goose bumps rose on her skin.

'I never got a letter from you, Emma.' His voice was low.

He really didn't know? Was he telling the truth? Could she trust him? A small tendril of hope unfurled in her chest but she pushed it down. Even if he was telling the truth, it wouldn't make any difference. He hadn't been a part of her life for a long time. You couldn't recapture the past; they'd both moved on. But knowing that it hadn't been deliberate made it easier to bear.

Emma ignored the shaky feeling in her knees and the warmth pooling low in her belly. 'The day you left for that football trip I got a call.' His blue eyes held hers. 'From home. I had no choice. My father died suddenly. I had to go home.'

'Oh, Em.' His expression softened and he took a step towards her. 'I'm so sorry.'

Emma took a deep breath. Her nerve endings skittered wildly as he stood close to her.

His voice was low and charged with emotion. 'I didn't know. Do you believe me?'

Emma pulled back and looked up at his blue eyes, no longer cold but filled with intensity. A fierce expression crossed his face.

'I need to know you believe me, Emma.' He ran his hand through his hair. 'Christ, what sort of a low life would that make me be if I'd known and not contacted you?'

'Yes. Yes, I do. It must have gone astray.' She nodded. 'I couldn't believe it when you didn't reply.' She turned sad eyes to him. 'But then all I could think was what your mother said.'

'What did she say?'

'That I didn't fit into your world. And the day I rang—'

'When did you ring? After you left?'

'Yes. A few days later.' Her voice firmed. 'She told me you and Polly were away together on the south coast and I knew you'd moved on.'

'She never told me you called. God, I can't believe it.'

'I asked her to tell you I called.'

'She never told me. And just to make it clear. I wasn't with Polly.' He shook his head. 'God, I'm so sorry. I can't believe it. Surely you know I would have come to you if I'd known. I would have been there for you.' Jeremy dropped his head and rested his forehead against hers. 'Tell me what happened.'

'It's a long story and it was a dreadful time for our family. Mum's been struggling for years and she's only recently starting to come through it.' He reached out and took her hand gently. As she looked down at his fingers, he lifted the other hand and cupped her cheek. She turned her face into his palm and closed her eyes, taking comfort from his touch. His hands were smooth and the fresh, clean smell of his skin overwhelmed her. The touch of another person was rare.

'You were away and Mum needed me.' Her voice broke

as the memory of that horrible day filled her. 'My sisters needed me. Dru had to deal with it by herself until Ellie and I got home. She was so strong.'

'And you never came back? You didn't ever want to come back?'

'Mum couldn't afford for me to go back to Sydney.'

The need to keep her distance disappeared as instinct kicked in. Five years away didn't matter anymore. Emma leaned into him and put her arms around his waist, resting her face against his chest. The beat of Jeremy's heart against her skin took her back to the days when he had loved her. The times he had held her like this, and the days when he had been there for her. The days when Jeremy had been the most important thing in her life.

Neither of them spoke for a full minute. The emotions surging through her were overwhelming. Confusion, happiness, doubt. Emma blinked and fought back the ache building behind her eyes. The contact was elemental. Memories flooded her mind and echoes of the love she'd once had for this man resonated through her.

But she shouldn't be feeling this way. That was in the past now. Sense won out and she took a step back.

Jeremy reached out a hand to her but she didn't take it.

'Oh no, you don't. I can see you over thinking like you always did,' he said. 'Stop it, Emma. Remember. Remember what we had. It was special.' He stood beside her and his scent was so familiar and comforting she was tempted to lean into him again.

'It was, Jeremy. It *was* special and it was a great time.' Her voice was sad. 'But you know we wouldn't have lasted, even without all of this. We're too different, our backgrounds, our beliefs, the way we see things. We would have parted eventually. Maybe at uni. Maybe later. We can't go back.' Her voice was sad, and a feeling of heaviness settled in her chest.

'No, Em, you're wrong.'

She ignored the disappointment in his voice. 'Why are you here, Jeremy? Why did you leave Sydney?'

Chapter 17

'I guess I'm looking for happiness. A cliché, I know, and I probably sound ungrateful, given how easy I had it.' Jeremy looked at Emma, drinking in the beauty of a face as familiar to him as his own. 'But I wasn't happy in Sydney. 'The social merry-go-round, the expectations, living up to the image. It wasn't for me. It was artificial and I was over it.'

He looked down at the little dog as he whimpered for attention. Leaning down Jeremy focused on rubbing the sleek black coat.

'After uni I worked for two years in emergency in St Vincent's then I went back to study last year. Did an MBA.'

'I'm pleased to hear that. I'm still surprised that you left Sydney.'

Teacups clattered as she put them on the table in front of him.

'Do you remember what they used to call Kings Cross?'

Emma nodded and pulled out a chair. 'The naughty patch. I did a short placement at St Vincent's in second year, remember?'

'I'd forgotten.'

'Two years is a long time to work at that pace.'

'I loved it at first. Stab wounds, gunshot injuries, alcohol-fuelled head traumas, drug overdoses, car crash casualties, and that was just a normal night. It was totally unpredictable.' He dropped his head into his hands for a moment. 'But after a while it lost its appeal. I guess I burned out and when there was a situation ... I ... realised I couldn't do it forever.'

'So here you are,' she said slowly.

'That's why I took the job way up here. A new direction. A new start.' He lifted his head. A small frown etched two small lines into her brow. 'And so far it's been everything I'd hoped for. Watching the way you guys work up here and comparing it to how we worked at St Vincent's —dealing with the immediate problem, never really connecting with the patient—well, it's motivated me.'

'So you're beginning to understand holistic medicine.' Emma's chair scraped back as she stood again. She poured hot water in to warm the pretty blue and white teapot.

'I guess I am. I know I'll be learning a lot from how you work at the hospital. And I'm excited about the Outreach work.'

Emma set the pot down in the middle of the table.

'Still a collector of bits and pieces, I see, Em?'

She smiled. 'Visitors get the fancy one. George and I use the old battered one over there. Still milk with two sugars?'

'Yes please.' He picked up a bark arrangement from the middle of the table and held it up to the light. Shades of colour from deep brown to a pale pink caught the light as he slowly turned it. Emma sat at the table and poured his tea and added the milk and sugar, just like she always had.

He lifted the cup and sipped the steaming liquid as an awkward silence settled between them. The kitchen was quiet apart from the ticking of a large old fashioned clock on the wall and the occasional snuffling of the little black dog that had gone to sleep on his feet.

'Em—'

'Jem—'

'You go first.' Her wide hazel eyes were full of life but despite the laugh her voice was hesitant.

'I just want to say how sorry I am to hear about your father.' He wouldn't share that he'd been envious of her family. Not that he'd ever met them, but he'd seen enough photos and overheard enough Sunday night phone calls to know that there was a lot of love there. 'What happened? A farm accident?'

He was surprised by the expression of raw grief that crossed her face.

'Dad was murdered. We only found that out this year.'

'Murdered? Jesus, Emma! What happened?'

'For a long time we thought he'd killed himself and it was hard to deal with. Mum would never accept that he'd suicided and she had all these conspiracy theories.' Emma took a deep breath. 'Ellie did some digging, and it turned out Mum was right all along. It was a guy who wanted Dad's land and he wouldn't sell.'

'It must have been horrible for you all to deal with.'

'It was. It's impacted on a lot of decisions each of us has made since then.' She put one hand to her lips looking to the window.

'Did your Mum keep the farm?'

He'd heard all about the mango farm where she'd grown up and how she and her younger sister couldn't wait to get away to the city when they were in their teens. Her childhood running wild in the outback had sounded idyllic. His had been so structured: the private schools, the piano lessons, the rugby coaching and rowing lessons.

Her face lit up in a smile and his heart beat a little faster. 'Ellie lives there now. She and her partner, Kane, have resurrected the mango farm and from all accounts, it's going well. They're getting married soon, and Dru will be home from Dubai for the wedding. I'm so looking forward to seeing them.'

'Dubai?'

'Yes, Dru lived with me in Townsville while I finished my medical degree at James Cook and she studied civil engineering. Just after I moved up here, she got offered a fabulous job in the Emirates. Anyway, that's enough about me.' Emma took a sip of tea 'Tell me about your new job.'

'I start officially on Monday. The four-wheel drive's on the way, and I'll be heading off to scout out some locations for clinics pretty much straight away.'

Emma's voice was dry. 'That's going to be hard, not having any local knowledge.'

'A lot of the preliminary work has been done for me. I've been reading up all week.'

'A big challenge going cold into an area you don't know.' Emma stared at him for a moment before she spoke. 'I want you to know I applied for the position too.'

'You did?' Surprise laced his voice. 'I thought you were settled into your clinic.'

'I am. I didn't think it through. To be honest, I think it was more about proving to myself that I was good enough to get it.'

Her eyes clouded. 'You are, Emma. And you know the

community so well. Did you get to interview?'

'I did. I'm still waiting for the feedback. I got a letter this week telling me I'd been unsuccessful. You know, if I'd been got it I think it would have been the wrong direction for me. I have enough patients here in town between the hospital and the clinic. And it would have meant a lot of time on the road, and I realise now that it is very much an administrative role and I hate that side of things.'

Jeremy remembered the conversation with the regional director and his stomach dropped. *Let's just say that up here in the north procedures can be a little unorthodox at times. It was my personal decision that the job went to a man.'*

Should he be honest or let it go? What would be achieved by telling Emma what had been said? And the director had asked him not to say anything. He felt guilty not telling her but he would leave it for the time being. Things were just settling between them and he didn't want to jeopardise the fragility of that.

'I'd be interested to hear what feedback you get,' he said carefully. 'And Emma, I have no doubt that you are more than good enough to take on anything you wanted to. And be great at it.'

'Thank you.' Her smile was genuine and another jolt of warmth hit his chest.

'So . . . where to now?' He stumbled over the words and cleared his throat.

'What do you mean?' Her brow wrinkled in a frown.

'Do you think we could be friends?'

'I guess so. We can try.'

'Can a friend ask if you and Troy are, you know. . .?'

He cut straight to the chase.

'I don't know. Maybe.' Emma stood up suddenly and the little dog shot out from beneath the table and began yapping.

He knew that she had retreated back into her shell. Jeremy took a deep breath, pushing away the disappointment.

We can't go back, she'd said.

He'd be seeing about that. But he'd take it slow. He knew Emma hated losing control and if she had an inkling of his intentions, she'd run. He'd settle into this town and into her life and see what happened.

Troy could go take a flying leap.

Jeremy stood and walked across with his cup, cursing himself for changing the mood. He tipped the remainder of the tea out and rinsed the cup. What had he expected? Sort out the past and she would jump back into his arms?

Emma let out a sigh as he kept his eyes on her. The window was open and the soft breeze lifted tendrils of hair around her face. His fingers itched to reach over and brush them back but he had no right. Her face softened as she looked away.

'I've got to go out today, so how are you getting back to Dalrymple?'

Leaning against the door frame, Jeremy relaxed and crossed his arms. 'You want the bad news?'

She frowned. 'What?'

'George said you'd drive me back to town. We collected his car from town so I need a lift. He drove me here and now he's gone bush for the day.'

'I should make you walk back.' Emma's laugh warmed his heart.

DAINTREE

Chapter 18

Daintree Rainforest

'It's beautiful up here.' Jeremy's arms rested on the roof of Emma's car as the vehicular ferry made its way across the Daintree River. She ignored the sculpted muscles that flexed beneath his T-shirt. On the way back to town, Jeremy had persuaded her to let him come along for the drive up to Wilma's place.

'Makes more sense than taking me south to town. Besides, I'll be company for you.'

'I suppose it does make sense. It's quite a long drive, though,' she said as they approached the T-intersection.

'I've got all day,' he said with a grin. 'Not a lot to do in my room at the pub.' If the truth be known, she appreciated having him with her. Troy's warning at the club last night had spooked her and knowing that there was a possibility of running into someone in the bush, the presence of a six-foot two male made her feel safer.

'And it'll be a good way for you to see where you'll be spending a lot of your time once you get on the road next week. She turned and pointed to the other side of the river. 'You'll get to know the road north very well. There'll be a lot of travel up to the Cape for you.'

Jeremy's smile widened and his teeth flashed white in the mid-morning sunshine. 'I'm looking forward to it.'

Emma took in the quiet serenity of the river. The sun was high in the sky and an early breeze had come up. Small waves kicked in the water as the outgoing tide pushed against the easterly wind. The ferry was full this morning as tourists and weekend travellers made their way north to Cape Tribulation.

'Isn't it a beautiful place?' she said.

'It's one of the most stunning places I've ever seen.'

'Look, a croc.' Emma pointed to the mudflats on the other side of the river.

'Awesome.' Jeremy's eyes were wide as the crocodile took off at a run and disappeared into the muddy water.

'And deadly. You make sure you look out for them when you're up the Cape.' She was looking forward to showing him the scenery on the drive north. 'What do you know about the Daintree and the rainforest?'

'Just what I've read about on the tourist sites. And that it's a World Heritage site.'

'Wait till you see the rainforest near Wilma's place. Gorges, tumbling rivers, pristine rainforest, and rugged mountains.' Her voice ran on and Jeremy smiled at her. 'There's just so much to see.'

'You love it here, don't you?'

'I do. It's sort of like the Territory because of the grandeur of the landscape but in a very different way. Did you know it's older than the Amazon? Over a hundred million years old.' Anticipation filled Emma at showing Jeremy some of the locations she loved. She knew he wouldn't be disappointed. 'And the animals and birds, the biodiversity is incredible. It's a unique place.'

'And criminal to think that someone might be interfering with the wildlife.' Jeremy said.

'Yes.' Emma sobered at the thought of what was

probably happening out there. 'I spoke to Troy about it last night and I feel more confident now. We don't have to worry.'

'Oh?' To Emma's surprise, Jeremy's expression darkened. 'Why's that?'

'Troy reassured me that National Parks and Wildlife are investigating it already.' Emma kept his warning about staying out of the rainforest to herself. It was enough to have George on her case without getting Jeremy more worried.

'That's good to hear.'

'Wilma will be pleased to hear it too. You know, she's taught me so much about the rainforest. What she knows is amazing.'

'Tell me about her. She sounds like an interesting woman.'

'She lives in an old cottage on land that has been in her family for a long time. She owns about three acres and apart from the road frontage; it's bounded by national park.'

The ferry was drawing close to the bank.

'Quick, back in the car. If you hold up the queue we'll bear Clive's wrath.'

'I'll tell you all about Wilma as we drive. She'll be a good contact for you for you getting to know the communities in the north.'

***

Jeremy relaxed as they headed north towards Cape Tribulation. Emma drove confidently as the road turned and wound back on itself in hairpin bends. He looked around as they passed beneath the thick canopy of trees. Every few kilomctrcs there was a break in the vegetation and an immense rainforest-covered peak would fill the gap in front of them

'Thornton Peak. No matter what time of day, or how clear the rest of the sky is, it's always topped with clouds.' Emma's voice was bright and cheery, and she'd kept the conversation general as she'd concentrated on the road. It was good to see her relaxed. Her wariness had disappeared now that they had cleared the air. Jeremy had managed to tamp down the anger that he'd felt at his mother's interfering. He suspected that she may well know something about the missing letter, too.

'That's where Troy works.' Emma's voice interrupted his thoughts.

He glanced across to the large colourful sign at the intersection ahead. *"Rainforest Tourist Centre: Explore from the forest floor to the canopy."*

'It's worth a visit. We could call in on the way back if you like.'

'Maybe another time.' Jeremy didn't particularly want to see Troy. 'One day when we can spend a full day there,' he added.

They travelled another half an hour before Emma pulled off the main road and turned into a narrow track.

It's a long way out here,' Jeremy commented.

'Do you know how much further you'll be driving to the Cape?'

'Yes. I do. I meant this is a long way for an elderly person to live out of town.'

'You'll find things are very different up here.' Emma negotiated the car along the bumpy track.

They followed the track for about fifty metres, the undergrowth brushing the side of her small car. She parked in a small clearing near a locked gate. Jeremy watched curiously as she crouched down and peered back towards the road.

'This is as far as we can drive. We have to walk the rest of the way in.' She reached into the back, grabbed a backpack and locked the car before directing him to a cleared narrow track leading down the hill. The rainforest encroached on each side of the narrow path but he could see a small timber house at the bottom of the hill. 'Do you think anyone could see the car parked in here from the main road?'

'I doubt it. Why do you ask?

'Nothing. Doesn't matter.' She shrugged and was quiet as they crossed to the gate.

Jeremy held out his hand as she went to climb over, but she pulled back when his fingers brushed hers.

'I'm fine, thanks.'

The track to the cottage wound down a hill. He was pleased he'd worn his running shoes as the incline was steep. 'You usually drive down here?'

'Only when it's not raining.' Emma grinned at him. 'So that means most of the summer, I have to walk in.'

'You said Wilma lives out here on her own. How does she manage?'

'She's got an old four-wheel drive truck. But I do worry about her. Her angina has been playing up a bit lately and it is a long way from town.'

The cottage looked deserted but Emma marched up to

the door and knocked. 'It's me, Emma.'

The door opened slowly and an elderly aboriginal woman ushered them in. Her eyes were kind but she stared at Jeremy intently when Emma introduced him.

Her small dark eyes raked him from head to toe and finally, she turned away and frowned at Emma.

'What are you doing out here again so soon?'

'I was worried about you. I wanted to come out and check on you after that business with the snakes. Jeremy came along to keep me company.' Emma opened her backpack and pulled out a blood pressure monitor. 'Plus I've got some news to ease your mind.'

'I'm all right. I feel good.' Wilma waved her away.

Jeremy leaned back against the sink and watched as the battle of wills developed.

'Please, Wilma.'

'No.'

'Have you been taking your medication?' Emma put the monitor back in her bag.

'My business.'

'Wilma!'

'When I need it.' She nodded at Jeremy. 'About time you got yourself a man.'

Emma's cheeks flushed. 'Jeremy's an old friend from Sydney. I wanted him to meet you because he'll be up this way a fair bit. He's the new doctor setting up the clinics on the Cape.

'Another doctor.' Finally, Wilma pointed to the table with a smile and he understood he'd been accepted. 'Sit down. I've just made some soup and bread.' She turned to

Emma 'So what news do you have?' Emma made her sit at the table and asked her where to find the soup bowls.

'I heard last night that the National Parks are onto the smuggling that we were talking about last night.

'That is good news.'

There was a steaming pot of vegetable broth on the stove, the delicious aroma wafting through the old house.

'At least you eat well,' Emma said as she put a bowl in front of Wilma.

'Of course I do. 'Jeremy, there's a hob of fresh bread in the bread bin.' Wilma pointed to an old-fashioned bread tin next to the stove and he walked over and lifted it out.

'So.' Emma pulled out her chair and sat across the table from Wilma. 'I heard Jock Newby gave you a hard time last time you were in town.'

'Who told you that?'

'One of the girls from the hospital saw him bail you up in the supermarket. She told me about it last night.'

'Who's Jock Newby?' Jeremy put his spoon down on the side of his bowl.

'Our local pharmacist.' Emma looked at him from beneath lowered lashes. 'He doesn't like alternative medicine either.'

'*Pfft*. That stupid man didn't worry me,' Wilma said before he could comment. 'Although he had some quite nasty things to say about you, Emma.'

'Yes, I heard that too.' Emma waved her hand before she picked up the soup spoon. 'But I'm not worried about him either.'

The elderly woman smiled as she turned to Jeremy.

'Emma knows the right stuff.'

'*You've* taught me most of what I know, Wilma.' Emma's cheeks had flushed at the compliment.

'Oh, and you forgot to take the sandpaper fig leaves with you yesterday.'

'I know, I realised that this morning.'

Jeremy listened as Wilma explained the process to Emma.

'Make sure you rub the leaves on the infected site until the skin is quite raw.'

He shook his head. There was a lot to learn up here. It was a big change. The holistic medicine he could understand, but it was going to take a while before he was convinced about this bush medicine.

Emma must have seen the doubt in his face. 'Why don't you come along with me next week and you can see me apply this to Mrs Abernethy's foot. I'll tell you about all of the topical creams we've used and the different treatments.'

Emma had a thought. 'Wilma, why don't you come with us? You can show Jeremy some of your remedies while I give you a good check-up. You can stay at my place for a few days while this smuggling business dies down.'

Despite Emma's offer, the old woman wouldn't budge. Wilma wouldn't leave her home and Jeremy and Emma had to get back to town.

It was mid-afternoon by the time they left. Jeremy carried the cardboard box that Wilma had filled with a variety of leaves and stems. The humidity had increased and he was perspiring by the time they reached the top of the hill.

'You'll get used to the heat.' She grinned at him as he

reached up with one hand to wipe his brow.

'There's a lot to get used to.'

The drive back was slower as there was a line of traffic ahead when they turned onto the main road. The afternoon sunlight filtered through the low branches of the trees and each time they crossed one of the narrow creeks, the polished rocks gleamed along the edges of the running water.

'There's a good chance we'll see a cassowary at this time of day. They've been known to kill and a male bird would attack if there were chicks or eggs close by.'

'Crocodiles, snakes and now you're telling me there are killer birds too?' He lightened his tone with a laugh. 'I'll keep an eye out for them.'

The afternoon light was fading and as Emma focused on a particularly winding part of the road, Jeremy took his fill looking at her face. A high forehead, softened by tendrils of hair that had escaped from her braid, met well-defined arched eyebrows. Her eyes were hazel, flecked with gold, wide and almond-shaped. He'd used to tease her about having cat's eyes. He'd forgotten that.

Her high cheekbones were slightly pink from their day out in the sun and fresh air. Her lips were rosy pink and full, and he remembered how he'd once traced them with his finger as they'd lain in bed. As he watched, the tip of her tongue peeked out and licked her top lip, and a sudden tightening in his groin made him look away.

'So where'— his voice cracked a little and he took a breath—'where do I look for these killer birds?'

A tourist sign indicated a lookout a couple of kilometres ahead.

'Want to stop and take a look? The Alexandra Lookout has a view to the north over some of the area you'll be travelling to. It will give you an idea of the terrain.'

'Sure.' Jeremy was pleased that she wasn't in an all-fired hurry to get rid of him. She'd been quiet since they passed the turnoff to the Rainforest Centre and he wondered if she was thinking about Troy.

She parked on the edge of the wide track and they walked across to a lookout. There was a fence at the edge of a steep drop. Beneath them, an extensive stand of low rainforest extended to the coast where it met sandy beaches and rocky headlands. To the south, the river wound in a silver trail until it reached the Coral Sea.

'Breathtaking, isn't it?' The wind caught her dress and pressed it against her, outlining her curves. A strand of her hair blew across his face and she reached up and removed it, her fingers brushing lightly against his lips. Jeremy was tempted to take her hand and hold it there but he fought the impulse. Clearing his throat, he lifted his head and took in the vista in front of them.

As they drove back towards the ferry, the lights of a police car flashed from the other side of the road.

'Karma.' Emma's voice was snarky as she gestured to the car pulled up in front of the police car.

Jeremy frowned. An older man was standing next to Craig, the policeman from the pub. As they flashed past, the older man was waving his arms.

'Obviously not happy about being booked,' he commented.

'That's Jock Newby, 'Emma said wryly. 'There'll be

hell to pay over that. He thinks he can do anything he likes.'

They didn't speak again all the way back to Dalrymple, apart from a conversation Emma struck up with the ferryman. She dropped Jeremy off at the pub with a quick wave as she drove off as a heavy shower of rain began to fall.

From the verandah outside his room on the first floor of the pub, he looked out over the tops of the palm trees rustling in the dark. A frog croaked in the distance. The shower of rain had washed everything clean. In a way, he felt cleansed too. He had direction; he was falling in love with this town and its people.

He had taken to Dalrymple already—he felt as though he was starting to belong. As he jogged each morning, someone would wave as they drove past him and the old fellow watering his lawn on the corner near the bakery would call out 'Good morning, Doc.'

All he had to do now was convince Emma that maybe they could work on more than friendship.

Slow and steady.

Today he'd had a glimpse of the woman he'd fallen in love with. He was hopeful that he might be able to rekindle that love.

DAINTREE

Chapter 19

Wednesday

The emergency department was busy when Jeremy arrived at the hospital early on Wednesday, but there was still no sign of Emma. He hadn't seen her since Sunday and wanted to tell her about the house he'd found. He'd called Jeff and he'd taken Jeremy out to a couple of properties at the beach, and on the Gorge Road yesterday afternoon. But his anticipation at seeing her disappeared in a flash when he saw the ambulance scream into the bay next to Emergency. Jenny looked at him curiously as he turned on his heel and went into his office as a cold feeling settled in his gut. They probably could have done with a hand but there was no way he could go in there.

He tried to focus on the paperwork on his desk and pulled up Google Maps on his computer to get a sense of the places that were listed as possible locations for the clinics but he couldn't focus. All he could do was wonder what was happening down in the emergency ward and push away the guilt at avoiding his duty. His stomach roiled as he visualised the nights he'd been in St Vincent's. Saving lives depended on teamwork and no one could afford to slink away. Every hand counted in those situations and he was disgusted by his cowardice.

Jenny came into his office with a coffee about ten o'clock and plonked herself down in the chair.

'Well, that was a busy start to the day.'

'What happened?' Jeremy put down the highlighter he'd

been using on the place names.

'First patient was a drug overdose. Stabilised and sent to Port Douglas.'

The room spun. Jeremy gripped the side of the desk, knocking her coffee over.

'Are you okay?' Jenny grabbed the cup and set it upright but coffee was running off the side of the desk onto the floor. He jumped up and grabbed some paper towel, and mopped up the liquid.

'Sorry. It didn't go on you, did it?

'No. I'm fine.' She gestured to the desk. 'Your papers are ruined.'

'It's okay. I can print them out again.'

'And then we had a cane worker in.' Jenny shook her head. 'He cut his leg with his machete, nicked the artery, wrapped his leg in a diesel-soaked flannelette shirt and drove himself in.'

Jeremy swallowed pushing back the ever-present guilt. 'Very busy down there.'

'That's not all. Within an hour we also had a couple with whiplash from a car accident on Ferry Road, and then to top it all off, a group of kids were brought in from the preschool. Vomited all over the place, and were fine again by the time their parents got here.'

'Hmm,' he said.

'We could have done with another pair of hands.' She looked at him squarely.

'I'm sorry. I was busy up here.' He injected a note of arrogance into his tone so she would think she had overstepped the mark but she held his gaze.

'I won't hold you up any longer, Doctor. I'll let you get back to your *work*.'

He knew he'd been judged and found wanting. As he turned back to his computer, his phone buzzed in his pocket and he pulled it out and glanced at the number with a grimace.

My father.

He didn't want to take the call but he stood and opened the door at the back of his small office. 'Hello, Dad.' He crossed to the low concrete wall that overlooked the lawn.

'Jeremy. We haven't talked since you left. It's almost two weeks.'

'I sent you a text to say I was here safely.'

'I know but it would have been nice to hear more about it. Nice part of the world. Your mother loves Port Douglas.'

'It is good up here. I've settled in well.' Jeremy looked out over the lawn. Rod was pushing an elderly resident in a wheelchair along the path and every so often he would stop and the woman would reach down and pick a flower.

'Anyway, we wanted to make sure you were okay.'

'Yes, all fine and looking forward to starting the job.'

His father's voice turned business-like. 'I have a proposition for you.' So this was not a social call.

'And that would be?' Two could play at this game. He made his voice as terse as his father's.

'We've decided to expand the practice. Your brothers and I are prepared to accommodate you.'

Jeremy couldn't help the laugh that rose to his lips. 'That's interesting. What if I'm not interested in being *accommodated*?'

'Don't be foolish, son. Show some gratitude. Stop dicking around up in Hicksville and come home. We're creating a place, especially for you.'

Jeremy raised his eyebrows. 'Dicking around, huh?' That expression was a long way from his father's usual language. 'I guess that's Brenton's phrase,' he commented wryly.

'He hit the nail on the head.'

'I didn't think Brenton would give two hoots about where I was. In fact, I know he'd prefer me to be elsewhere. Probably even further away than *Hicksville*.'

'Be that as it may, your place is here at the family practice and as I said I—we—are can make room for you. With any speciality that you would like to practise in.'

'I've found where I want to be, Dad. A good combination of medical administration and clinical practice, Dad. And in a rural setting.'

'We can wait until you get this out of your system. I've got the first option on the suite next door to our rooms and in six months you can come back and set up in the family practice.'

'No.' Jeremy clenched his jaw. He took a deep breath and looked out at the trees in the hospital grounds. Rod and the patient had disappeared. Brightly-coloured birds hung upside down in the huge bottlebrush trees as they drank the honey from the red flowers. Their squawking contrasted with the muted hum of traffic on the highway a block away. He felt his serenity returning. He refused to let his father's attitude upset him. 'Thanks, but no. I'm not interested.'

'I don't expect you to make a decision immediately. It

will take you a while to decide what specialisation you want to follow.'

Jeremy rolled his eyes. It was as though he hadn't spoken.

'And I have enough connections to get you out of your contract. The old boys' club has a long reach.'

Jeremy could just picture his father tapping his nose and adjusting the old school tie. 'I'm sure it has. Thanks for your call, Dad. I hope everyone is well down there. I have patients waiting. Goodbye.'

He pressed disconnect before his father could reply and tucked the phone back into his pocket. As he leaned back against the wall—there were no patients waiting—Emma walked out of the small building in front of him, pushing another wheelchair. Her braid fell over her shoulder as she leaned forward to speak to the elderly woman in the chair. Her laugh reached him as he watched her, and a rush of warmth pierced his chest.

Emma was wheeling the chair into the pathology room along the corridor and he could hear her talking to the nurse. He walked slowly up the corridor and smiled at her when came out.

'You look happy.' Emma pushed the empty chair into the corner.

'Good morning, Doctor Porter. I am.'

'What were you doing this morning? We could have done with you in Emergency.'

'Ah, I was busy.'

She flashed him a curious look.

'Have you got time to go over to the aged care building?

Mrs Abernethy's been asking for that good-looking young man to come and see her all night. I'm about to treat her toe infection with the fig leaves and I thought you might find it interesting.'

'Sure. She's a sweetheart. Thinks I'm her son. Come to the staff room and I'll shout you a coffee on the way.'

Emma followed him down to the small kitchen near his office. 'Dementia is a cruel thing. She is such a sweetie. They all are.' Her words were punctuated by a yawn.

'Late night?' He knew she was watching him as he crossed to the corner of the room and switched on the jug.

'Bowser kept me up most of the night scratching at the door. We had a bit of a scare with a snake last week and I'm reluctant to let him outside after dark.' Emma folded her arms and settled into the chair. 'It's not like him to carry on all night though. I was a bit worried that there was something— or someone—snooping around.'

'Ever had any problems over there?'

Emma's forehead wrinkled. 'No, not really. George generally keeps an eye on the place when I'm not there but—'

'But what?'

'I thought I'd shut the back door when I left yesterday morning and it was wide open when I got home last night. I probably forgot to shut it but it made me a bit jumpy all night. She pointed to the jug. 'Water's boiled.'

'Make sure you lock it next time.' He placed a mug of coffee beside her and straddled the desk chair.

'So, I have a favour to ask.'

She looked at him curiously. 'Yes?'

'I've found a place to stay and I'm moving out in a few

days. Want to help me move?'

'Where to? Wonga Beach?' She closed her eyes and sighed as she took the first sip. 'Perfect. Thank you. That's what I needed.'

'No. I've rented a small house on the road out to the Gorge. If you're free, it'd be nice to have some company when I unpack on Sunday.'

She looked at him and began to shake her head but he held his hand up. 'As a friend, Emma. I'm not putting any pressure on you. Really, I could do with a hand. And I could do with a friend.'

'I'll see what I'm doing. That's all I can promise.'

'And—this is where the real favour comes in—I've ordered a heap of furniture from a catalogue . . . and I'm sure you'll remember my handyman skills?'

'Mr Useless who couldn't even change a light bulb till I showed him the difference between an Edison screw and a bayonet cap? I sure do.' She grinned at the shared memory. 'So what needs doing?'

'Ah, the furniture is coming in a flat pack.'

The peal of laughter that came from Emma's lips sent warmth rushing through his veins. She put her cup on the table and waved her hand. 'I guess I can help you out. But there's a catch.'

'And that is?' Her eyes were dancing with mischief. It was his Emma of old times.

'Help us with the setting up at the park on Saturday.'

Jeremy frowned and put his finger to his lips with a mock frown. He had no intention of telling her that Jeff had already asked him and he'd agreed to help. 'Hmm . . . well, I suppose . . . yes, okay, I guess I could.'

'Good. We have a deal' She stood and smoothed her hands down her navy work trousers. 'Come on, let's get to work. I'm due at the clinic soon.'

'While I think of it I wanted to let you know . . . I'm heading up to Cooktown tomorrow and staying overnight.'

'If you think Dalrymple's a frontier town, wait till you see Cooktown. Is the four-wheel drive here for you?'

He nodded. 'It arrived yesterday.'

'Are you taking the main highway to Cooktown?

'No, I'm expected at Quarantine Bay mid-morning so it's the coast road.'

'That road is really bad once it gets onto the Bloomfield Track. Have you had much experience in a four-wheel drive vehicle?'

'What? You think I only know how to drive a flash car on a freeway?'

She lifted her chin. 'In a word, yes.'

He regarded her steadily. 'There's a lot you don't know about me now, Emma Porter. And who knows, you might enjoy finding out.'

The *hmpph* she gave him reminded him of old George, and he smothered the grin that threatened.

'Well, just be careful on that road.'

'Yes, ma'am.'

'I'll see you at the park early Saturday morning if I don't see you before.' She flicked her braid over her shoulder. 'Which house are you renting on the Gorge Road?'

'It's on the last corner before you turn off the Gorge road.'

Her eyes widened. 'Are there two big Poinciana trees in the front yard?

'There are two big trees but I'm not sure what they're called. They've got orange flowers.'

'That's a lovely place. Albert and Lorna James are both in care here now. It'll be good to have somebody looking after it. You can meet them after I've done Mrs Abernethy's treatment.'

Jeremy was smiling as they headed over to the aged care building. It was the first time he and Emma had managed a conversation without descending into an argument. A good start. And he'd see her both days of the weekend. *And* she was worrying about him.

Perhaps he had a chance after all.

***

Emma was thoughtful as she walked back across to the main building. She'd left Jeremy chatting to the James who'd been delighted to hear the new doctor was going to rent their house. The hospital was quiet and only the distant sounds from the kitchen reached her as lunch was prepared for the patients. Jenny had had a quiet word to her about Jeremy's avoidance of the emergency ward this morning and she was disappointed in him. He had to learn the expectations of a rural hospital if he was going to be accepted. It was all very well to be popular and social but he had to pull his weight. He needed to have some of that Sydney doctor attitude rubbed off.

This was not the time to worry about Jeremy. She had her own patients to attend to. They were her priority. Talking about the Outreach work with Jeremy on the weekend had made her realise she hadn't given enough thought to what the job would have meant. Three or four days on the road some weeks would have impacted the clinic too much, but she still had reservations about his ability to manage it.

She found it hard to accept that he had made such a drastic change to his life. He'd listed the reasons, but it was very different to what he was used to. What would he think when he pulled up outside the old Quarantine Bay pub and was shown the small room that they were planning to use as a clinic?

Time would tell.

How long would it be before he got sick of life up here and missed Sydney? She'd gotten used to having him around very quickly. She realised she'd miss him if he left. Back to where he had everything he wanted...and the best of everything. Not flat-pack furniture and an outside loo.

She grinned, wondering if he had noticed the outhouse at the old James' house.

Chapter 20

Thursday – Daintree Rainforest

Jeremy was the first to drive onto the vehicular ferry and he decided to stay in the car for the short trip across the river. The brand new Land Cruiser's air-con had kicked into cool and he didn't want to get hot and sweaty before his first stop. A grin tugged at his mouth as he looked down at his suit. Emma would have laughed at him—he was seriously overdressed—but it was his first official visit to Cooktown and the other towns up the Cape, so he wanted to make a good impression.

The ferryman tapped the window and he wound it down to show him the twelve-month pass that had come with the vehicle's paperwork. A gust of tropical air immediately filled the cabin.

'You're the bloke who was with Doctor Emma on the weekend.'

'Yes, Doctor Jeremy Langford.'

'Ah, another doctor.' The man held his hand out. 'Clive Montgomery. Welcome. You going up to see old Wilma the Witch, are ya?'

Jeremy shook his head with a frown. 'No. I'm heading up to Quarantine Bay today.'

'Okay. Watch that road. Shame to get such a shiny car dirty. Where you from? Cairns?'

'No, Sydney.'

'Ah.'

Jeremy sensed he'd been found wanting. Again.

He paid due care as he headed north. It was so *green* up here—the trees, the ferns and the rainforest canopy. It was peaceful and so different to the cityscape he was used to. He could feel the tension leaving him as he drove. He'd checked out the map and had decided to take a coffee break at Cape Tribulation before he hit the Bloomfield track. After Emma's warning, he'd Googled the area, and checked the Shire Council website for current road conditions and he knew what to expect. The track was subject to seasonal flooding, slips, loss of traction, potholes and fallen trees and the warning was clear. If it's raining, don't drive on it.

The conditions didn't faze him at all. When he'd applied for the Outreach position he'd undertaken a four-wheel-drive course in the Blue Mountains and was confident he could tackle anything the Daintree Rainforest threw his way.

He drove past the lookout where he'd stood with Emma the other day. She was in his thoughts as he drove along. When he could, he'd tell her what had happened in Sydney and why he found it difficult to work in emergency care.

He stared ahead at the mountain looming over the gap in the canopy. Truth was, he was the one who had delivered the most judgement on himself. If he'd listened to a patient with the same problem, he would have told them to go to counselling, but for some reason, he'd been unable to do what he knew was right.

'You're running away,' his father had said when he'd first told him about the move to North Queensland. 'Face it, son.'

Hell, maybe it *was* running away, but he liked this life

so far. Emma being here had been an unexpected bonus. Now to see if his new job shaped up as well as he was expecting . . .

He slowed the vehicle down as the road began to wind up through the mountains. The sealed section narrowed and some of the curves were almost one hundred and eighty-degree bends. He passed the Rainforest Tourist Centre where Troy worked and most of the traffic behind him turned off down that road.

Two small creek crossings posed no problem for the high four-wheel drive. The tyres gripped the stones firmly and the water splashed no higher than the running board. He wondered what they'd be like in the wet season if the creeks were already running after the small shower of rain they'd had last night.

He reached down and turned the radio on, and scanned the channels until he found a station with music. Then he settled in to enjoy the drive up to the Cape. He turned the music up loud as a country and western song came across the air. 'Can't take the country out of the boy,' the singer crooned.

But I will take the city out of the boy, he thought with a grin.

Thornton Peak appeared ahead in the gap in the canopy and the road began to climb another hill. The car slowed as he reached a line of traffic stopped at the top. He looked ahead, wondering if there'd been an accident, and jumped as the small UHF radio mounted on the base of the dash cracked into life.

'Six to go south and all clear, mate.'

Roadworks.

Jeremy looked down curiously at the radio. He'd have to learn how to use that.

The traffic began to move and he waved at the lollipop man who was holding the sign to slow. The man waved back at him. The cars ahead of him accelerated, but Jeremy kept his speed down as he approached a muddy four-wheel drive parked on the side of the road. As he drew closer, the driver's door opened and Troy Greaves climbed out.

Jeremy pulled over and parked the car before climbing out. He'd take the opportunity to talk to Troy.

'Hi, Troy.'

'G'day, Jeremy. What are you doing out in the wilds?'

Jeremy leaned back against his car. 'I'm heading up the Bloomfield Track a ways. We're looking at establishing a clinic up there so I'm on a bit of an exploration foray. What about you?' He nodded to the backpack. 'Looks like you're off for a hike.'

Troy nodded. 'Yes. Parks and Wildlife were planning on putting a walking track in here, but they're not so sure about it now so I'm going for a look.' He beamed at Jeremy. 'It's good to be out of the office and not dealing with tourists for the day. Shame you've got your day planned. It's a good stroll in to the peak. Emma loved it when I took her in a few weeks back.'

"Yeah, she brought me out to the rainforest on Saturday. Great scenery.'

Troy's eyes narrowed. 'Saturday?'

Jeremy nodded. He wanted Troy to know that he wasn't the only one that Emma spent time with. 'She needed some stuff for her bush medicine. It was interesting. Anyway, I'd better keep going.'

As he turned away a tendril of smoke through the treetops caught Jeremy's attention. 'Not a fire in there, is there?'

'No, there's a private house in there.' Troy frowned. 'An Aboriginal woman lives there. She makes our job hard sometimes.'

Jeremy looked around and recognised the spot where Emma had turned off the other day. 'How's that?'

'We have the difficult situation of a privately owned narrow band of three acres from here to Thornton Peak . . . totally surrounded by national park.' His voice held a note of frustration. 'National Parks have to get her permission every time they want to access parts of the rainforest. The main track to Thornton Peak crosses the back of her property. And she isn't always co-operative.'

Another vehicle pulled up and Jeremy turned around, surprised to see the police car.

Craig Anderson stepped out. 'Troy.' He ignored Jeremy.

'Morning, Craig.' Troy frowned. 'You're a long way from your patch.'

The policeman shook his head. 'We look after the whole road from Dalrymple to Cape Tribulation. Those backpackers up at the old pub were apparently on the grog last night and Sarge asked me to come up here and read the riot act. Again.'

'Understaffed like everything else up here.' Troy replied, knowingly.

'What brings you up this way, Doc?'

So he does know who I am, Jeremy thought.

Even though his words were friendly, the policeman's voice was laced with hostility. Jeremy had wondered if he'd remember their encounter the night he'd manhandled Emma. He obviously had.

'Working.' He nodded curtly to Craig. 'And I'd best be off. I've got a long drive ahead.'

Troy gave him a wave and headed for the track but Craig stood by the police car staring at him as Jeremy walked to his vehicle.

He drove away, the gloss taken off his morning. The policeman was obnoxious but he could deal with that. When Emma had come back in from the verandah at the club the other night with Troy she'd seemed troubled. And she brought him up frequently in conversation.

It was Troy that he was more worried about and what his feelings were for Emma.

Chapter 21

Friday

Despite being busy both here and at the hospital, Emma had missed having Jeremy around. More than once she wondered how he was coping with the rough roads up the Cape. The last couple of days had flown by with the clinic at full pace and a tummy bug doing the rounds of the school. The preschool kids who'd ended up in emergency the other day had shared the virus with their siblings. It seemed half the kids in town had come down with it. Mid-afternoon Friday, she walked out into the waiting room relieved to see there was only one woman waiting with a young boy.

She'd let her admin assistant leave early. Lily was in a panic about her face-painting stall at Rainbow Day; there was some issue with the delivery of fairy glitter.

'Thank you, Doctor Em. Oh my God, I just couldn't bear it if we had no glitter.' Lily jumped up from the reception desk with a huge smile on her face. 'The little kids would be devastated.' She put her hand to her chest in a dramatic gesture and Emma waved her away with a smile.

'Go. We can't have devastation on Rainbow Day.'

Lily grabbed her in a hug on the way past. 'Have I told you today you're the best boss ever, Doctor Em?'

'No need to suck up, I said you can go. Now get out of here before I change my mind. How many appointments to go?'

'This is the last. I've taken their details. Her name is Fleur.'

It seemed as though the whole town was preparing for Rainbow Day at the park tomorrow. Only the last few of the tummy bug patients had come in today

'Okay, go and do what you have to do. I'll lock up here after I see this pair and have an early mark too.'

'Mwah.' Lily blew her a kiss as she tottered off on her three-inch wedge heels. 'You're a darling. See you tomorrow. I'm so excited!'

With a smile, Emma turned to the young woman in the waiting room. She was unfamiliar to her, and she ushered her and the young boy into the consulting room. 'Come in, Fleur.' She leaned down to the small boy. 'What's your name?'

"Mason.' He had a slight lisp. One hand was on his stomach and she gave him a sympathetic smile. 'Sore tummy, Mason?'

He turned wide eyes up to her and nodded.

It was the same virus that had been doing the rounds and she gave the young mum instructions for rehydration and pain relief for the little boy.

'You have a little rest there while I talk to Mummy.' She left the little boy on the examination table.

The young woman looked at her with concern. 'What else is wrong?'

'Nothing. He's fine. I wanted to ask you how you are.'

'Me? I'm fine.' Her lip trembled and her eyes shone with threatening tears.

'You don't look well. You're very dark under the eyes.'

'I'm tired. I've got a new bub, and with Mason here being sick—' She put a shaking hand to her face as tears rolled down her cheeks. 'I just can't cope.'

Emma leaned forward and took Fleur's hand. 'I haven't seen you around town. Are you local?'

She shook her head. 'No, we're up here on holidays. We're out at the caravan park at Wonga Beach, and that makes it even harder. My husband is off fishing every day and I'm stuck in a van with the kids.' Her voice got louder. 'And now with Masie sick, I can't do it anymore.

'Have you talked to your own doctor about how you've been feeling?'

She nodded. 'Yes. He prescribed anti-depressants but I don't want to take them anymore. I flushed them down the toilet. I'd rather feel like this than how they made me feel. It was like I was looking through glass.'

Emma listened sympathetically. 'Do you know there are more natural ways to treat post-partum depression?

'No. What sort of things? Herbal tablets and stuff?'

'No. There are other therapies we use. I've used it with a couple of my patients and we've seen great results and very quickly.'

Fleur's eyes widened. 'Tell me about it.'

Emma reached across to her shelf and selected the leaflets she was looking for. 'There's a combination of therapies we can implement. Folic acid or Vitamin B9 which you can start taking straight away, a course of acupuncture and an increase to your daily exercise. There's also an adjunct therapy called 'bright light therapy' which has had great results.'

'Oh, but we're going home tomorrow.' She looked across at the little boy who was now dozing on the examination table. 'That is, if he's well enough for the drive back to Cairns,'

'I can give you the name of a colleague down there who'll take you through the program if you're interested.' Emma was pleased to see Fleur's eyes brighten.

'Oh yes, please.'

Once Fleur and Mason had left, Emma tidied up the examination room, checked the supplies and lifted the lid on the glass bowl where the cocky apple bark was breaking down ready for the infusion. She was looking forward to showing Jeremy how successful the fig leaf abrasion had been on the fungal infection. When she'd checked on Mrs Abernethy this morning, her skin was almost clear. The sweet smell of the cocky apple drifted up to her and she thought of Wilma. She picked up the phone on her desk in the clinic and dialled her number. She'd been uneasy about Wilma ever since she'd refused to come back into town. She'd been short of breath and Emma knew that she only took her heart medication when the pain was almost unbearable. She glanced at her watch. It was still early enough to drive out and check on her and be back by dark.

The phone picked up on the first ring but the voice was hesitant. 'Hello.'

'Hi, Wilma. It's me, Emma.'

'Hello, Emma.'

'I thought I might come out for a drive. Do you need anything from town?'

'No, thank you. And don't bother coming out, I'm fine. Waste of a trip.'

Emma pulled up Wilma's chart on the computer screen as she held the phone to her ear. 'How much heart medication have you got left?'

Silence.

'Wilma?'

'I have plenty.'

Emma stifled a sigh. 'You haven't been taking it, have you?'

'I don't need it.'

I'm coming for a drive. Are you sure there's nothing you need?'

'No.' Her voice was quiet.

'I'll see you in a couple of hours.'

The visit to Wilma's was frustrating. Her lips were pale and she was short of breath when she opened the door for Emma but she refused to be properly examined, and wouldn't come back to the hospital.

'How about a cup of tea before I head back into town then?'

Wilma went to stand but Emma put a gentle hand on her shoulder.' I'll get it. I should know where everything is by now. It's almost like my second home.'

Once the pot of tea was brewing on the table, Emma pulled out the chair beside Wilma.

'Now I'm going to be blunt with you. I'm not prepared to sit back and let you get sick because of some stubborn reason that I can't understand.'

Wilma reached for the teapot and poured her tea without looking at Emma but her lips were set.

'I'm talking to you as a practitioner, but more as a friend. Wilma, you've taught me so much. I'm not going to turn up here one day and find you cold on the floor.'

Wilma lifted her chin and held Emma's eyes.

'You have to listen to me. Otherwise, I'm going to insist that you are admitted. I'll cross a professional line here and call an ambulance and have you carted off to the hospital. I'll say you're incapable of making the decision yourself.'

Wilma sat back and folded her arms. 'If that's what it's going to take, that's what I'll do.'

Wilma reached for the box of Corlanor sitting in the middle of the table and snapped it open. She popped one of the small tablets out of the foil and placed it in her mouth.

Emma smiled as relief coursed through her. 'Good. Now can I have your word that you'll keep taking them?'

'Yes. I'll take them.'

Emma's voice was gentle. Sometimes we have to take pharmaceutical drugs. You know that as well as I do.'

'Now what do you say about you coming back with me and you can come to the Rainbow Day tomorrow?'

Wilma folded her arms. 'I'll be there anyway. I've got a stall booked.'

Emma was surprised. It was the first Wilma had mentioned it. 'Are you up to it?'

'I am.' The woman's gaze was steady.

'What are you selling? Have you been baking?'

Wilma laughed, and Emma was pleased to see the stubbornness had disappeared.

'No. All sorts of interesting things. You'll have to come and have a look tomorrow.'

'I will.'

'It's time I was going,' Emma finished her cup of tea and stood. 'Your next tablet is due in four hours and then another one when you go to bed.'

'Yes, Doctor.' Wilma's voice was meek but there was a twinkle in her eye. "Give us a hug, love.'

Emma hugged her back and headed up the hill to the car.

The last shards of sunlight filtered through the trees and motes of dust hung like lace in the shadows. It would be dark by the time she got to the ferry and she had an early start tomorrow.

As she drove, she wondered how Jeremy had gone up north, and whether he was back at the pub yet. She tried to push him from her mind and focus on the organisation for tomorrow's fundraiser. This year, all she had to do was check that everyone with a job turned up and have a thank you speech ready. Jeff was in charge of getting the tents and setting them up, and he and Cissy were running the coffee stall.

But she couldn't stop thinking about Jeremy. Worrying how he'd gone on that road and whether he'd known to take spray to keep away the mosquitoes. Dengue fever was a problem up here. Cook town was such a different town and once he'd got to the small settlement of Quarantine Bay he would have been in an entirely unfamiliar world. She was looking forward to hearing what he thought.

Emma glanced left as something moving at the edge of the forest caught her eye. A possum scurried into the bush. As she turned her attention back to the road, she gasped and hit the brakes. A line of cars was stopped in the middle of the road in front of her. For a moment she didn't think the car was going to pull up; the brake pedal felt spongy beneath her foot. She pulled up only centimetres from the last car at the end of the line.

She peered through the windscreen in the failing light. Three tourists with cameras were standing at the front car. There was a flash of movement as a cassowary burst out of the low scrub and ran along the edge of the road. The photographers raised their cameras, snapping madly. Emma reached for her phone, wound the window down and took a photo as the large bird ran past her car only a couple of metres away.

That was the first time she'd seen a cassowary in the wild; the tourists who were out of their cars obviously didn't know what a dangerous creature they were. The traffic moved off slowly and she started the car again. Darkness had fallen swiftly and as the last car disappeared around the bend she flicked the headlights onto high beam. The road was a series of tortuous curves and hills descending to the Daintree River. She focused on her driving, wondering how Jeremy had handled the four-wheel-drive on the Bloomfield Track.

Jeremy. She had to get him out of her thoughts.

A small nocturnal creature suddenly ran out onto the road in front of the car and Emma pressed the brakes.

Again they felt strange beneath her foot, and the car did not slow at all this time. Emma wrenched the wheel and the small creature scurried out of the way with a whisker to spare. As the next curve approached she eased her foot back onto the brake, but this time, the pedal went right to the floor. She flicked a worried glance at the speedometer. She was only doing seventy kilometres an hour but that was still too fast to take the approaching curve.

She told herself to stay calm. The worst thing she could do was panic. As she tried to pump the useless pedal, she downshifted into low gear. Keeping her eyes on the road ahead, she reached for the park brake and slowly pulled it up, remembering the driving lessons Dad had given all of them back on the farm in their teens. The rear wheels squealed as the car skewed slightly to the wrong side of the road, but she adjusted the steering and the car slowed enough to take the curve. Thank goodness there was nothing coming towards her.

She let out the breath she'd been holding and pulled the park brake a little more. The car slowed a fraction more but a tighter, almost hairpin bend was fast approaching. Emma flicked on her hazard lights and checking that nothing was approaching, moving the steering wheel from left to right and back again, trying to slow the car even more.

Not enough. The car was going to go straight through the curve at this speed. At the last moment, she yanked the park brake to its full extension and the back of the car skewed around as the car slowed Sliding across the narrow bitumen, the headlights lit the heavily timbered forest. Emma yanked the wheel to the left as a large gum tree loomed ahead.

DAINTREE

Chapter 22

Friday evening - Cape Tribulation Road

It had been a successful few days. As Emma had predicted, the pub at Quarantine Bay had been full of patients waiting to meet him. No one had been ill, apart from a couple of children with an earache, thank god. Most of the locals had just wanted a yarn.

He'd spent two nights at the hotel in Cooktown and had made the most of the time writing up his report on the viability of Quarantine Bay for a clinic. Even though he'd been busy, he'd still found himself thinking about Emma. He'd missed her. He was looking forward to seeing her at this fundraiser tomorrow, and to being part of the community activities. He was sure, with it being an environmental thing, Troy was sure to be a big part of it, but he'd have to deal with that. Emma would be passionate about the fundraising, Troy or no Troy.

Maybe she'd missed having him around too. Maybe he was kidding himself.

The road hummed beneath the wheels of the Land Cruiser as he got closer to the ferry crossing and home. Yes, home. After almost two weeks, he felt more settled here than he had felt since his days at university. Being based at Dalrymple Hospital was an added bonus to the Outreach work.

Emma had worried about him driving on the Bloomfield Track, but he'd enjoyed the four-wheel driving and was proud of how he'd handled the challenges. The road narrowed and he slowed the car as a bright flashing light ahead caught his eye. There had been road works all the way this afternoon and he was surprised to see them still on the job. But as he got closer, his eyes narrowed. He realised that the light was coming from the side of the road.

Shit. It was a car's hazard lights. A small red car. And the vehicle was hard up against a tree.

His blood ran cold. *Emma.*

Jeremy flicked his own hazard lights on and pulled carefully to the side of the road. He flung the door open and jumped down from his seat.

Holding his breath, he pushed his way through the low scrub, not giving a thought to snakes or wildlife as the long, rough grass caught on his suit. He ran to the driver's side and peered into the car, the interior lit garishly by the flashing orange of the hazard lights.

It was empty.

Horrific visions of injured drivers wandering away from the site of car accidents tumbled through his head. He'd attended a particularly nasty accident on an isolated road in the outback when he'd been out at Bourke. Three passengers had been airlifted to Sydney but it had been two days before they'd found the driver's body two kilometres into the bush.

He cupped his hands around his mouth and yelled, 'Emma!'

A loud bang and a muffled 'effing hell' came from the front of the car. He leaned forward as her head appeared over the front of the bonnet.

'That hurt.' She sat back down, rubbing her head.

Jeremy hurried around to the front and dropped down beside her as she pulled herself up on the front bumper bar.

'No, sit back down. Where are you hurt?' He held her shoulders gently, scanning her face and body for any visible injuries.

'Only my head where I just banged it under the car when you called me,' she said crossly. She looked up at him, her face smeared with oil and her hair full of small twigs.

'Did you get thrown out when you hit the tree? Christ, Emma, you scared ten years off my life.'

'No, I climbed under there to see if I could back it out. Bu the car is wedged on a tree stump.' She ran her hand over her face, grimacing as it came away covered with foul-smelling brake oil. 'I wasn't hurt at all, so there's no need to panic.' She glanced across at the passenger side that was crumpled in and her voice broke. 'I'm just so thankful that Wilma wouldn't come with me.'

'I still want to check you out. Tip your head back.' Jeremy held her face gently as he checked her pupils. He was calmer now that she seemed to be relatively unhurt.

'I'm okay. I managed to slow it down enough that the airbags didn't go off, thank goodness. I've seen the skin abrasions and black eyes they can cause.' She pulled away from his hold. 'I'm all right. I'm just angry at myself. I've been so busy I haven't had my car serviced for over a year and the brakes failed.'

'Come on, I'll get you back to town.'

'Can you get the boot open? There's some stuff I need out of there for tomorrow.'

'Sure.' Jeremy opened the boot and carried the box back

to his vehicle while Emma leaned against her car and waited.

He held his hand out and glanced back at the car. He'd be surprised if it wasn't a write-off.

The satisfaction that he felt when she leaned into him was mixed with the worry of how much worse it could have been.

Chapter 23

Saturday – Rainbow Day – Dalrymple

They drove by the police station after calling into the garage and arranging for her car to be towed in. It was locked up and in darkness.

'I'll report it tomorrow. I'll have to for my insurance.' Emma ran her hand through her hair in frustration. 'When I can find a spare minute.'

She shook her head as Jeremy turned on the left indicator at the street past the lights.

'Take me straight to the village please.'

Jeremy shook his head. 'I want to check you out thoroughly . . . '

'No.' Her voice was emphatic. 'I'll admit it shook me up, but honestly by the time I went into the scrub the car was crawling. There's no need. I'm fine.'

She took a deep breath and held her hands together as he headed along the road to the village. 'So how was your trip?'

'It was an eye-opener.' He shot her a grin and Emma was taken aback by the little tingle that ran through her.

'But it was great.' His voice was full of enthusiasm. 'I met with the elders, had a few 'yarns' and treated half a dozen patients. I'm looking forward to the next trip.'

'I'm pleased.'

'I fell in love with Cooktown. How would you feel about going up there one weekend and showing me around?'

'Maybe.' She turned and looked out into the darkness. She was getting used to Jeremy being around and if she was honest it was a lot better than what she'd anticipated when he'd first turned up at the pub two weeks ago. It would be fun to show him around.

Maybe.

She insisted on being dropped at George's. Jeremy wasn't keen but once she convinced him she was okay and he extracted a promise that she would ring if she felt ill, he headed back to Dalrymple. He also offered to take Wilma's box to the park for her in the morning.

Emma had a restless night. Flashes of car accident victims she had treated in emergency and the possible injuries she could have sustained—or worse— if she'd not been able to slow down came to her every time she closed her eyes. The only way to block it was to remember Jeremy's gentle hands as he'd examined her. When she finally went to sleep, she dreamed that Wilma was in the car with her and woke up in the early hours covered in a lather of perspiration. She was sure she'd heard a vehicle and a plane after that but when she'd got up and peered through the kitchen window there was no sign of anything over the river. Whether it was a dream or just an overactive imagination, whatever it was had her seeing shadows wherever she went.

The third time she woke it was after seven and she shot out of bed and hurried around getting ready. Emma dug deep into the wardrobe and found her favourite long white pants and a short-sleeved red top. A shell necklace and a pair of dangly earrings, a spray of perfume and she was ready. She would be much later getting into town than she'd planned.

George had no problem lending her his old beat-up ute to get there.

'Just treat the old girl, gently.' He grinned at her. She felt a rush of affection. George was wearing a pair of blue-striped flannel pyjamas. He'd healed well and his bruises were almost gone but his cheeks were unshaven. 'I'll grab a lift in later *if* I decide to come in.'

'You have to come. The whole district will be there.' Emma took the keys and climbed up into the old ute. '*Ugh*, what's that smell?'

His grin got wider. 'I picked up a dead roo yesterday.'

Emma leaned out the window. 'Don't you dare think about eating it. How many times do I have to tell you about the parasites and diseases?'

George just grinned at her and she shook her head. 'I'll see you in town.'

'We'll see. Too many people for me in one place.'

The smell of brewing coffee tickled Emma's nose as she parked the ute in the hospital car park and walked to the end of the main street. The highway was gridlocked with traffic as locals, tourists and passers-by fought for the few remaining car parks. Rainbow Day was usually well attended and she knew that by mid-morning the highway would have cars parked all the way across the bridge to the north side of town. The large park was at the end of the main street and fronted the highway along one side. She loved these days and she loved this town. The way the community pulled together never failed to impress her.

She was pleased to see that Jeff's team had set up the tents and all of the stalls were set up and already stocked with a variety of fresh produce, preserves and craft goods. There were already queues at most of them as people vied for the best deals of the day. The first half of the day was for the stalls. The organised events didn't begin until lunchtime.

She knew she'd find Jeff and Cissy in the coffee tent. They always manned the portable coffee machine that the local church used to raise funds. She lifted the flap and poked her head in. 'Sorry I'm so late, guys. Jeff, you've done a great job. Clever move putting the coffee near the kids' stuff.'

'Thanks. We had lots of willing helpers, and yes many happy parents are keeping us busy.' Jeff's voice was concerned. 'Are you okay? Jeremy was here at sun up and he told us what happened.'

'I'm fine. I'll tell you about it later. I'd love a coffee when you get a chance please, Cissy. No rush. Double shot.' She was going to need an energy boost to see the day out. 'Do you guys need a hand?

'No, all good here. Come back in five and I'll have it ready,' Cissy called over her shoulder.

Emma wandered around, pleased to see how many stalls there were this year. Forming a committee to organise the day had been the best thing she'd ever done. Last year, she had run herself ragged. This year the load was shared.

'Coffee's ready, Em.' Cissy called her as she walked back to the tent. 'Can you give me a hand for half an hour?' 'Thanks.' Emma closed her eyes and inhaled the coffee that Cissy handed to her. 'No problem. Where's Jeff?'

'There's a problem with the PA system. He won't be long, I hope.' She rubbed a hand over her eyes and flicked a glance at the long queue.

'You make the coffee and I'll take the orders.' Emma said.

'Thanks, you're a doll. Coffees are all four dollars, and cakes and biscuits are two dollars each. The paper bags are under the till.'

Emma worked steadily taking orders and slipping slices of homemade cake and biscuits into the small white bags until there was a bit of a lull in the queue. She chatted to the locals, and many of her patients walked over to say hello. Her tiredness lifted and she began to enjoy herself.

'Phew, that was busy.' She picked up and drank the last of her now cold coffee.

'Thanks, Em. Really appreciate it. I'll make you another one.'

The flap on the back of the tent lifted and Jeff slipped under.

'Hi, darling. All sorted?' Cissy went over and hugged her husband and Emma waited by the counter.

'Sorry, I took so long. All fixed now. It was a simple fix but bloody Sergeant Smith held me up. 'He thinks he's in charge today and he's changed all the order of the events his afternoon.'

'I'll go and see what I can sort out. Thanks, Jeff. Like I said you guys have done an awesome job.'

Cissy came back over to the counter. 'Thanks for your help, Em. You still feeling okay?'

'I'm fine.'

'What time's the tug-of-war?' Cissy called out after Emma as she walked away.

'It was three o'clock.' Emma smiled. 'I'll check there's

been no change. I hope everyone has their teams sorted.

She wandered through the crowd sipping her coffee, returning smiles and stopping for the occasional chat. The last stall of the first row was particularly busy and she caught a glimpse of a long white braid as the woman behind the counter turned to reach for a jar on the makeshift shelf at the side of the front table.

'Wilma!'

'Hello, Emma.' Her smile was wide today and her skin colour was good.

Emma wrinkled her nose as the pleasant smells mixed around her.

An array of soaps, salves and small bottles were lined neatly on the table.

'How's it going?' Emma glanced up at the sign above the counter. *Daintree Delights. Natural Remedies*.

'I've almost sold out of soap.' Wilma's lined face was bright with happiness.

'You look much better.' Emma smiled as she reached for a dark bottle with a colourful label.

'Took my medication like you said.'

'*Mr Bogeyman*? And *The Monster Cure*?' Emma chuckled as she read the labels on the small bottles.

'Gets rid of bad dreams for the little ones.' Wilma's smile widened as Emma picked up a pink bottle. 'That's sold well too.'

Emma put it to her nose and sniffed. '*Lavender Oil Love Potion*? Smells good.'

Wilma tapped the side of her nose. 'Lavender oil and a secret ingredient. Might give you a bottle.'

Emma put the bottle down with a chuckle.

'When you called in last night, I forgot to tell you I had a visitor the other day.' Wilma said.

'A visitor?'

'Troy rainforest centre called in to introduce himself. He seems very nice. They've decided not to put the walk in near my place because of some palm cockatoos that are out there.'

'Troy? He said he was going to call in. That's great news.'

She shot Emma a secretive smile. 'He said he knew you. Seemed quite smitten. When he realised we were friends, he wanted to know all about you and how often you came out to see me. So you got yourself two fellas?' Wilma's eyes were dancing and Emma laughed. 'Maybe you don't need that lavender potion after all.'

'No, not me. No fellas. Troy was probably just happy because I was the one who told him about those cockatoos. And Jeremy is just an old friend.' She reached over and gave Wilma a hug. 'I am so happy to see you out here and looking a lot more relaxed.'

They were interrupted by a couple of women who picked up the soaps and sniffed them.

She smiled. So Troy had been asking about her. As Wilma took the sale, Emma left and made her way back to the centre of the park. The jumping castle was covered with children jumping and squealing.

A group of women stood by the coffee tent which had been placed close by the children's activities to provide for the parents.

The white plastic chairs and tables were full of locals

and tourists sipping coffee. As Emma walked past the squealing children she caught a glimpse of sandy hair just before Jeremy's laugh reached her. A fluttering feeling stirred in her stomach and her pulse quickened. She stood to the side of the tent and watched as he laughed and talked to the group around him. *Holding court* was the term that sprang to her mind. It was good to see him at ease. Today he had dispensed with the designer labels and she was sure it was a white Bonds T-shirt that was tucked into a pair of faded Levi jeans. She focused her attention on him. The T-shirt clung to his chest and her pulse kicked up another notch.

The women around him seemed entranced

He lifted his head and caught sight of her. The flutters in her stomach pooled in her lower belly.

'Excuse me.' He left the group of young women and took Emma's arm guiding her to the side of the tent. 'How are you this morning?'

'I'm good, but I will admit to not sleeping well.'

'You look beautiful, Em.' He reached over and touched her necklace. 'Is that the one I bought for you?'

'It is.' She held his gaze, confusion swirling through her as her legs got a bit shaky. God, this was Jeremy, not Troy. But she couldn't help the grin as Wilma's words flitted into her thoughts. *Two fellas.*

Well, she'd enjoy it today. It would make a change from working hard and having none.

'Jeremy, got a minute?' Jeff called over from the coffee machine, holding up an empty milk carton.

'Looks like you're needed. I'll see you later.' She gave him a quick smile and turned on her heel, legs still tingling.

After she'd got the milk for Jeff from the mobile cool room, she headed across to a small office next to the council building. Inside, the floats were being distributed, and takings put away securely.

'How's it going?'

Jenny was behind the desk taking her turn on the roster that Emma had set up last week. She flashed a bright smile. 'What a morning. This is going to be our best yet. Apparently, there's a caravan muster up at the Cape and they've all come down for the day. They've even entered a grey nomie team in the tug-of-war.'

'So how many teams do we have?'

'Would you believe sixteen entries at one hundred dollars per team? Sixteen hundred dollars raised just from the tug-of-war alone! You've excelled yourself this year, Emma.'

Emma fanned her cheeks. 'Don't be silly. It's a whole town effort. Even Wilma's down there with a stall.'

Jenny gave her a sly grin. 'Did you see old George?'

'Nope. Do I want to?'

'He's got a little stall down the back. He's selling knives and axes.'

'He's what? The old bugger was whinging about coming into town.' She grinned as she remembered George criticising Rainbow Day as a damn fool idea. 'I remember when he said we didn't need any more tourists in *our* rainforest, God love him. Can I get you anything, Jenny?'

'I'd kill for a coffee.'

'How about I take over here and you can go for a wander.'

'You're a sweetie, Em.' Jenny stepped out and hugged

her. 'There's plenty of change in the safe if any of the stallholders come in.'

'Thanks, I'll be right.'

She walked around the counter and sat on the stool, casting her eyes down the list of figures that Jenny had tallied up. A very successful morning so far. The Gorge committee would be flush this year.

*****

The door pushed open and Emma looked up. She stifled a groan as she met the pursed lips of Jock Newby.

'Doctor Porter,' His voice was almost a grunt. 'Who's in charge here?'

'Is there a problem, Mr Newby?'

He drew himself to his full height and puffed his chest to show her how important he was. 'Who's in charge?'

'I guess I am.' Emma straightened her shoulders. He really was the most difficult man but she had to live and work in the same town so there was no point antagonising him.

'That woman selling those quackery creams and remedies. Does she have a license?'

Emma played dumb. 'What woman?'

'You know who I mean. Wilma Randall. Who knows what's in that stuff she brews out in the bush? It's not legal. We have standards you know.'

'It's not a problem, Mr Newby. All the rules and regulations have been followed for the day and for the stallholders.' She crossed her fingers behind her back. She didn't know how legal it was for George to be selling knives and axes but he wasn't complaining about that.

'I want to see it.'

'See what?'

'Her registration.'

'I really don't think that is any of your business.' Emma's voice was cold. She held her temper. She knew Wilma was licensed as a complementary practitioner and furthermore had RTO status to run courses.

He leaned forward and put his face close to hers. 'It's bad enough that we have you performing your hocus pocus in the town without you encouraging more of it. Ridiculous that you go into the rainforest picking leaves. You should be using your time to look after your patients better.'

Before she could reply, the door opened and Jeremy walked in. He crossed the room and Newby stepped back. Emma clenched her hands in her lap, aware that her cheeks were flushed with anger. She concentrated on keeping herself calm and pushing back the angry words that hovered on her lips.

'Dr Langford. Have you met Mr Newby yet? Our local pharmacist.'

'I have.' Jeremy nodded courteously. 'Good morning, Jock. How are you?'

Jock Newby glared at her and swept past Jeremy without returning his greeting. He called back to her as he shoved the door open. 'It won't be the end of this.'

Jeremy looked after him. 'What was all that about?'
'He was asking about Wilma's license. Don't worry. Jock's had a bee in his bonnet about me ever since I came to town and now he's trying to take it out on her.'

'Seems like a nasty type.'

'He has a problem with our therapies. Close-minded, that's what he is. Anyway, enough of that, not your worry.' She looked up as Jenny opened the door and came in with a cup in each hand.

'One for you too, Em. Thanks for holding the fort. Jock been giving you a hard time?'

'He wanted to know if Wilma was a registered practitioner.'

'Everything is in that folder. It's all good, so stop worrying about him.'

Jeremy was close behind her and Emma took a step to the side. Jen picked up her coffee. "I'll be buzzing by the end of the day!'

Jenny looked from one to the other and winked at Emma.

'Looking good today, Doctor Langford,' she said.

Emma giggled. 'We have a new pin-up boy.'

She was pleased to see him blush.

***

By the time the events had started, the crowds had thinned. Most of the stallholders had packed up, as their goods sold and the tourists meandered back to their resorts and caravan parks. The grandstand began to fill and a crowd of parents cheered from the sidelines as the sack race began. There were a half dozen novelty events for the local children before the tug-of-war heats.

Emma stood beside the grandstand was ticking off the tug-of-war teams on the list that Jeff had handed over.

'I need a word, Doctor Em.' She turned at the gruff

voice.'

'Sell all your knives, did you?'

George pulled a wad of notes from his pocket. 'And don't worry. I paid my stall fee.'

'You old bugger. You told me you weren't even coming.'

'Changed my mind. Besides, I wanted to have a look at your car over at Reg's garage.' He took her arm and pulled her out of earshot of the people walking towards the grandstand. Emma frowned as George looked around and lowered his voice.

'You've been pissing someone off big time. I told you to stay away from the rainforest.'

'What are you talking about?'

He let go of her arm. 'I went to the garage to see your car. You sure made a mess of it.'

'Yes, I think it will be a write-off. I haven't had time to report it yet. I'll have a word to the Sergeant before the tug-of-war heats.

'Reg said your brake line was cut.'

'What?' Emma put her hand to her mouth. 'Is he sure?'

'One hundred percent. He showed me. It was a clean-cut.'

Emma closed her eyes as fear trickled through her. 'He's saying someone deliberately tampered with my car?'

'Yes. And it's because you were out there poking your nose into that bird business. I told you to stay away from the forest, didn't I?'

Everyone had, she thought.

'I told you it was dangerous. You're lucky you didn't

bloody kill yourself when you ran off the road,' George persisted.

Emma bit her lip. 'He's got to be wrong. It could have been a rock or something.'

'It was cut, Emma. Sliced through cleanly. I saw it.' He patted his pocket and pulled out a wad of nicotine gum. 'I told you to stay out of it.'

'I'm going to tell Sergeant Smith. He's over there waiting for the tug-of-war to start.' She handed the clipboard to George. 'Hold this for me. I'll be back in a minute.'

George's eyes widened and his voice shook. 'You can't go telling the police anything. I already told you that.'

'I have to. I've got to report my accident for my insurance, and I'm going to tell him what Reg said too.'

'No, Emma!' Agitation filled George's voice. 'Those men mean business. And they won't care who you are. Woman doctor or not.'

'Which men?'

He stared at her and as she watched his shoulders slump as he came to a decision. 'It's that copper.'

'Which copper.'

'That Anderson bloke.'

'Are you sure?'

'I recognised his voice after he hit me.' George nodded.

Emma's skin crawled with revulsion. Not only was Craig a sleaze, it looked like he was involved in something criminal. She was surprised to see a glint of tears in George's eyes as he looked up at her. 'I was stupid. They snuck up on me, but I heard them talking when they thought I was out to it. Whatever you know, you have to keep it quiet.' He squeezed her hand hard.

'I can't promise that, George. These men are breaking the law and they have a helpless old woman terrified. And they assaulted you. It could have been much worse too.'

'Yeah, but he *is* the fucking law.' His voice was full of disgust.

'Are you absolutely sure it was Craig Anderson?'

'Yes. He got bit by a bird. Check his finger and you'll know I'm telling the truth.'

It hit Emma like a steam train. Craig's finger had been bandaged when she'd seen him up at Wilma's last Friday. She put her hand to her eyes. 'Oh no, and I asked him to keep an eye on Wilma. You said you heard 'they' snuck up on you. How many?'

'I don't know. I only heard one other bloke speak. I didn't recognise his voice but he seemed to be the boss.'

Emma tried to shake free the fear that had settled in her chest. 'Stay here. I won't be long.'

'Doctor Em, please. No!'

She shook off George's hand and strode around the edge of the grassed area. She barely heard the laughter and the screaming of the children running in the race. She bit her lip thinking of how much she would say. Troy had been right. He'd said there were locals involved but he'd said he'd already spoken to the sergeant about being discrete.

Sergeant Smith was on the footpath. Despite the heat, he was wearing a jacket and tie, and his cheeks were ruddier than usual. A small dark cigar was clamped between his lips. Emma wrinkled her nose at the bitter smell and he waved the smoke away.

'Sorry, Doc. Keeps the mossies away' He didn't look apologetic and kept smoking as he regarded her. 'Are you ready for me over there?'

She glanced over at the park. The children's races were still going. 'Soon.'

'I won't be long.' He bent down and ground the stub into the grass.

'I wanted to have a quick word if I may.'

'Sure. But I'm pretty right. I've got the rules here.' He tapped the pocket of his jacket.'

Emma folded her arms. 'It's not about the tug-of-war although I did want to check we're still on for 3 pm. It's about my car.'

He frowned. 'Yeah, 3 pm it is. What about your car?'

'I had a bit of trouble with my brakes last night out on the Cape Tribulation Road. I ran off the road and my car was pretty banged up. Reg reckons it was deliberate. He said they were tampered with.'

'You okay? 'The sergeant stared at her for a moment and then shook his head. 'Bloody kids.'

'What kids?' Emma jumped as a high pitched squeal came over the PA.

'You park in town? At your clinic?'

'I do.'

He turned away and coughed into his hand. 'It's not the first time this has happened in the car parks this week. It's happened to others. We're looking into it.'

'So you don't believe I was targeted deliberately?'

'I doubt it, Doc. Just random stupid behaviour. Lots of that in kids these days.' He buttoned his jacket and straightened his tie, full of self-importance. 'Don't worry, it's under control.' He narrowed his eyes and looked at her. 'Looks like they're ready for me over there. 'Anything else bothering you?'

'No. Thanks for your time.' Emma turned and headed back across the park. George had followed her some of the way and he was leaning against his ute. As she approached him he turned away and spat out a wad of nicotine gum onto the grass.

'George!'

'Bloody stuff tastes foul.'

'So you've told me many times. But since you've stopped smoking, I haven't heard you coughing as much.' She held her hand out for the clipboard.

'So what did he say?'

'It's nothing to worry about.'

Emma and George sprang apart as a shadow fell across them.

It was Jeremy, who looked curiously between the two of them. 'You two look serious. Everything okay? Not crook again are you, George?'

'Nothing that a durrie wouldn't fix.' George slunk away.

Emma grabbed Jeremy's arm. 'I need to talk to you.'

'Come on doc, we're ready.' Jeremy looked around as someone called him from the door of the change room.

'The team's getting changed to go out. Can it wait?

'Okay.' Emma chewed her lip.

'You okay?'

'Not really.'

Jeremy took her arm and frowned. 'Are you ill? Is your

head okay?'

Emma waved her arm. 'No, it's not that. I'll talk to you later.'

'Okay. Now seeing as you made me go in this, I came over to make sure you at least cheer me on.'

'Oh, I'll be there with bells on.' They hurried towards the grandstand together.

'Different to what you're used to, Jeremy?'

'It is.' His mouth tipped in a smile.

They reached the base of the steps. The 1930s grandstand was almost full; children squealed as they ran along the old seats playing hide and seek. The elderly residents from the aged care facility had been set up in the shade along the front of the stand.

'How about a kiss for luck?' Jeremy held her fingers firmly in his and gently tugged her towards him.

She shook her head.

'Old time's sake then?'

She held his eyes steadily for a long moment, ignoring the flutter in her lower belly. 'Don't push it, Jem. I'll kiss the whole team if you win the cup. That will have to do.'

Disappointment clouded his eyes as he dropped her hand. 'I guess it will.'

She watched as he walked away, the denim jeans hugging his butt and the white T-shirt defining his broad shoulders and muscular back. Heads turned as he walked past. Even to people who didn't know him, he had a presence and he'd been quickly accepted by the community. He'd been talking to someone different every time she'd passed him today.

Emma climbed the stairs and forced her thoughts back to the problem in hand.

Was Craig really involved in the smuggling? Was it really him who had hit George? She shivered as she remembered she'd told him about Wilma. Emma looked across the lush green grass of the park below when she reached the top of the stairs. George *had* to be mistaken.

If he was involved Craig wouldn't have sent her into the police station to talk to Sergeant Smith.

Chapter 24

Emma settled into the front row of the grandstand next to Jenny and Judy. The hospital was manned with a skeleton staff today. She pushed the worry about Craig to one side as she watched the next team coming out of the change room below them.

Judy leaned over to Emma. 'The Council beat the bank team and this is the second heat.'

Sergeant Smith held up his hand as both teams grabbed the rope. His deep voice boomed over the microphone. 'Pick up the rope,' he called.

The second heat was decided. Hoots of appreciation filled the air as the next teams emerged from the change room. The boys from the Rural Fire Service had come out in their Speedos and brought an appreciative smile to many faces. A few female hands were fanning cheeks amongst screams of laughter.

Even Jeff had stripped down despite his portly physique. Cissy hurried up the steps and joined them.

'Oh my goodness, how embarrassing. I'll never live it down,' she said.

'It's great to see everyone in the spirit of the day.' Emma bumped her with her shoulder. 'For a middle-aged bloke, he's looking pretty good, Cis.'

The girls cheered as the grey nomies team ran out. They were dressed conservatively in black shorts and yellow T-shirts and the RFS guys quickly pulled them over the line.

There was much back-slapping and congratulations as the visitors conceded defeat. To Emma's fleeting disappointment the medical team ran out and competed in white coats. Jeremy stood a head taller than the rest of the team and Emma cheered as they beat the town team.

Within half an hour, the heats and the semi-finals were over. The girls let out a whoop. The medical team were to face up to the Rural Fire Service for the final.

Cissy fanned herself with the program. 'Well, I don't know who to cheer for!'

The firemen ran from the change room. They'd changed into their fire uniforms for the final and the crowd erupted in a huge cheer. The firemen lined up and waited in the centre of the field and the PA crackled as someone turned up the volume.

Out swaggered the medical team to the words of 'Wild Thing'. The doctors, paramedics and wardsmen postured and hammed it up for the crowd.

Emma caught her breath. How much had Jeremy had to do with the choice of song? That had been his nickname for her in those heady early days. Those lazy sex-fuelled afternoons when they were supposed to be studying.

'Wild thing,' he'd whispered against her hair as they'd caught their breath in her bed.

Now Jeremy stood in the middle of the oval, dressed in a pair of jeans that sat low on his slim hips.

And nothing else.

No shirt.

No shoes.

Just jeans and wraparound sunglasses and a glorious expanse of tanned, muscled chest that brought a collective gasp from the crowd around her.

Each of the men wore the same, but Jeremy was the only one Emma had eyes for. She bit her lip and tried to focus on the rest of the team as they danced up to the firemen.

'The RFS is one short,' Jenny said.

'I wasn't counting,' Cissy said drily. 'Too busy perving on the new doc. Don't tell Jeff. Looks like Troy hasn't turned up.'

Emma started. She hadn't seen Troy all day and hadn't even given him a thought.

'You all right there, Em?' Jenny's eyes were dancing.

'Yes, why?'

'You're very flushed and you keep looking at that scrumptious man.'

'Who? Jeremy?'

Jenny slapped her sides in laughter. 'Oh girlfriend, you are so obvious. Then she drew in her breath on a gasp. 'Look, there's Troy now.'

'I didn't think he was going to turn up,' Cissy said.

Troy ran out from the change room and joined the firemen's team. Unlike the rest of them, he was dressed in a pair of Speedos and heavy boots.

'Looks like they didn't tell him about the costume change,' Emma said. She stared at Troy and sighed. Not a flutter, not one physiological reaction. All she wanted to do was look at Jeremy, damn it.

'Let's go down where they can hear us cheering. Cissy stood and headed for the stairs.

The three women followed her down the steps to the grass verge closest to the area that had been marked out for the competition.

'That's not fair. That bloke's got boots on,' someone called from the crowd. 'Everyone else is bare-footed.'

'Who's looking at his boots?' Cissy murmured.

Emma pushed her shoulder gently. 'Control yourself, you're a married woman.'

'Doesn't mean I can't appreciate the goods on display.'

'Wait,' Sergeant Smith boomed. 'Please remove your shoes, sir.'

Troy sat on the grass and slowly removed his boots. The medicos heckled him, but he grinned and shrugged as if to say it was worth a try.

Sergeant Smith pointed to the boots on the grass and a young boy ran out and collected them.

'Now, the rules may need to be repeated.' He held the microphone to his mouth.

Emma rolled her eyes. 'He can't help himself, can he?'

'He's the same everywhere. Give him a microphone and you can't shut him up.' Cissy rolled her eyes. 'Loves the sound of his own voice.'

'This red mark on the rope needs to be at a perpendicular angle to the exact centre point on the ground, before the commencement of the game. There are two white marks exactly thirteen feet from the red mark on both sides of the rope. The game is won when—'

'We know the rules!'

'You already told us!'

'Here they go.' Cissy grabbed Emma's arm.

'Pick up the rope,' Sergeant Smith called.

Both teams picked up the rope and every man leaned back.

'Pull.'

The crowd erupted in a roar as the men pulled. The medical team had the upper hand from the outset.

'Come on, Jeremy,' Emma called. 'Pull!'

She forced herself to admire the muscles rippling in Troy's broad chest. He looked up and grinned at her. 'Go, Troy.'

She shrugged when Cissy looked at her.

'Gotta be fair.' Emma held her breath as the firemen dug deep and the medicos lost a couple of feet. Their bodies were at an angle of thirty degrees to the ground.

She jumped up and down beside Cissy, screaming. 'Jeremy - pull!'

Each team gained a little ground and then gave it back as the other pulled strongly. Finally, with a deep roar, the medical team put in a supreme effort, and the firemen fell to the ground as the white mark on the rope crossed the centre.

'Yay! We won!' Emma jumped up and down with the other women. They all ran onto the field as the medicos climbed the small stage that had been set up on the side.

Sergeant Smith picked up the trophy and held it to his burly chest as he grasped the microphone with his other hand. 'For the third year running, the hospital team has won the annual Dalrymple Gorge Preservation Fund tug-of-war. I'd like to tell you a little bit about the town. I've lived here for ten years and as you know I'm president of the Rotary club—'

'Give it a break, Sarge,' someone called from the crowd.

'Just present the trophy. The guys deserve a beer.'

Jeff popped a bottle of champagne and sprayed the

winning team. The sergeant jumped back and dropped the microphone. He shoved the trophy at Jeremy before he hurried down the steps with a disgusted look on his face.

Emma caught Jeremy's eye as he held the trophy up with a huge grin. She gave him a thumbs up.

The men headed for the change rooms to get dressed and the crowd dispersed quickly. Emma headed off to help with the clean-up.

'Come over here, Emma. I came to collect.' The deep, familiar voice sent a little frisson of warmth down her back.

She turned slowly. Jeff and Jeremy had caught her up. Jeremy was still shirtless and he lifted his sunglasses with a grin. 'Come on.'

'Well done, both teams. Commiserations, Jeff. Medicos keep the trophy. Three years in a row. Great job!' Emma knew she was babbling but she could hardly take her eyes off Jeremy's bare chest. She tried to focus on his sunglasses, which he dangled by his side.

'We did good, didn't we? Good song too, hey Em?'

She forced herself to look up at him. His smile was innocent but his eyes were dancing. 'You're playing dirty, Jem.'.

'So . . . I believe I was promised a victory kiss?'

Emma stood quickly on her toes and brushed a kiss against Jeremy's smooth cheek.

'Oh, no, you don't get off so lightly.' He grabbed her by the waist and pulled her close. His sunglasses dropped from his hand and bounced on the grass beside the tent.

Jeff's chuckle was the last thing she was aware of before Jeremy's warm lips claimed hers. Her thoughts stuttered to a halt and she lifted her hands to his bare shoulders to push him away, but somehow found herself holding him in a tight grip. His hands slid up her back and a low moan sounded in her throat. Her fingers brushed against his neck and he deepened the kiss. As the blood hummed in her ears, Emma moved closer to his bare chest, her eyes closed, lost in the moment.

Danger, delight and reluctance warred with the desire to lose herself in his arms . . . in his kiss. For one wild moment, it didn't matter where they were. Emma drew a shuddering breath and pulled away when Cissy's amused voice reached her.

'Shall I call the rest of the medicos over for their kisses too?'

Raising a shaky hand to tuck back her hair, Emma focused on keeping her voice calm, looking anywhere but at Jeremy.

'That one was for the whole team.' Her voice was husky. She cleared her throat, clasping her hands together and struggling for calm.

'Okay, boys. Fun's over. Go and get dressed. The official thank yous are about to start.' Cissy saved her from any further embarrassment. 'Well done, Emma. Jenny said we've raised more than thirty thousand dollars this year.'

'A top effort.' Jeremy's voice was quiet.

Emma shook herself out of her dreamy state. She had to get over this before she went on stage to make her thank you speech. If the smile on Jeremy's face was anything to go by, he knew exactly what she was thinking.

'How about a night out to celebrate? Drinks at the Federal?' Jeff looked from Emma to Jeremy.

'A pass for me, but thanks, Jeff. I've got some things I have to do.'

Emma would have loved to go to the pub but she knew it would put her in Jeremy's company for the night. She was helping him move tomorrow so a bit of distance was needed. Time to pull back a bit. Her reaction to his kiss had been a timely warning.

'Come on, you guys. All the helpers up on stage in fifteen minutes so we can wind this up.' Emma's voice was brisk.

Chapter 25

Things to do? Emma was obviously trying her best to avoid him. Jeremy was disappointed, but still looking forward to having her to himself tomorrow. That would be better than sharing her with the crowd at the pub.

'I'll just come for a quick drink, Jeff. I've got a big day tomorrow.' He glanced at Emma as he spoke. 'Moving house, remember? You said you'd help.'

'I almost forgot. Do you still need me?' Her voice was tinged with reluctance.

'Oh, yes. I sure do.' Jeremy looked around and rubbed his hands together. 'So how can I help with this cleanup?'

'You could put a shirt on first. That way we might get some more work out of the other helpers,' Cissy said drily. 'But come on over to the stage first. You've been a part of the team today too.'

He looked down with a grin. In all the excitement of winning and kissing Emma, he'd forgotten he'd shed his shirt for the tug-of-war. He picked up his sunglasses and headed for the change room. Troy was in there getting dressed.

'Great day.' Jeremy pulled his T-shirt over his head.

'Yeah, can't beat these country towns, can you, mate? A huge amount of money raised in such a small place.' Troy picked up and his bag and looked at Jeremy curiously. 'You and the doc got something going on?'

Jeremy pulled his T-shirt down. 'Why do you ask? You interested?'

Troy smiled coolly. 'Could be. You seem to be pretty

good friends.'

'Yep, we go way back.' Jeremy kept his tone noncommittal. Troy could interpret that however he liked. 'Shout you a drink after the official bit?' He injected friendliness into his tone.

'Sure, why not.'

They strolled out together and he looked around for Emma but she'd disappeared. Cissy was walking across the grass towards the car park carrying a bag of rubbish.

'I'll take that over for you.' Troy reached out for the garbage bag.

'Thanks,' Cissy said.

'Where's Emma gone?' Jeremy asked.

'She was worried about Wilma Randall. She noticed she was a bit pale when she was packing up and went to check on her.

'I saw Jock Newby giving her a hard time when I arrived.'

'He's a pain in the arse.' Cissy grimaced.

'What's his prob—'

'Help me! Get the paramedics!' The shout came from the car park.

Emma. Jeremy's blood ran cold.

He took off towards the car park, calling back to Troy over his shoulder. 'Quickly, call the paramedics over here.' Cissy ran beside him.

By the time Cissy and Jeremy reached Emma, the siren was wailing.

Emma was leaning into an old Land Rover and Wilma was inside. Emma was supporting her head against the seat with one hand as she searched for a pulse with the other.

'Wilma! Can you hear me?'

No response.

'The paramedics are here.' Jeremy leaned in beside Emma. 'Here. I'll support her shoulders and you and Cissy take her legs while we get her out of the car.'

They managed to get Wilma on the grass by the time the ambulance pulled up. Emma started the chest compressions and Jeremy tipped Wilma's head back as Tony, one of the paramedics put the defibrillator on the grass beside them.

'Clear please, doctors. We've got her now.'

Emma leaned back against Jeremy as the paramedics worked on Wilma.

'No breathing. No pulse.'

Jeremy held her shoulders steady as they watched Tony attach the electrode pads to Wilma's chest while the other paramedic continued the CPR.

'Rightio. Clear.' Tony's voice was clear as he issued the command and then pressed the shock button. 'We've got a pulse,' he called over his shoulder.

'Quick, we need to get her across to emergency. At least it's not far,' Emma's voice shook.

Jeremy's hands tensed on her shoulders. *Emergency.*

"We'll meet you over there, Doctors. There's a skeleton staff over there. You'll be needed.   We'll take her over now.'

Jeremy glanced into Wilma's car. The keys were in the ignition. 'Jump in, I'll drive. We'll get there quicker if we take her car over.'

The highway traffic pulled aside as the ambulance's wail screamed across the two blocks to the hospital. By the time it had pulled up in the emergency bay, Jeremy had parked the car, and Emma and Cissy ran with him to the emergency door. The familiar cold feeling crawled into his throat and he swallowed it down.

Shit. How could a room have such an effect on him? He tried desperately to keep it together.

***

Five minutes later they'd all changed into hospital scrubs and cleaned up. Jeremy stood behind Emma as she pulled open the curtain of the cubicle. His legs were trembling and his throat was dry, and his heart thudded hard. Chris Shannon was on duty and he glanced up at them briefly as he inserted an IV line into Wilma's arm. 'We're going okay. She's resumed spontaneous circulation but is still unconscious.'

He handed over to the nurse once the line was in. 'Emma, she's your patient, isn't she? Fill me in on her background.'

'Long history of circulation problems. Angina and a partially blocked valve awaiting a stent insertion. She's on ivabradine but has a history of not taking it regularly.' Her voice shook. 'I was at her place last night and I was hard on her. She's started taking it again in the last twelve hours.'

'That probably saved her.'

'Thank God.'

Jeremy stepped outside the cubicle and left Emma with Chris as they planned a treatment regime until Wilma could be safely moved to the coronary unit in Cairns.

'Dalrymple?' The radio crackled and Cissy walked over and picked up the handset.

'Dalrymple Emergency. Go ahead.'

Dread closed Jeremy's throat as the paramedic spoke. 'Drug overdose on the way in. Patient was unresponsive, difficulty with breathing. We're ten minutes out.'

He had to get out of here before he made an absolute fool of himself. The room closed in on him as Emma stepped from the cubicle. 'I'll stay, Cissy. Wilma's stable.'

Jeremy moved quickly to the door. 'I'll see you tomorrow.'

Emma's eyes opened wide and she frowned at him. 'You're leaving?'

'Yes. You don't need me. Not my role here. Under control.' His voice cracked and he barely got the words out. 'Hope Wilma's okay.'

Emma put her hand on to his arm. 'Are you all right?'

As she spoke, a drop of perspiration ran down his cheek. He shook her hand off and dug for his handkerchief to wipe his brow.

'Jeremy? You're very pale.'

'I'm fine. Just do your job.' Jeremy looked away from Emma's shocked and angry expression and backed away from the cubicle. Bright lights hovered at the edge of his vision. He gagged, and lifted his hand to his mouth as he fled from the emergency room. Pulling the scrubs off, he flung them into the basket at the door and pushed open the outside door. He stepped into the driveway where the ambulance was parked and lifted his arms up against the wall. Resting his head on the backs of his hands, he took deep breaths. It took a long time for his heart rate to return to normal and the nausea to pass.

Slowly, he became aware of the sounds around him. Traffic hummed along the highway, and a car started up in the car park. He looked around. There was no one else around and he shoved himself away from the wall and walked over to the bench seat on the edge of the lawn overlooking the aged care facility.

The high-pitched wail of the ambulance siren reached him as he stared at the brick building, now bathed in the afternoon sunlight. The air was thick and syrupy and the cloying smell of sugar cane filled his nose as the ambulance came to a halt in the bay outside the emergency room.

He was kidding himself to think he could stay in a medical career. If this was going to happen to him every time he was in an emergency ward, it would be life-threatening. He already had one death on his conscience and he wouldn't risk it again.

The blue sky was bright and he let the soft afternoon breeze dry the remnants of perspiration on his face. The gurney's wheels scraped on the concrete path as the paramedics pushed it to the door, but Jeremy wouldn't look at it.

Instead, he leaned forward, dropping his hands loosely between his knees and stared at the grass. He had to get away.

Away from the hospital. Away from emergencies. Away from critical care. He could cope with the Outreach position and doing clinic work, but he needed an office somewhere else. He had finally realised it was only the emergency ward where he came undone. He'd coped fine with George's emergency and Wilma's heart attack but as soon as he was in the ward everything went to shit.

If he was expected to be in the hospital and be available for emergency work, he'd move on. Somewhere else, away from anything to do with medicine. He had his MBA to fall back on. He pushed himself to his feet and walked slowly back to the hotel. He remembered Jeff's invitation to drinks, but he was in no mood for company tonight.

He blocked the thought of Emma and the doctors working together in the emergency room. Trying to save another life.

They'd be better off without him.

Chapter 26

The paramedics had the patient with suspected psycho-stimulant toxicity stabilised by the time they reached the hospital. The young man was conscious when they examined him and it was clear he was in no immediate danger. Another local victim of the ice epidemic in the Daintree.

Emma returned to the cubicle where Wilma lay staring at the ceiling. She was drowsy, but aware enough to be argumentative and Emma wouldn't leave until she was sure that her patient was stable and responding to the drugs Chris Shannon had administered.

'I'll come back first thing in the morning before they take you down to Cairns.'

'I don't want to go to another hospital.' The elderly woman's face was lined and her eyes were bloodshot.

'We won't send you down there until we see how you are in the morning. We'll discuss it then.' She lifted the old woman's hand in hers. 'That was a very close call. If you'd been at your place . . .'

'If I'd been at home it would have been my time. I'm ready for it, Emma.' Wilma squeezed Emma's hand and set her lips in a straight line.

Emma frowned. 'You're not going to die anytime soon.'

'Please don't worry about me,' she said quietly.

She nodded reluctantly as Wilma tried to sit up and she pushed her back gently. 'Okay. Now settle down and I'll come see you in the morning.'

'Thank you.' Wilma's thin hand reached out for her. 'Emma. I'm sorry.'

'What for?'

'For not listening to you.'

Emma leaned over and let her lips brush against Wilma's forehead. Maybe it was unprofessional, but she considered the old woman a friend as much as a patient. 'It's okay. I'm sorry for being so hard on you too. You know I just care about you.'

She pushed opened the door and took a deep breath. Darkness had fallen while she was inside and the night was quiet and still. A shadow moved outside the door and she put her hand to her chest.

'I guess you want a lift home, Doctor Em?'

'Oh George. You startled me. But yes, thanks. You're a champ to wait for me.'

'Is Wilma going to be okay?'

'I hope so. We'll have to run some more tests' She followed him to the old ute and climbed up into the passenger seat. 'Do you mind stopping by the pub on the way home?'

'Hard day, hey?'

'Yes.'

It had been a horrid day. Well no, not completely, to be fair.

The huge amount of money they'd raised at the Rainbow Day and the community spirit there had filled her with pride. The response from locals and tourists had been great. Looking at Jeremy with his shirt off—that had been another high point. Her lips tilted in a smile. But the rest of the day had sucked, and Jeremy's behaviour at the hospital had annoyed her.

George changed gears noisily and turned the corner,

parking outside the back door of the pub.

'I won't be long. I just want to talk to Doctor Langford for a minute.'

'Take your time. I like the new doc too.' This time he threw a smile her way and she rolled her eyes at him. She was disappointed in Jeremy. If he wanted to be a rural doctor, he was going to have to shed some of that arrogance. It was time he realised that everyone pulled together up here in the small hospital.

She opened the door to the bar and waved to Rod before turning to the steps that led up to the guest rooms. She was halfway up when she realised she didn't know which room was Jeremy's.

'Rod, which room is Jer . . . uh, Doctor Langford's?'

'Number three, but he's not up there.' Rod pointed to the door. 'He headed off in his running gear about an hour ago.'

'Oh, okay. Thanks.' Emma ignored the disappointment that tugged at her, but at least if he'd gone for a run, he was okay. She'd talk to him tomorrow. 'Can you tell him I called in and I'll see him in the morning?'

'Sure will,' Rod said with a wink. 'Nice guy that doc.'

Seemed like everyone liked the new doc. And that there was a bit of gossip around after that public kiss. But he'd upset her when he'd left emergency tonight, even if he hadn't been feeling well.

George dropped her off at the boat ramp and waited until she was safely across to the other side in her punt.

Poor little Bowser flung himself at her when she opened the gate at the top of the two back steps. She'd left him secure on the porch all day, still wary of letting him out near the river when she wasn't home. He took off with a yap and lifted his leg on every fence post along the side of the house, before trotting back to her as she filled his bowl with kibble.

'Sorry, little man.' She ruffled his soft fur and yawned. 'If I'd known I was going to be so late, I would have taken you to town too.'

The house was dark, but there was a cool breeze blowing down the hall. The hair on Emma's arms lifted. She'd never felt uneasy living alone before and she was angry that she was jumpy tonight. She reached over for the light switch and flicked it on, bathing the front half of the house in bright light.

No movement, no sound greeted her. Cautiously, she walked slowly down the hall, pausing outside each door and looking into the two bedrooms and the bathroom. They were all empty and everything seemed to be in its place. As it should be.

She jumped as a gust of wind slammed the door back against the hallway wall. She reached for it and gripped the edge as she peered around the front. The small front yard was deserted and there were no vehicles in sight. Bowser stood quietly beside her.

She pushed the door closed and turned the key firmly to lock it, her hands shaking. Leaning against the door, she listened to her heart thudding. Knowing that someone had tampered with her car scared her. For the first time, she didn't feel safe in Crooked Cottage.

Chapter 27

Saturday night – Dalrymple

The run hadn't helped Jeremy's peace of mind. Normally if he pushed himself, he could make himself forget the memories. But being in emergency tonight had brought the past slamming back with a vengeance. He pushed open the door of the hotel and crossed the empty room to the bar. Rod was just closing up.

'Soda water?' Rod reached for a glass, but Jeremy shook his head and pointed to the doorway that led to the bottle shop at the side of the pub.

'Bottle shop still serving?'

'Sure is. What can I get you?'

'A bottle of Glenfiddich. Put it on my bill, please.'

'Celebrating your last night, doc?'

Jeremy forced a smile onto his face. 'Yeah, something like that.' It was his business, and his alone, if he intended drinking himself into a dreamless state tonight. Rod disappeared into the other room and came back with the requested bottle, but he was on for a chat.

'Nice place you've got yourself out there on the Gorge Road.' He leaned his elbows on the counter and nodded. 'Looks like you've settled into Dalrymple real well.'

'Yes.' Jeremy picked up the bottle. Everything in this town was everybody's business, it seemed. What was attractive to him only this morning, now breached his privacy and he forced a polite tone to his voice.

Rod took the hint that he wasn't in the mood for

conversation. 'Well, I won't keep you.' He picked up his cleaning cloth. 'Oh, I almost forgot. Emma came in. She said to tell you she'd see you tomorrow.

'Thanks.' He picked up the bottle and headed for the stairs.

Three hours later, Jeremy was sitting on the verandah, enjoying the feel of the warm, tropical air on his skin. The cloying smell of the sugarcane surrounded him as the night deepened. He'd pulled the pin when the bottle was half empty. No need to poison himself. His father's proposition was uppermost in his mind tonight. He'd called twice more this week and Jeremy had given him short shrift.

'Your place is here in Sydney,' his father had said when Jeremy had declined the offer for the third time. 'With your family.'

Family? It was impossible to believe that Brenton would ever want him back in the city. Jeremy's actions, or his lack of action, had destroyed a part of their family. The loss would always be a part of the relationship.

He reached for the bottle and poured another two fingers of whisky into the small glass. So much for stopping. He threw it back in one gulp, appreciating the cruel burn as it seared his throat.

In the short time he'd spent in the emergency room tonight, it had become quite clear that he'd been kidding himself. As long as he was involved in any health career, he would always be expected to help in an emergency. That was the oath he had taken.

'I will not be ashamed to say 'I know not,' nor will I fail to call in my colleagues when the skills of another are needed

for a patient's recovery.'

It didn't say anything about walking out when he should have helped.

His thoughts blurred and ran together and Jeremy welcomed the fuzziness. After tonight it would be it quite clear to anyone at the hospital that he wasn't to be relied on. After kissing Emma this afternoon, he'd briefly indulged the hope that they might be able to get together, but he'd been kidding himself if he thought rekindling that relationship could make everything better.

He slammed the glass onto the table. Lifting his hands to his face, he rubbed his eyes.

It was time for him to face the truth. He had to deal with it.

Or leave.

He was kidding himself now and letting himself wallow in self-pity.

He had an opportunity to make a life up here with Emma if she'd have him. And by God, he wasn't going to let that dark place in his heart drag him down again.

In the short time he'd been here, he had become a part of the community. That was an entirely new experience for him and one that he was appreciating more each day.

Emma was a big part of his entry into this world. He was valued here as a person, not because of what sort of car he drove or where he lived or where he was seen dining or socialising.

He pushed himself to his feet and opened the door to go inside. The lights of a vehicle blinded him as it turned the corner and headed down towards the mill on the next block.

With a shrug, he closed the door, kicked off his running shoes and stretched out on the bed.

***

Daintree Village

After a quick shower and a toasted sandwich, Emma fell into bed. Although she was tired, sleep eluded her as her mind raced from one thing to another. Had someone been in her house? Was it just a coincidence that her brake line had been cut? She jumped at every noise as the old house settled and creaked in the dark.

And what about that kiss with Jem? She had to put aside her feelings for him or she was in for heartache—and she wasn't going to let that happen. She thumped the pillow and rolled over, remembering the disdain on his mother's face. She hadn't been good enough then, and if being a doctor meant she might be more acceptable now, she didn't want a bar of that.

And there was Wilma—Emma was worried about her chances. She'd called the hospital and been reassured that she was sleeping, but her heart was in a bad way. She didn't like the way Wilma had been talking tonight. It seemed as though she had given up, and with the elderly that was often the thing that tipped the balance between life and death.

She thumped the pillow again and kicked off the sheet. The humidity was building as summer approached and this small house didn't have an air conditioner. She reached over and turned on the overhead fan to stir the air.

In the end, she gave up trying to get to sleep and padded out to the kitchen and put the kettle on, before digging deep in the cupboard for a chamomile tea bag, one of Wilma's blends. Jock Newby flashed into her head; he'd probably say it was more of her hocus pocus. Damned fool; Jenny had told her that he'd confronted Wilma at her car. She suspected it had been the stress of that confrontation that had set Wilma's blood pressure soaring and sent her into cardiac arrest. There's been no sign of him as they'd worked on Wilma. Why was he going on about it so much? She poured the boiling water and let the bag steep.

Tomorrow was going to be a challenge. Spending the day with Jeremy in his rented house, helping him put his furniture together would test her will power, but she was determined not to give in. She stood at the sink in the darkness looking out over the river. The new moon was rising, but only a sliver lit the dark sky to the east. An arc of bright light swept the treetops high in the paddock across the river as a vehicle turned off the village road. Emma narrowed her eyes and gripped the edge of the sink as the low noise of a plane's engine reached her. She glanced at the clock. It was the same as last time: almost 4.00 am.

Right. This time she was going to find out exactly what was going on over there. If she saw Craig there, it would be confirmation that he was involved.

Emma hurried into the bedroom and Bowser gave a little snuffle from the end of her bed as she reached for her jeans and slipped them on over her pyjama bottoms. She waited until he tucked his nose down again and settled back to sleep. Without making any noise, she picked up a pair of socks and closed the bedroom door behind her. Grabbing her slip-on leather boots, she opened the back door and stepped onto the porch.

The vehicle lights had disappeared but she could just make out voices across the narrow river. As she watched, a flicker of torchlight pointed skywards briefly. She kept to the shadows as she walked slowly down to the edge of the river, keeping an eye out for snakes. In the dim light from the sliver of the moon, she saw that the river was high. Noiselessly she slid the punt away from the bank and jumped in.

The tide swung it around and rocked it gently from side to side as Emma lay down and reached up for the rope with one hand. Moving across the dark channel towards the other side of the river, the only sound was the occasional quiet slap of water on the side of the punt. She shivered, wondering what was moving in the water beneath her. The punt hit the bank on the village side with a small bump and she sat up slowly; her eyes now fully accustomed to the dark.

She climbed out and slipped the rope on the bow of the punt around the steel post at the edge of the narrow boat ramp. Keeping to the deep shadows beneath the trees and watching where she was putting her feet, she made her way along the bank until she reached the edge of the paddock where the vehicle was parked. The drone of the plane's engine slowly got louder and two streams of torchlight pointed to the sky to guide it in. A small bump and the engine cut as it cruised along the narrow paddock.

She crept along further, trying to listen to the low voices. It sounded like there was two of them on the ground waiting for the plane. She gripped the edge of the overhanging bank above her head and slowly stretched to the tips of her toes. With a stifled gasp, she pulled back; the vehicle was only a stone's throw from where she was standing. Lights flashed around and over her head to the other side of the river and she held her breath as they played across the wall of her cottage. Her kitchen window was clearly lit and she could see the shelves on the back wall. They would have seen her standing there the last time they were here. Footsteps approached the bank and she dropped to a crouch and put her hands over her face.

'It's all quiet tonight.' She heard the creaking of a door and the thud of something hitting the ground.

'Good. There's been too much interest around here in the last few days.' The voice was muffled and although it was familiar she couldn't place it. She was pretty sure George had been mistaken. But if it wasn't Craig, who was it?

'How many have you got for me?'

'Just the one pair.'

'Hardly worth the bloody trip.' Emma tipped her head to the side waiting for the response.

'You'll want to take care of these ones. It's a rare set. Ninety thou for the pair.'

'Fuckin' hell! What are they, gold-plated?'

'Don't you worry about it, just deliver them. Make sure they're X-rayed before you hand them over. We don't want them breeding this lot over there. And make sure the money goes in within forty-eight hours. Okay, then. Help me with the rest of these.'

The men moved away from her and the voices faded. Emma edged forward, trying to hear the rest of the exchange. The riverbank crumbled beneath her feet and there was a soft splash as a clod of earth hit the water.

'What was that?'

'Just a bird or something. Hurry up and get those boxes unloaded.'

'I'm going to see. That piece across the river was watching us the other night.'

'Don't worry, I've got the doc sorted.'

Emma drew in a breath. Whoever they were, they knew who she was.

'Is she there tonight?'

The man laughed. 'With the other doc, if he got lucky.

Emma pressed herself back into the tangle of tree roots in the bank, trying not to think of what else might be in there with her. A cobweb stuck to her face and she closed her eyes as something ran lightly across her forehead. Footsteps rustled in the grass above her head and a shaft of torchlight highlighted her house again and swept down to the edge of the river beneath her backyard. The bitter smell of a cigar drifted down to her hiding place and she stifled a gasp.

'It's all right. She's not home, the punt's on this side. Maybe the lucky bugger did score tonight.' Now that he was closer, she recognised the voice. It was Sergeant Smith. And the smell of the cigar smoke confirmed it.

She held her breath as the light played along the edge of the water only a metre from where the toe of her boots was dug into the mud to stop her sliding into the river. Eventually he seemed satisfied and his footsteps receded. She listened as more boxes landed on the ground.

A few minutes later, a door slammed and the plane's engine hummed to life again. She waited as it took off, watching as it circled over the low rainforest to the west of her house, staring at the blinking lights until they disappeared into the night sky.

All was quiet above her; no sound of movement or of a vehicle starting up. But then a movement further along the bank set a pair of ducks squawking into the night air, breaking the silence with their raucous cries. She risked leaning out and glanced along the bank, and pulled back quickly as she saw the bright red tip of a cigarette glowing in the dark. He was still there. A car door slammed.

'Anderson. After you drop me off unload those boxes into the shed at the back of your place.'

'No, I'm going to move this lot to the shed at the police station.' Craig's voice was clear now as he moved along the bank directly above her hiding place.

'Who the fuck do you think you are, boy? Smith's voice was belligerent.

'My wife is moving up here. I don't want her to see them. I'm on my last warning with her with the drugs.'

'I don't give a flying fuck if the bloody Queen of Sheba is moving here. You do not make the decisions in this game. You don't know how close you came to getting into big trouble down in Brisbane, dickhead. It would only take one phone call to your uncle and we can pull all of that nasty business up again. Not only will you be out of a job but you'd be inside before you know it.'

'But—'

'You might think you're more than a player in this game, but you do as you're told. And keep your mouth shut.'

'I can't.'

'You fucking will. Do I make myself clear?' His voice

rose and there was a flutter of wings as a couple of birds took off from the bank above Emma.

'Yes.' Craig's voice was sullen.

'Yes what?'

'Yes, sir.'

'Don't mess with me. If you bugger this up, I'll make you wish you'd never heard of this town. I don't care who your uncle is.' Emma's heart was thudding painfully and her throat ached with the effort of holding her breath and trying not to move as insects crawled over her hands and up her arms. Finally they moved away and a door slammed and the vehicle moved away towards the village. Waiting till all was quiet, she brushed frantically at her arms and pushed out of the wet tangle of roots. She climbed up the bank and peered over to an empty dark paddock.

She put a shaking hand to her forehead. It was the two policemen who were involved. They'd assaulted George and now she knew for sure that her brakes had been tampered with.

Smith was in it up to his neck and she'd told him about George and Wilma. Emma began to walk back to the punt. She should have listened to Troy and George and kept her mouth shut.

Chapter 28

Sunday

The low overhanging grey sky matched Emma's mood when she woke the next morning. Heavy clouds were scudding across the sky and small whitecaps stood high in the brown muddy river as the wind pushed the water against the tide. Bowser was scratching at the door demanding to be let out and she climbed wearily out of bed, resisting the temptation to bury her head and let the world go by. There were calls she had to make and promises to keep, no matter how much she had on her mind. She fed Bowser and called the hospital, frowning as Judy spoke of Wilma's difficult night.

'Greg has decided not to move her to Cairns until her blood pressure settles. He's been with her most of the night.'

'Is she better this morning?' Emma bit her lip, hoping that George had remembered he was driving her to town. Not having a car was going to make things hard but that was the least of her worries today.

'She's quite calm now, and pleased to still be here.'

'Okay, please let her know I'll be there soon.'

The second call she made was to the rainforest centre. She had to talk to Troy and let him know what she'd seen.

'Good morning. Rainforest Tourist Centre.'

'Troy Greaves please.' She walked over and opened the door and let Bowser back in.

'I'm sorry. Troy's not at the centre today. Can someone else help you?'

'No,' Emma said. 'It's personal. Do you have a mobile number where I can reach him?' Emma realised how little she knew about Troy. She didn't even know if he lived in town, and she'd never had his mobile number – he'd always called her.

'I'm sorry. I can't give out personal numbers.'

'It's essential that I speak to him today.' Emma's voice firmed. 'It's Doctor Emma Porter from the hospital and I really must speak to him.'

'Just a moment, Doctor Porter.' The woman's voice was muffled as she put her hand over the phone.

Emma tapped her foot impatiently as she waited for her to come back.

'I'm sorry, I can't give you his number but I can take your number and ask him to call you. He's down in Cairns for the day.'

'Thank you. Please tell him it's a matter of urgency.' Emma gave her mobile number and disconnected.'

Bowser snuggled his head into her lap and she ruffled his fur. 'Bowsie, what am I going to do?' Her voice shook and she brushed away the tears that threatened to spill.

By the time Emma had showered and pulled the punt across the river, George was out the front of his old house waiting for her.

'Where to?' He chewed on his gum and a scowl split his face.

'What are you so happy about today?'

'Didn't get much sleep.'

Emma looked at him curiously. 'Why? Did something keep you awake?'

'Like what?' He turned an innocent look her way.

'Nothing, doesn't matter.' Emma walked around to the passenger door.

'Mightn't to you.' His voice was gruff. 'But that was a damn fool thing you did last night. I saw you come across the river.'

Emma's head flew up and her eyes narrowed. 'Did the plane wake you up?'

'No. I couldn't sleep. I heard the punt scrape when you pulled it up.'

'It's not the first time the plane's been there. Have you heard it before?'

'No, I haven't. You scared ten year's growth off me, Em. I just about had me own heart attack watching you, making sure you got back safe to your place.'

'I know who it is.' Her voice was flat.

'You saw him?

'I saw *them*. Craig and Sergeant Smith.'

He stared at her, tight-lipped. 'I'm not surprised. I told you not to go to the cops. What are you going to do about it?'

'I'm going to tell Troy and he can hand it over to the National Parks guys.'

'I'm so bloody cranky at you, Emma. You could have got yourself killed last night not to mention your car accident.' George held the steering wheel tightly and didn't speak again as they drove into town.

'Just be bloody careful today, okay?' He dropped her off at the front of the hospital and drove off before she could even thank him for the lift. As soon as she checked on Wilma, she'd go to the pub and help Jeremy with his move. The

274

thought of being alone with him in his new house brought butterflies to her stomach. She told herself it was only because her nerves were shot by what she'd found out. She gripped her mobile tightly waiting for Troy to call but the phone stayed silent.

Wilma was pleased to see Emma.

'Emma, if I'm in here for a while, can you please ask George to check up on my place occasionally. Feed the ducks and the chooks?'

'I'm sure he will.'

'And Emma? Can you do something for me too? '

'Of course.' She smoothed back Wilma's hair from her forehead. She looked tired but her blood pressure was stable.

'I need a few things from home. It looks like I'm going to be away a while.' The elderly woman pulled a face. 'I guess I do need to listen to the doctors a bit more.'

'You do.' Emma smiled.' What do you need?'

Wilma told her where to find her clean clothes and what toiletries she needed. 'There's no rush. Just when you can. And take that young man of yours with you. I still worry about what's going on out there.'

'I will.' Emma didn't mention what she knew nor did she correct Wilma about the 'young man' comment. And there was no way she'd go out there by herself again.

Emma pushed open the side door of the pub and waved to Rod as she crossed the bar to the stairs and headed for the top floor. She stepped onto the wide graceful verandah. The old timber floor was covering in orange petals from the Poinciana tree that grew on the footpath outside. The door to Room Three was pulled shut and the curtains were drawn. A half-empty bottle of scotch and a single glass were sitting on the small table outside the door.

Frowning, she tapped on the glass door, but there was no answer.

'Jeremy?' She rapped her knuckles harder this time. 'Are you in there?'

Maybe he'd gone to the house without her. She glanced down at watch. She'd said mid-morning and it was only just after ten-thirty.

Knocking again, she stepped back and waited, watching the busy highway as the traffic passed through the small town. A muffled bang and a groan came from within and Emma hurried back to the door.

'Jeremy? Are you in there?'

'Go away.'

'What's wrong? Are you sick?' She cast a dubious glance down at the bottle on the table. During the night she'd put his leaving down to not feeling well, prepared to give him the benefit of the doubt.

'No, I'm fine. I'm having a sleep in.'

Emma pursed her lips and folded her arms. 'I came to town especially to help you move. But I'm happy to leave. I can find plenty to do on a Sunday off,' she yelled through the door. 'What's it to be?'

The glass panels shook as the door was wrenched open, and Jeremy stood in the doorway scowling at her. She looked him up and down and fixed on the bare stomach in front of her. His jeans were unbuttoned and his chest was bare. Her temper was momentarily forgotten as she dropped her eyes to the narrow V of golden hair that disappeared below the open zipper. Her mouth dried and she snapped it shut as she glared at him.

There was safety in temper. If not she'd be too tempted put her hands on that warm bare skin. His eyes were bleary and his hair was tousled and he looked about eighteen years old. The smell of stale alcohol wafted off him.

'You know, I've just about had enough of being scowled at by cranky men this morning.' She inclined her head to the bottle and glass. 'But I guess it's the alcohol talking and the smooth, suave Doctor Langford that the town loves has taken a break?'

'Well, you're in a fine mood this morning too.' The first glimmer of a smile tilted his mouth. 'At least I can blame a hangover. What's your excuse?' He rubbed his hand through his hair in frustration. 'I'm sorry. Is it Wilma, is she all right?'

'Yes. But still not out of the woods.'

'I'm sorry, Em. A tough night coming to terms with some things I needed to.' He looked miserable.

'Do you still want me to help?'

'Can you put up with me being shitty?'

'I guess I can. Now go and take a shower. You look like you need one. I'll go and rustle up a couple of coffees. And you think you've had a tough night? Wait till you hear about mine.'

'What?' His brow lowered in a frown and he winced.

'I found out who's involved in the smuggling. And who assaulted George. And I need to tell you about my car too.'

'Who and what about it?'

'I'll fill you in when I get back. Now go and have a shower.' She looked down at her phone willing it to ring. 'I'll be back in five minutes.'

By the time Emma returned from the bakery with three croissants and two strong coffees, Jeremy was sitting at the table on the verandah. She'd avoided the police station and kept a nervous eye out for either of the police cars as she'd walked along the main road to the bakery. Her phone stayed silent. The scotch and the glass were gone and he was showered, clean-shaven, and dressed in a pair of jeans and a clean white T-shirt. He no longer looked like a man who'd demolished half a bottle of whisky.

He reached for one of the paper bags as she held out his coffee. 'You're a lifesaver.'

'So are you going to tell me what happened to you last night?' She wagged a finger at him. 'And don't try to deny it. You took off from the hospital as though someone was after you, and then drank yourself silly by the look of things.'

'I'm okay.' He ran his hand through his damp hair but he didn't meet her eyes.

Emma sipped her coffee as he chewed on the croissant. She put the other bags on the table beside him.

'Don't you want one?'

'No, I bought three for you. I remember you always had a ravenous appetite after a night on the town.'

'You're a sweetheart. I'm sorry I was cranky.' He looked up at her and reached up for her hand. 'Thanks for the breakfast. Now what did you find out last night?'

Emma pulled her hand away and reached for the empty bag.

'It's both of them from the police station.'

'What?' Jeremy's eyes widened.

'It's Craig *and* Sergeant Smith. They assaulted George and it was obviously them out at Wilma's.

'Jesus, are you sure? How did you find out?'

Emma waved her hand. She'd had enough grief from George about last night. What Jeremy didn't know wouldn't hurt him.

'Trust me. I'm sure. I've left a message for Troy. As soon as he rings he can let the national parks guys know.' Emma dropped her head into her hands. 'Can you believe it? I don't know who to trust anymore.'

'Do we need to call someone? Let someone else know? And what about your car?'

'The brake line was cut. It was deliberate.'

'What! You need to tell the police. Shit you can't.'

'I already have but Smith brushed it off. I should have known he was fobbing me off. Troy can handle it. He has the connections.' Emma closed her eyes as Jeremy cupped her cheek with his hand.

'Jesus, Em. You could have been killed. Are you okay?'

She let out a sigh. 'I'm all right. It's just been a hard couple of weeks.'

'It has. How's Wilma this morning?

'She's not being moved to Cairns yet.'

'That's good news. She must be responding to the drugs.'

'She is.'

'Look, I knew you all had it under control last night. You didn't need me, but I'm sorry I took off in such a hurry.'

'You want to talk about it?'

Jeremy took in a deep breath and stood. 'Come on, let's

get out of here. You happy to drink your coffee while we head out to the house?'

'I'd be happier if you let me drive and you drink *your* coffee.'

A rueful grin crossed his face. 'Yeah. I didn't think of that. Not a good example if I get booked for drink-driving. Where's that other croissant?'

'Get your stuff first.'

Jeremy bought out a couple of suitcases and Emma smothered a grin.

Always organised. Always neat and everything in its place.

She drove the Outreach Land Cruiser through town and turned right onto the Gorge Road. It was only a five-minute drive out of town. It was good to be doing something normal. She sighed as she turned into the driveway of the property he was renting. The grass was long and the flowerbeds were choked with weeds.

'How sad. Albert and Lorna always kept this garden immaculate.'

'Guess I've got my work cut out for me.'

She shot him a curious glance. 'So you are going to move in? I was starting to wonder.'

He held her eyes steadily and she pushed away the little frisson that stirred in her belly.

'Yes. I might have a couple of things on my mind but I'm not a quitter. Besides, I'm not renting it—'

'For long?' Emma finished the sentence for him but was surprised to see him shake his head.

'If you let me finish, I was going to say, I'm not renting

it. Well, I am, until settlement. I've bought it. When I spoke to Lorna and Albert, I realised that they needed the money to stay in the aged care facility. And—'he shrugged—'if I move on I can always rent it out.'

Surprise shot through Emma. It was the last place she would have expected him to live. She couldn't help herself. 'Not what you're used to. You'd better do some renovations before your mother—your family—come to visit. But it was a lovely thing to do.'

'I don't expect they'll visit.' His tone was terse and very un-Jeremy like.

'Why not?'

'You nailed it. It's not a five star resort.'

He opened his door, and came around and opened the driver's side door while Emma gathered up the empty coffee cups and brushed the croissant crumbs off the seat. Their fingers brushed briefly but she ignored the tickle at her nerve endings.

Emma had always loved this house. It was an original Queenslander, situated high to let the cool breeze circulate underneath. In the days those houses were built, there was no air conditioning to ease the topical heat. The long straight staircase leading up to a closed in front verandah was shaded by the overhanging branches of the Poinciana trees on either side.

'Needs some work,' she commented. The white paint was peeling and in a couple of places the guttering had detached from the tin roof. Palm trees shaded it from the north and the lawn was long and lush.

She followed him along the driveway. The house was

surrounded by vacant land and Emma shivered as the grass rustled on the paddock on the other side of the fence. 'Watch out where you're walking. You'll have to get someone in to mow this soon–I'm surprised the agency let it get this long. The snakes are on the move already.' She tipped her head to the side. 'Are you really sure you want to live out here?'

'I know it's a challenge, but it's one I'm ready to take up.' This time he grinned, and it was good to see his lips tip in a smile. 'It will be good to have my own place and I'm looking forward to learning some building skills.'

Emma couldn't help the laugh that bubbled up from her chest.

'That'll be fun to watch.'

'Would you believe it's my first foray into living independently? Not like you, living in that little flat in Surry Hills when you were seventeen.' The miasma of gloom surrounding him had disappeared. 'Twenty-eight and I finally have my own place.'

'You know it's only got an outside loo, don't you?'

'Yep. Part of the rustic appeal.' His blue eyes bored into hers.

'You might think I'm playing at being the country doctor. I told you I wasn't happy with the life I was living before, and it's time for a whole new start. It's going to be hard—in many ways but—' he stopped at the end of the driveway and took her hands in his— 'I want you to think about being a part of it.'

Her whole body was trembling with restrained emotion. How easy would it be to fall into his arms and pretend they could take up where they left off?

'I can't make you any promises I can't keep, Jeremy.' She pulled her hands out of his and strode up the stairs. 'We're a fine pair,' she muttered under her breath as he followed her up onto the front porch.

Chapter 29

The delivery man from the furniture store in Port Douglas had unloaded the flat pack boxes onto the porch and Jeremy regarded them with some suspicion. How could all that neat furniture be stored in three piles of flat rectangular boxes? The problem at hand—the furniture assembly—was filling his mind nicely and the darkness of last night was receding with each step they took around his new house. Having Emma beside him was a bonus that was improving his mood.

'I wish Troy would ring. I can't settle until he knows and starts things moving.' Emma had been holding her phone since they'd left the pub. 'I feel so frustrated. I don't know where else to go. It's hard to know who to trust.'

'It all seems very murky. With the two of them being in the police force will make it interesting.'

'They'll have to answer to the assault on George and the tampering with my car as well. I won't let it go. As soon as the police—or whoever it is investigating—arrive, I can tell them what I heard.' Emma bit her lip and picked up the first flat pack.'

'Heard?' Unease flooded through Jeremy. 'What did you hear?'

'I heard them talking about storing something in the garage at the police residence.' Emma mumbled as she ripped open the box.

'So where did you overhear this?'

'Don't worry about it. As soon as Troy rings, I can

relax.' Emma glanced across at the phone on the floor beside her. She sat in the middle of the half-opened boxes and pushed a strand of loose hair back. Jeremy decided not to push the issue. He'd find out later what she was talking about.

'It's good to see you looking a bit happier.' Emma shot him an affectionate glance as they opened the last box.

He glanced over at her, trying to ignore the spark that fired in him every time he got a whiff of her perfume. Her skin was glowing and she had her hair pulled high into that swishy ponytail thing that he'd always loved. She wore a pair of cut-off denim shorts and he caught a glimpse of her soft curves outlined by the black singlet top as her over-shirt fluttered open when she leaned forward.

'A bed. One table, eight chairs, a desk, a coffee table. She looked at the pieces on the floor in front of them. 'This shouldn't take long.'

'It would have taken me all weekend.'

Her laugh stirred his blood, but it was the words that followed that had the most effect on him.

'We both know what you're like with your hands, don't we, Jem? Just as well you never wanted to be a surgeon.'

A soft pink flush stained her cheeks. He saw the moment that she read what he was thinking.

'I thought I was pretty good with my hands once.' He kept his voice soft and her blush deepened as she held his gaze.

'Well, those days are long past.' She rubbed her hands together and looked around. 'Did you get set of Allen keys?'

'I did.'

Well, she couldn't stop him looking at her rounded

bottom in those hip-hugging shorts as she bent to open the first box.

It took longer than he'd thought to put it all together. Even Emma had frowned at some of the directions. It was good to hear her laugh as she read some of the Chinese literal translations.

'Are these for real? Or is it supposed to be funny?' She giggled as she turned the assembly sheet the other way.

Jeremy's contribution consisted of holding and passing as Emma directed. Finally the table and chairs were set up in the kitchen, and the desk and coffee table were together in the living room. Emma grunted at him. He passed the bag of screws over with his spare hand as he held the final corner of the bed frame above the floor. She turned the Allen key and screwed the bed head on.

Finally she stepped back. 'You can let go now.' She looked around the room. It opened onto a verandah that ran around three sides of the house. Lacy curtains hung either side of the double cedar doors that opened onto the verandah. An old cane lounge setting was up against the wall beneath the window. 'Here, cut the plastic off the mattress and we'll get it on the bed.'

Together they picked up the king-size mattress and levered it so it was over the bed frame. Jeremy pushed his end and it nestled neatly in the recess at the top.

'All done. Have you got any sheets? I'll give you a hand to make it.'

Jeremy headed out to the car. He'd left the park yesterday for a quick shop at the local co-op and bought some essentials and left them in the boot.

He opened the packet of sheets as he walked through the door.

'Ugh. You could have at least washed them; they'll be as stiff as a board.'

He raised an eyebrow and a blush ran up her neck. She moved around to the other side of the bed, then flicked the bottom sheet over the mattress. As she stretched to tuck the far corner in, she over-balanced and fell along the top of the mattress.

She rolled over and lay there staring up at him and the vulnerability on her face banished the last shreds of determination that Jeremy had held onto. He dropped onto the bed beside her.

And then he was kissing her, his mouth hot and hard against hers as their playful love turned to passion. Teeth clashing, tongues dancing, delicious heat and power flowed through her.

He lifted his arms from the bed and pulled off his T-shirt at the same time that her fingers found the zipper of his jeans.

'I've wanted to do this ever since you ran out in your jeans and sunnies yesterday,' she said.

He dipped his head and placed his lips against her neck, his bare chest warm against her chest. 'And I've been wanting to do this since that beautiful hippie woman walked into the pub a couple of weeks ago and stole my heart back in one breath.'

'Too many clothes,' he muttered as she lifted her hips. He slid off her shorts and panties in one swift movement. He pulled her T-shirt over her head. Emma placed her hands against his bare chest. His heart beat hard and fast beneath her fingers.

There were no more words. She gasped as she took him inside her. She rocked beneath him and the heat coiled in her belly built into an exquisite wave of pleasure. And then the wave broke.

It had been a long time since anything had felt so right.

***

'Do you know how much I missed you, Em?' He lay beside her, his face shadowed in the dying light of the afternoon. Emma's breath caught in her throat as he stared at her. The look in his eyes told her exactly how much.

'I tried to fill the gap when you left, but I was never able to.' His voice broke and her heart clenched in her chest.

Emma reached up and smoothed his hair back from his forehead.

'What happened last night?' She could barely say the words. 'I know something's wrong. The way you were at the hospital. And you never used to drink like that.'

Jeremy turned and sat on the edge of the bed, his bare back to her. Emma rolled over and sat beside him, comfortable in her nakedness. She picked up his hand, running her thumb over his warm skin.

'When I met you, you were my entry into a whole new world. I was me, and you loved me for what I was—not as a Langford. God Emma, when you left I missed you so much.'

Tears filled her eyes as his fingers gripped hers, and her voice was a whisper. 'It was the same for me. With everything that was going on back home after Dad died, for a while I thought I'd die without you there to talk to me, to support me. And knowing—thinking—you didn't want me anymore made it so much harder.'

'But we've made it, haven't we? We both did what we had to do. I'm so proud of what you've achieved. A strong independent woman, highly respected by your community.' He reached out and tipped up her chin so that she had to meet his eyes. 'I still love you, Em. Nothing's changed. There's just been some time apart in the middle. I want you to think about that. If you think we still have something that can work.'

She opened her mouth and he shook his head. 'No, don't answer me yet. I have to tell you what really brought me here. I don't want any more secrets between us.'

Emma sighed as Jeremy stood and pulled his jeans back on. He passed her shorts and T-shirt over to her. Once she was dressed he moved up onto the bed and leaned against the bed head with his legs stretched out. He pulled her over and settled her between his thighs; her back pressing against his chest. She closed her eyes and he lowered his head and rested his forehead on her shoulder.

His breath was warm against her neck.

'You remember my niece. Brianna?'

She nodded.

'She was still a child when you left. But as she got older, she made some poor choices. She got in with a different group of kids.' His voice shook and she sensed it was anger rather than grief that made it tremble.

Emma sat back and let him talk.

'Brenton and Sally tried their best. I spoke to Brianna and she assured me she wasn't into drugs. And I believed her.

But one night she went to an outdoor concert at the Domain. She took an ecstasy table that had DXM in it. We found that out after . . . afterwards.'

Emma waited. She suspected what was coming. DXM–dextromethorphan–was often used by teenagers as a kind of hallucinogen and had dangerous side effects.

The skin on her shoulder was cool where Jeremy's forehead had rested. He'd lifted it away.

'What happened?'

Guilt was washing off him in waves. His fingers were clenched and his voice was quiet.

'At St Vincent's drug overdoses and ice-fuelled rages were commonplace; we saw them every night. I should have been able to handle one more.'

He was quiet for a while and Emma squeezed his hand.

'I was with another patient when they brought her in.'

By now, he was gulping in deep breaths and Emma twisted around to face him. Up on her knees she put her hands on either side of his face.

'Calm down. Just tell me slowly what happened. Take a deep breath.'

'I should have been able to do more.' Jeremy shuddered. 'I should have been able to save her.'

She put her arms around him and held him as though she would never let him go.

***

He closed his eyes and let the events of that night play through his mind like a movie. It helped him detach and helped him find the words to tell Emma what is had been like. The horror and the grief, the words he'd had to find when he'd gone to find Brenton and tell him his only child had died under Jeremy's watch.

'It was a quiet Sunday night. . .' he began.

They'd had three shoulder dislocations after an afternoon of the usual sporting injuries and then the paramedics had radioed in. 'We've got an adverse drug reaction. Three minutes out.'

The team had mobilised in readiness for the ambulance. Being registrar on duty, Jeremy was in charge of airway management.

'The paramedic came over to see me.' He kept his voice level.

He'd directed the two medical students to follow him as the doors flew open and the other paramedics wheeled the trolley in. The pink curtain around the cubicle had snapped open and the first team members lifted the patient onto the gurney.

'Convulsing . . . and her body temperature is off the scale. We've given her oxygen and administered Midazolam for the seizures but there's been little response.' The paramedic's voice was urgent. 'She's got a friend in the front of the ambulance but we can't get a lot of sense out of her. We picked them up at the concert over at The Domain. No ID. All we have is her first name. Brianna.'

Jeremy's head had flown up as a cold premonition seized him. He pushed the curtain aside and walked across to the gurney. The young woman's face was obscured by the medical team working frantically, but as soon as he saw the white-blonde hair, he knew it was his niece. He watched for a few seconds, satisfied that the team had the resuscitation and the airway management under control. He knew it was vital for her chances that they find out what she had taken. He swung around to speak to the young girl that the other paramedic had now brought in. It was Laura Delaney, Brianna's best friend.

He dropped to his haunches in front of the plastic chair, fighting for calm. Digging deep to that place where he could be detached, setting aside the knowledge that it was his brother's daughter who was critically ill only a few metres away.

'They must feel confident in you. They must feel safe with you. There must be a relationship of trust.' The words of the professor and the drug counsellors flowed through his mind. He'd put them into practice on many nights in emergency; he needed to remember them now.

'Laura. It's me. Jeremy. Brianna's uncle.' He reached out and lifted up the curtain of the girl's hair. Her eyes were wide and scared, and her nose was running.

At least she was coherent. 'Jeremy. Oh, thank God. It's you.' She burst into noisy tears and her frail shoulders shook as she sobbed. 'I'm so scared. Brianna's eyes rolled back and she passed out. I couldn't wake her up and I. . .I didn't know what to do. So I called triple zero.'

'You did the right thing, sweetheart. But now you can help even more. You have to tell me what Brianna took. Do you know what it was?'

A glimmer of something flickered in her eyes and he firmed his voice. 'It's very important that you tell us. It will help us save her life.'

Rebecca's voice hitched. 'It was only one tablet.'

'What sort of tablet?'

'Ecstasy. We all took one but Brianna was the only one who got sick. She started vomiting and then she was really thirsty and she drank so much water but she kept vomiting and vomiting.' She started to sob again. 'And then she went all rigid. I was so scared.'

Jeremy looked across to the medical student beside him. 'Please take Laura over there.' He gestured to the cubicle where a nurse was waiting before he ran over to the cubicle where they were working on Brianna.

'It's ecstasy. He caught the eye of the doctor who had taken over the intubation while he spoke to Laura. 'And you need to know she's my niece.'

'There's a high risk of regurgitation. She was with us for a moment and she's trying to pull the tube out.' Jeremy looked over just as Brianna's eyes flew open and her head arched back.

'She's arresting!' the nurse yelled

'Defibrillate.' The doctor's instruction was calm but the sense of urgency was second nature to this team.

Christopher, the medical student who'd been shadowing him all night, gripped his arms and pulled Jeremy back as the assistant registrar applied the first sternum paddle under Brianna's right clavicle. The senior nurse turned on the defibrillator screen.

Helplessness flooded him; he had to do something. He stepped forward but the student held him back and spoke quietly.

'No, doctor. You know the policy.'

He shoved the guy's hand away. 'I have to do

something.'

'They're doing all they can. It's the same as you would do.' He could still see the dark eyes of the student as he gripped his arm.

They worked frantically but the noise in the room faded to a hollow buzz. All Jeremy could hear was the beeping of the machine as Brianna flatlined. His eyes were fixed on the green line that ran continuously along the bottom of the screen.

It was too late.

Chapter 30

Daintree Village – just on dark, Sunday.

George woke with a start and sat up, frowning as someone pounded on his front door. He'd been dozing in front of the evening news.

'Fire! There's a fire over at the doc's house.' His neighbour's voice got louder. 'George, come and help us. Quick.'

'Bloody hell!' He leapt from the lounge, pulled on his boots and wrenched open the door. An orange glow reflected on the water with a macabre light and Bowser was running back and forth along the edge of the riverbank, his distressed barks echoing eerily across the water.

Jim from next door was already heading to the two fishing boats lining the bank, followed by another two neighbours who had been roused by his yells. George directed his gaze to the boat ramp. Emma's punt was on this side of the river.

He hadn't seen her since dropping her at the hospital that morning. Maybe she'd stayed at the clinic in town. He ran his hand over his face. But maybe she'd got a lift home. There was a chance she was inside.

'Did you call the fire brigade?' he yelled as he ran for the punt.

'It's on the way. And I called the ambos too. Grab some buckets. It's too far for a hose to reach. We'll have to do our best till they get here.'

Within minutes the two boats were heading across the narrow channel but George was first over there. The punt scraped onto the concrete pad he'd laid for Emma last summer.

'He could hear Bowser's frenzied barking. She must be inside if the dog was. His breath hitched and a dull ache lodged in his throat as he ran to the house. The flames were now licking along the guttering of the roof on the river side. He ran up the back steps, the flames on the post sizzling as the first bucket of river water hit them. He turned; the men had already formed a chain and were passing buckets of water from the river to the house.

Acrid smoke burned his eyes as he pushed open the gate at the top of the steps.

'Emma! Doctor Em!' Bowser was yipping on the other side of the door.

The flames were snapping and crackling around the back door and the timber groaned as the beams on the verandah threatened to give way. George pulled his shirt off, wrapped it around his hands, and reached for the door knob.

'Fuck,' he yelled as the skin on his fingers blistered through the fabric. He put his shoulder to the door and pushed but the door wouldn't budge. 'Someone help me. She might be inside.'

There was a horrendous creak as the main roof beam succumbed to the flames.

Chapter 31

Emma held Jeremy to her as he let out the grief that he'd been holding in for so many months. For an hour they lay there quietly and he shared his feelings. He talked about his family and of his disillusionment with medicine when Brianna had died that horrendous night last summer. The investigation into her death had found no blame and the medical staff—including Jeremy—had done all they could to save her. She smoothed his hair and held him tightly as he talked and talked.

'So why do you feel as though the blame is on your shoulders?'

'I should have recognised the serotonin toxicity.'

Emma shook her head. 'Look at me, Jem.'

He lifted his head and his eyes were bleak.

'There is no doubt that it was a dreadful tragedy. You say there was no blame found? You know that there is no way you could have diagnosed that without knowing *exactly* what she had ingested.'

'I know that. But I carry this enormous guilt. I was there. I was there next to my niece when she died. And I couldn't save her. I'm sure my family blame me.'

'If they do, they shouldn't. Have you been to counselling?'

'No. I haven't been able to talk to anyone.'

'Is that why you left Sydney?'

'It was part of the reason.'

Then he told her of his father's calls offering him a place back in Macquarie Street and of his reluctance to go into the family practice. 'I've never belonged there. I've been happier up here for the past two weeks than I have since our days at uni.'

She was quiet and still.

'What's wrong?' He lifted his head.

'Are you sure it's the right move for you?'

'It is. I know Dad only wants the best for me. Or what he sees as right.' Those blue eyes held hers. 'But this is what I want. What I need.'

'You're sure, then.'

'Hey, I bought a house. I'm here to stay.'

Cautious optimism filled Emma. She leaned towards him, letting that little tendril of hope open to his warmth a little more.

She reached down and picked her phone up from the floor. 'Nothing from Troy. I wonder if he got the message?'

A frown crossed Jeremy's brow and she reached up and smoothed her fingers along the lines in his skin.

'Tell me about Troy,' he said.

Emma shrugged. 'I think he was interested, but I was trying too hard. When you arrived—'

She shrugged and his surprised expression was followed by a relieved smile when she finished. 'After you arrived, I couldn't summon up enough interest. He's a nice guy.' Unease replaced the contentment she was feeling. 'I just wish he'd ring and I could talk to him.'

Her stomach rumbled and Jeremy smiled.

'I hope you've got food here, because we're not exactly in the middle of town,' she said.

'Nothing, I'm afraid. Not even a croissant crumb.' His

laugh was low and deep. 'If you want to eat, we'll have to go to town . . . or back to your place.'

'I'll have to go home. It's late and poor Bowser's still outside.' She put her hand to her head. 'And with everything that's been going on, I haven't fed the frogs for a couple of days.'

'Come on, then. I'll run you home.'

Chapter 32

The road was quiet as they turned towards the village. Emma glanced at Jeremy as he changed back a gear as they approached the creek crossing ahead.

'You're really getting used to the roads up here, aren't you?'

'I am.' His grin was wide.

'What about the rest of the things you'll have to deal with? How are you going to cope with them?'

'Like what?'

'The wet season, the bad roads, the leeches, the mould . . .'

'You're painting an attractive picture, Em.'

'Can you really stay somewhere so different to Sydney?'

'I love it here. It's alive. Even with the frogs and the leeches and the rain.'

He reached over and picked up her hand after he'd negotiated the creek crossing. 'And I don't think I told you before. 'I love *you*, Em.'

There was an eerie red glow on the horizon as they followed the river along to the village. Jeremy listened quietly as she told him about going across the river last night.

'Emma, you are going to get yourself hurt one day if you don't think before you act.' Jeremy looked at her in disbelief. 'I can't believe you did that.'

'Don't you start. George has already given me a serve.'

'I did think Craig was a bit unstable that first night in the pub. I'd bet he's an addict.'

A bright red glow lit the sky ahead as they got closer to the village.

'Burning the sugar cane?' Jeremy looked to the west as they turned onto the side road.

'It's a bit late in the season for that.'

As they crested the last hill, Emma saw the flashing lights of a fire engine parked down near the river. And then the whole scene revealed itself.

'Oh God. It's my place.' Shadowy figures were moving back and forth across her yard, ferrying buckets to the fire. But it was clearly in vain. The dark flickered with an orange light as the inferno devoured her house.

Dread closed her throat as Jeremy parked the car. 'Bowser! Jeremy, hurry. I left him locked inside.' She flung the door open and ran down to the riverbank.

The punt was on the other side of the river and Jeremy pulled on the rope to bring it across.

'Quickly, Jeremy!'

Emma waited with her hands to her mouth. Her breath hitched and she tried to focus on steadying her breathing. The small punt was almost to the bank when sirens blared through the night air and an ambulance arrived, followed closely by a police car with its blue lights flashing. The ambulance came to a sudden stop. Doors slammed and the paramedics hurried down the hill.

'Thank God, Emma. We got a call saying they thought you were inside.' Tony pointed across the river. 'The other ambulance has gone across river on the ferry to get to the house side. George tried to get inside.'

Her legs buckled and Tony grabbed for her the same

time. Jeremy dropped the rope and ran back to her.

'No, no. I'm all right. Get the punt.' Her voice broke as a sob caught in her throat. 'Where's George?'

Tony held her arm firmly. 'They said he's all right. I think that's him over by the fence.'

She looked across the river. The smoke was swirling around the yard but as she searched, she saw George sitting back against the fence post clutching her little black dog to his chest.

'Oh, thank God.'

Tony let go of her and walked back to the ambulance and she hurried down to the water's edge. The punt had almost reached this side. A police car pulled up beside it, the macabre blue light giving the paramedics a ghoulish appearance. Emma held her breath waiting to see whether it was Craig or the sergeant. It was Craig who got out of the car and ran down to the water.

'Are you all right, Emma?'

'I'm fine.' She turned to Jeremy. 'Take me over to George.'

'It's an old place. Probably the wiring.' Craig's face was in the shadows as he glared at her as if it was her fault. 'I told you to get it checked.'

'What wiring? What the hell are you talking about?' Emma took a step back but Craig took her arm in a firm grip.

'Let her go.' Jeremy's voice was cold. Emma gave him a warning look. She didn't want Craig to know they were on to him.

He dropped her arm. 'That night when I stayed over—' he stared coldly at Jeremy '—one of your power points caught fire. Surely you remember that?'

Emma closed her mouth and narrowed her eyes. Craig was lying through his teeth; he'd never once been in her house at night. They'd never had that conversation. She turned her back to the policeman and stepped into the punt.

'I want to get to George.'

'We'll come over after you.' One of the paramedics pushed the punt away from the bank as Jeremy jumped in behind her. Emma sat with her arms wrapped around her stomach. Smoke swirled over the water; the acrid smell caught in her throat and made her eyes water. She leaned forward, disbelief flooding though her as she watched the flames licking around the roof of her home.

Jeremy pulled the punt quickly across the narrow river. 'Hang in there, Em.' He reached over in the flickering light with his free hand and squeezed her shoulder as she sat on the narrow wooden seat. The concern in his voice brought the pricking of unshed tears to her eyes and she nodded mutely.

Voices reached them, interspersed with Bowser's barks. Two of George's neighbours were waiting for them as the punt scraped onto the concrete ramp.

'George!' One of them yelled. 'It's all right. Doctor Emma's here. She's not in there!'

The tears finally sprang from Emma's eyes as she jumped out. Ignoring the burning house, she ran across to George. She crouched down beside him. His face was blackened by smoke and he was holding tightly onto Bowser's collar. Torchlight played across his face and she could see the wet tracks where tears had run down his cheeks.

She put her arm around his neck and pulled him close.

He smelled of smoke and his rough skin was scratchy against her face. 'Oh, my god, George. Are you hurt?

'I thought you were in there, Em. I couldn't get the door open and then the roof crashed in.'

'How did you get Bowser?'

'The back door came open when the roof caved in and he shot out.' He held the little dog out to her. His tail's singed but apart from that he was a lucky little fellow.'

Emma took Bowser and hugged him to her chest as he tried to lick her face. 'Oh, Bowsie, are you all right?'

George's voice broke again. 'I thought you were inside.'

'I'm okay.' She held her voice steady, trying not to think of the destruction in front of them. Almost everything she owned was inside her cottage. 'The ambos are coming across now. I think they need to take a look at you.'

'I'm okay. Just a bit of a blister on my hand when I grabbed the door handle.' He jutted his chin out. 'They'll just want to take me to that damn hospital again and I ain't going.'

Emma leaned back and held Bowser to her, assessing George without making it too obvious. His right hand was wrapped in a shirt and he held it against this bare chest.

'I'll see if I can get you a blanket or something. Although I don't know where.' She looked up at Jeremy, and gratitude filled her as he pulled his T-shirt over his head and tucked it around the older man's shoulders.

'Thank you.' She pushed herself to her feet and leaned into Jeremy as his arm went around her. 'You're making a habit of giving your shirts to George.' Her voice broke and Jeremy pulled her closer.

She blinked at the surreal scene in front of her. The

firemen had come across in the punt and had joined her neighbours as they passed bucket after bucket of river water along the human chain. There was nothing more they could do. The river was too wide for their hoses to reach from the fire engine parked on the other side.

Jeremy held her close. 'Do you really think it was a wiring issue?'

'No.' Emma's temper fired. 'Craig's never even been to my place at night. I spent one night at his place, which I've regretted every day since, but that was all.'

Jeremy's arms relaxed a little as he held her and she watched Craig across the river. He stood apart from the small crowd looking at the burning house.

'There's not much that can be done. I don't think there's much of anything left around here.' Jeremy's calm voice soothed her a little. She followed his gaze as it moved to the house as another piece of the roof crashed to the ground.

'It's all right. Everyone's okay. Apart from my poor frogs.' She pursed her lips together as her knees trembled. There would be time to fall to pieces later. She wouldn't think of all of her personal possessions that had gone up in smoke. *Not now*. 'The chooks are far enough away and. . .no. . nobody's been hurt.'

George's querulous voice reached her and she caught the eye of the paramedic leaning over him. 'No. Bugger off. Doctor Em can take a look at me.

'It's okay, Tony. I'll take a look at him myself.'

Tony passed them a blanket and George handed Jeremy's shirt back.

***

Two hours later, all that remained of Emma's house was a pile of smouldering embers. They were sitting on the back verandah of George's house across the river watching the firemen put tape around the fence line. Despite the warm night, and the blanket wrapped around her, Emma was cold.

'There'll be an investigation.' She glanced at Jeremy

'What? They think some bastard lit the fire?' George's voice was still a bit shaky.

'The RFS guy said it's routine.' She swallowed. If it hadn't been for Jeremy, she would have been in the house when the fire started. The cold spread through her body and she started to shake.

Jeremy hadn't left her side and he tucked the blanket more tightly around her. 'We need to find you a bed so you can get some sleep.

'George, you look knackered too,' he said.

Jeremy left his hand on her shoulder and she reached up and squeezed it. He had examined George and allayed her fears. His blood pressure was fine, and Jeremy had tended to the burns on his hands. Emma had been trembling too much to be any use.

A shaky smile crossed her lips. 'I guess the clinic's going to be home for a while. At least I have some clothes there, and my laptop, and I keep all my personal documents in the safe there.'

'No. I'll take you back to my place. We'll pick up some food in the morning.' Jeremy took her hand and pulled her to her feet. 'Thanks for the tea and toast, George. We were actually on our way to Emma's for dinner when we saw the fire.'

'A bit late for dinner.' George narrowed his eyes and looked down at their entwined fingers. His lips stretched in a wide grin. ''bout time you had someone else to look out for you, Doctor Em. I'm getting a bit sick of bailing you out of trouble.'

'You do look after me very well. Now you get some sleep and I'll see you soon.' Emma bent and brushed her lips across his unshaven cheek. 'And thank you for looking after Bowser for me. And for saving his life.'

'Never mind about that. You make sure you let your mum know about the fire too. You don't want her reading about it in the paper.'

'I will.'

'I'll see you tomorrow.'

Emma leaned her head back on the headrest and closed her eyes as they drove back to Dalrymple. The dark paddocks whizzed past and the river was black and dark. The sky had clouded over and the moon appeared briefly through the scudding clouds. Thoughts churned through her mind and a cold vice of fear clutched her chest. Seeing Craig there had unsettled her. His bizarre comment about the power point had unsettled her. It was too much of a coincidence.

'Try to get some rest, Em. I can hear you thinking from here.' Jeremy reached over and touched her hand.

'How did Craig know about the fire?' she said.

'I guess it would have been on the police radio.' Jeremy glanced at her. 'I do find it a bit suspicious in light of everything else.' Another shiver went thought Emma. She couldn't get warm.

She turned to look at Jeremy His profile was in darkness, lit only by the instruments on the dash, and she couldn't see his expression but the tone of his voice said it all.

'If you're right it was attempted murder.' He took his eyes briefly from the road.

Chapter 33

Monday-Dalrymple

Waking up in Jeremy's arms helped Emma calm herself, and by the time they'd showered, and were getting ready to head to town, she was feeling calmer.

'I'll have to pick up some things from the clinic if I'm going to stay out here.' She zipped up the shorts she'd worn all day yesterday and looked down ruefully at the T-shirt that still held an aroma of smoke. 'And do some clothes shopping in town.'

'But first, I'm going to call Troy. What time is it?'

'Just after eight.'

Emma pulled the number up on her phone and dialled the rainforest centre.

The phone clicked over to a message. 'The hours of the Daintree Rainforest Centre are nine am till—'

Emma disconnected.

'No luck?' Jeremy held his hand out.

'I'll try from town.'

'Okay. Em?'

She looked up at him.

His voice was hesitant. "How would you feel about staying here? At least until you get sorted. I hate the thought of you staying at the clinic.'

'There are conditions.' Emma let a smile cross her face.

'Oh yeah?'

'You get some groceries in, and buy a washing machine.'

He tilted her chin and brushed a kiss across her lips. 'Washing machine, fridge, television, Xbox—' he looked at her innocently as she shook her head '—and a heap of other stuff is coming this afternoon. I've got a meeting at the hospital this morning I can't get out of. The state manager of the Outreach Program is driving up from Cairns and then I'll come back here while I wait for the delivery. What do you want to do?

'I want to go and see Wilma. And I'll have to call Lily and get her to cancel my appointments.' Emma was finding it hard to focus. 'And I have to ring Mum.'

'Ring your mum now. I'll get the car out of the shed.' Jeremy pulled her close again and she pressed her cheek against his chest. The cotton of his short-sleeved shirt was crisp against her skin.

'Thank you,' she whispered.

'What for?' His words rumbled through his chest against her ear.

'Just for being you.' Emma reached up and pressed her lips against his. 'You make me smile.'

'Just as well.' His mouth moved under hers.

She stepped back when he pulled away and picked up his car keys.

'But if we don't leave soon, you'll have to support me because I'll be out of a job if I miss this meeting.'

'What time is it?'

'Nine. But I want to go through my notes first. That was the plan for yesterday afternoon after you put my furniture together.'

His cheeky grin sent a shaft of warmth heading low.

'Get going, then.' She waved him away and pulled out her phone. She pressed the shortcut to the mother's number.

'Emma! You must have read my mind.' Her mother's voice was brighter every time they spoke lately. Mum had had a tough enough time over the past few years and Emma was reluctant to give her a new reason to worry. 'I was going to call you as soon as we finished breakfast.' Her voice was more than bright; it was full of suppressed excitement.

'We?' Emma frowned. Who could possibly be there at this hour of the morning; it was barely seven-thirty.

'I had a surprise visitor last night and I was going to ring to see if you could put us up next weekend.'

'Who?'

'Your sister!'

'Ellie? She's over from the Territory?' Guilt flooded through Emma. She'd been so preoccupied with everything; she hadn't called either of her sisters for a couple of weeks. And she'd considered that if Ellie heard that Jeremy was back in her life, she'd have plenty to say about that. Emma had wanted to sort out her feelings without any input from her forthright sister.

'No, not Ellie. Your baby sister!'

'What? Dru's home from Dubai?' Emma's eyes widened. She caught Jeremy's gaze as he opened the screen door. He paused and raised his eyebrows.

'Yes, Dru. She came knocking on the door last night and it was such a lovely surprise. I'll put her on.' Mum's voice was full of excitement.

'Mum—' Before she could say why she'd called, the husky tones of her younger sister's voice filled her ears.

'Hey, Em.'

'Dru. What a surprise.' Emma swallowed as emotion clogged her throat. She'd thought the fire hadn't left her too fragile, but now her voice shook as she tried to speak. 'What... what ... are you doing back in the country? And how long are you here for?'

'Long story. I'm home for good.'

'Really? But that's wonderful.' Emma brushed away the tears that filled her eyes.

Bloody stupid, crying on the phone. When Jeremy's arms went around her, she couldn't hold back the sob that broke from her throat. She shook her head and put her hand over her mouth as tears rolled down her face.

***

Jeremy took the phone from Emma's trembling hand.

'Hello? Em, are you there? You, okay?' The husky voice was anxious.

'Hello, this is Jeremy Langford. Em's just a bit upset. There's been a bit of an incident.'

Emma leaned against him as he explained to her sister about the fire, and reassured her that no one had been hurt.

'Are you sure Emma is okay?'

'Yes. She's going to be okay. A bit of shock but she's coping.'

'We'll drive up today.' Her sister's voice was full of concern.

'How about we come down to Port Douglas instead this afternoon? I think it would do Emma good to get away. There's been a fair bit going on here and it's long past time for me to meet Emma's family.'

Emma smiled at him through her tears as he organised the visit.

They drove into town and Jeremy parked out the front of the hospital. Emma waited as he locked the car and they walked into the hospital together. 'I'm going to see Wilma and then I'll wait for you in the staff room.'

She'd braided her hair this morning. Light mauve shadows circled her eyes and her fair skin was paler than usual.

'If you're sure you're okay?' Jeremy stared at the gold flecks in her hazel eyes as a surge of need hit him square in the chest.

'I'll make this meeting a quick one. I don't like leaving you. He reached for her hand. 'See you soon?'

Emma nodded and he watched as she walked down the corridor towards the stairs.

He was still waiting for the director to arrive when Emma pushed open the door to his small office. Her brow was wrinkled in a frown and he jumped to his feet. 'What's wrong?'

'It's okay.' She waved to his desk. 'I'm sorry to interrupt your work. Wilma's good but she's being moved to Cairns this afternoon, and she needs a few things from her place. Can you take me out there after your meeting?'

'Let's go now.' He reached over and picked up his keys.

'But what about your meeting? Isn't that guy flying up specially to meet with you?'

'Yes, he is. But yours and Wilma's wellbeing is way more important. I'll call him. He can sightsee in Dalrymple for the morning.'

'That'll fill in ten minutes or so,' she said.

He chuckled at her wry grin. 'Come on, the quicker we get back, the more chance I've got of pacifying him.' He pulled out his phone to postpone his meeting as he followed Emma to the car park.

Chapter 34

Daintree rainforest

A huge bank of cloud moved in from the Coral Sea as the vehicular ferry crossed the river. The wind was pushing against the tide and the crossing was rough as the ferry sliced through the rough waves.

'Rain's not far off,' Clive called through the window. Emma acknowledged him with a wave.

'Looks like it's already raining further north.' She pointed to the dark cloud mass blocking the view of the peaks ahead as they followed the main road. The wind increased and the trees above them swayed.

'Wet season's hitting with a vengeance today,' Jeremy said. He switched the wipers on when the first drops hit the windscreen. 'I've got to get used to these seasons. Reading about it is nothing like being here.'

'Wait till February. That's when the humidity kicks in.' She reached over and touched his hand. 'I can't believe you postponed your meeting with the state manager.'

'Priorities.' Jeremy smiled as he squeezed her fingers.

Emma pulled out her phone and tried the rainforest centre again. Finally the call was picked up and she asked for Troy, only to be told that he was unavailable. She left another message for him to call her urgently, frustrated that she'd been unable to speak to him.

'I know he's busy.' She tapped her fingers against her leg. 'But it's making me so angry. I feel as though they're just getting away with it.'

'Don't worry. We'll get it sorted today. If needs be, we'll drive back out to the centre this afternoon.' Jeremy's voice was calm.

Inside the high vehicle Emma felt cocooned. The pounding of the rain on the roof of the car left them in their own isolated world and enhanced the intimacy.

Her eyes lingered on Jeremy's profile as he concentrated on the winding road. A couple of times he had to slow down to dodge fallen branches as the weather deteriorated.

He frowned as he peered ahead. For the first time in so long, Emma felt safe.

Jeremy coming back into her life had removed the emptiness that she'd carried within since Dad had died and she'd left Sydney. She knew could even cope with the loss of her house with him by her side. She smiled. Despite the events on the last week, things were looking up.

***

Finally, they turned off the main road onto the narrow track that led to Wilma's place.

'Gate's already open.' Jeremy slowed the car. The puddles on the dirt track indicated that it had been raining heavily.

Emma frowned. The gate was clipped to the fence post with a short length of chain, and the large padlock was sitting on top of the wooden fence post. It looked like the chain had been cut. Wilma had given her the key to unlock it so she wouldn't have to carry her things back down to the road. She narrowed her eyes at the tyre tracks in the soft mud ahead of them.

'They've been back here.' Fear crept into her voice.

The motor roared as Jeremy accelerated up the hill past the gate and Emma gasped as the wheels of the large Toyota spun in the mud. A couple of trees flashed past her window as the vehicle slewed around and then stopped. The tyres struggled for purchase and the motor roared again but the large four-wheel drive didn't move.

'Sorry, that was a bit close for comfort. I think the back wheels have dropped off the edge of the track.' Jeremy frowned and reached down to put the vehicle into four-wheel drive. He accelerated slowly but the back wheels spun on the wet undergrowth.

'Damn. You can't miss your meeting. There's no phone service from here.' Emma glanced at her watch. 'It's taken us longer to get up here than I thought it would. If we're going to be late we can call from Wilma's phone though.'

'It's not till twelve. I'll make it if we hurry back. Look, I'll winch it out while you run down and get Wilma's stuff. We'll be quicker that way. And I'll keep an eye out for anyone. There's no sign of anyone and if you hear a car get straight back up here. Okay?'

'Don't worry, I will.' Emma looked down the hill towards Wilma's cottage. 'There's no one there. They must have gone into the forest. Or they've already gone.' She tipped her head to the side and looked at him curiously. 'Do you know how to use the winch?'

'Do I hear a silent *city boy* in your tone?' He raised an eyebrow at her.

'Just checking.'

Jeremy opened the door and came around to her side. He held a hand for her to climb down. He then led her to the front of the four-wheel drive where Emma spied the large hook on the front bull bar.

'Ah, fully equipped.' She looked up at the green canopy above. 'At least the rain's stopped for a while.'

The smells of the wet rainforest surrounded them and the quiet was broken by the creaking of branches as they dipped beneath the weight of the rain. The moisture dripping onto the decaying mulch stirred up an aroma of sodden leaves and wet fungi.

Jeremy dropped her hand and unhooked the winch rope. He crossed the narrow track and looped it around a large tree trunk on the other side.

'Okay, looks like you've got that under control. I'll go down and get Wilma's things. When you get it out, drive down to the house. There's more room to turn around there. If we hurry, you'll be back in plenty of time.'

Emma hurried down the track towards Wilma's house, taking care on the slippery leaves covering the mud. At one point she heard a muttered curse behind her as the winch rope slipped down the tree. She stopped and looked back, but Jeremy waved to her to keep going. She kept her eyes ahead on the track from Wilma's house into the rainforest.

A strong gust of wind hit as she pushed open the door of Wilma's house and flicked on the light. With it came another heavy rain shower and she glanced up the hill. The noise of the wind and the rain covered the sound of the engine, but she was pleased to see that Jeremy was back in the car and it was inching forward slowly. He'd be down here in a minute or two. She stepped inside and jumped when the wind caught the door and slammed it behind her.

Wilma's kitchen was cold and empty. The fire in the stove had long gone out; a scattering of ash covered the stone-flagged floor in front of it. A light film of damp covered the kitchen bench tops, but Emma resisted picking up the cloth and wiping it down. She'd come back up and air the place before Wilma was discharged.

She walked over to the kitchen table and glanced at the unopened boxes of medication. She shook her head.

Events of the past few weeks, and her refusal to take her medication had all contributed to the tension that resulted in her heart turn. The theft of her snakes had been the beginning of her nervousness and Emma was determined to set that right so Wilma had no reason to be frightened when she came home.

Soon, hopefully.

Emma turned and headed for the hall. She'd not been past the kitchen but Wilma had told her where to look for her clothes and toiletries. She flicked the hall light on.

Emma jumped as a board creaked up the dark hallway. It was the house moving in the wind. She'd been jittery ever since Wilma had told her about the snakes in the spare room. That was another job to do after she'd collected some clothes and toiletries. Wilma had asked her to check the snakes assuring her that it was safe.

'Just check that the light is still on,' she'd said.

Emma would peek into the room but she had no intention of going anywhere near them.

She swallowed and tried to push her nerves aside, but then a loud clap of thunder shook the house and the light went out. The sky had darkened and very little light came in through the small windows. She dug into her pocket for her phone and flicked on the flashlight app. Shadows flickered in the hall as she shone the light ahead looking for the first door on the left—Wilma's bedroom. The door was shut and as she pushed it open. She crossed to the chest of drawers next to the door and pulled open the top drawer as Wilma had instructed.

A chain rattled outside. Emma crossed to the window, expecting got see Jeremy parked in the small yard. She put her hand to her mouth and her skin crawled. There was see a white ute parked at the back of the house. She hadn't noticed it on the way in because it was around the other side of the house.

A man stepped out of the back shed and looked up the hill. The motor of Jeremy's four wheel drive was roaring as he accelerated. A rain hood covered his head and she couldn't see his face. As she watched, he walked across and carefully placed two white plastic pipes like the one she had seen in the cocky apple grove in the back of the ute. He kept looking up the hill to where the Land Cruiser was revving loudly.

Suddenly he lifted his head and looked directly at the window where she was standing. Emma gasped and stepped quickly to the side, dropping her phone to her side. Her hand was shaking.

It was Troy. Panic filled her; she didn't know what was worse. If he drove up the hill he would come across Jeremy; if he came into the house he would find her.

She leaned forward and peered through the side of the window, taking care not to step out of the darkness. Her heart was pounding and she gagged as her stomach hit the bottom of her throat.

Shit. Looking down, she realised that the light from her phone app was reflecting on the glass. Oh God, she hoped that wasn't what had caught his attention.

Her hands shook as she shoved the phone into her pocket as she ran back to the kitchen. Where was Jeremy? If he came down to the house, maybe they could bluff it together and then head for town and figure it out. Who to tell? What to do?

The handle on the back door rattled and Emma jumped. Biting her lip to keep from making any sound, she glanced at the door, wondering foolishly if she had time to lock it, and knowing she didn't. All she could hope was that he hadn't seen her at the window. The door handle turned slowly and with a muffled cry, she turned on her tiptoes and ran back into the narrow hall.

Facing the cage full of snakes would be easier than confronting *him.*

The lowlife lying bastard.

Shivering with fear, she wrapped her arms around her chest as she ran into the room opposite Wilma's bedroom. There was an archway like in an old Queenslander, open to let the air flow through. She looked around in the dim light but there was nowhere to hide. The room was empty.

The silence was shattered as the back door of the house slammed shut and a gust of wind blew down the hall. The wind had picked up again and the trees creaked and branches rubbed on the guttering. She ran across the room to the window on tiptoe, her feet making no sound on the timber floor.

Her body was rigid, every nerve ending tingling as

adrenaline coursed through her. If she could get out before he came up the hallway, she could climb out and run up the hill to Jeremy. Please God. Let him have the car off the bank.

Turning her back to the doorway, she reached for the frame, ready to pull the sash up and climb out.

As she pulled frantically at the heavy timber window base, a hand snaked around her neck and pulled her back against a solid chest. A woody cologne filled her nostrils.

She screamed as he pressed his hand over her mouth. She bit down in a reflex movement, her teeth scraping on a ring.

Troy grunted in pain.

She pulled away as he dropped his arm. Emma ran across to the other side of the small room, turned and backed up against the wall. There was just enough light for her to see his face. With shaking hands, she turned her phone on and hit the light and held it up.

'Put the phone down, Emma.'

She gasped as he walked towards her slowly.

'Troy? Thank God, it's you.' She would play dumb. It was the only way she was going to get out of here. 'God, you frightened me. If I'd known it was you, I wouldn't have run. What are you doing here? I. . .I've been trying to call you since yesterday.'

He shook his head slowly. 'I know. I'm sorry, Emma.'

'Sorry? About what?'

'I have to do this.'

'Do what?' She raised a shaking hand to her lips and almost gagged when she smelt his aftershave on her fingers.

He walked over to her slowly, his face garishly lit by the

flashlight app.

'Give me your phone.' His voice was hard.

'Troy, you're scaring me.' She pressed her back against the wall and looked at him. 'What are you doing? I need to tell you what I found out.'

'Oh don't worry, Emma. I know what you want to tell me. I know you've figured it out.' The look that crossed his face filled Emma with terror. 'A fucking shame that the airstrip is across from your place, isn't it?' He smiled at her and ice crept through her veins. 'I owe you big time though.'

'What for?

Jeremy, where are you? She had to keep him talking.

'Why do you owe me, Troy?'

'For telling me about the palm cockatoos.'

Fear coursed through her as she stared at him silently. Hyperawareness flooded Emma's senses. The wind whistled through the roof and the trees brushed against each other. The smell of the rain. The cold running through her veins. Snakes slithering against each other somewhere in this house.

She took a step forward, fighting to keep her voice level. 'Can we discuss this sensibly?'

Her shoulders sagged with relief when he walked past her, but he turned and grabbed her arm before she could run to the window. 'The time for being sensible has long gone.' Troy's fingers pressed into her forearm as he led her along the hall. Emma threw a hopeless glance at the back door as they passed the kitchen.

He grabbed the phone from her hand and shone it into a small room. Emma gasped as four pairs of cold, reptilian eyes stared unblinkingly at her through the glass of their tank. The bottom of the tank was filled with short sticks and a tree branch leaned against the back glass wall. A soft light illuminated the tank from above.

'I'll be honest with you. Snakebite isn't a pleasant way to die,' he said in a conversational tone. 'I'm sorry it has come to this.' His voice was soft. 'Ever since you saw us at the airstrip that first night, I knew it would end this way. It's ironic that it's up to me to deal with you. The sarge didn't do a good enough job on your brakes, Craig stuffed up last night. You were supposed to be in the house. And Jock Newby was supposed to intimidate you and the old woman.'

'Jock Newby?' Emma whispered.

'Ah, not so clever after all, Emma. You didn't figure that one out?'

'Figure what out?' She was so scared it hurt to breathe.

'Jock supplies the drugs we used for sedation. But never mind that. Coming here today was very thoughtful of you. I was wondering how I was going to stop you. You've just made it so much easier for me.'

Emma straightened her shoulders and took a deep breath. 'I promise you. I didn't see a thing. I didn't even know it was you.'

'Not going to work, Emma. You know if you weren't so honest, we could have been good together. For a while there, I thought it might have worked out. I'm going to be a very rich man soon.'

'I won't tell anyone.' She was clutching at straws; trying to delay him. Hoping, praying for Jeremy to get down here. Her voice shook. 'You don't have to do this.'

His head flew up as the back door opened with a bang.

'Emma! Where are you? There's a car out the back!'
Jeremy. Thank God.

Emma screamed as Troy pushed her towards the glass case holding the snakes and then disappeared back out into the hallway, slamming the door behind him. She fought to keep her balance but her right shoulder hit the glass and the case toppled off its wooden stand.

'Jeremy! Look out! He's coming.' Her scream mingled with the shattering of glass as the case smashed to the floor. She heard yelling and a loud crash from the kitchen, and then all was quiet. A soft swishing noise rose from the leaves on the wooden floor and Emma remembered the speed of the taipan she'd seen in her backyard.

On all fours, she backed away, crab-like, from the mess of broken glass and small branches now scattered on the floor. Her heart was pounding in her chest, and her hands shook uncontrollably as she pushed herself to her feet. She widened her eyes in the dim light and her mouth dried as she waited for a snake to strike. She held her breath, trying to hear what was happening in the kitchen.

Was Jeremy all right? Why was it so quiet? Why were there no voices?

But there was nothing—no sound, no voices. She bit her cheek, fighting the whimper that rose in her chest. Not game to cry out again for fear of moving the air and attracting the snakes, she pressed her back against the closed door, searching for the handle.

The cold metal of the door knob slipped beneath her sweating palms and she turned it slowly. Ever so slowly.

The door creaked open and she stepped quickly to the

side, scratching her arm on the sharp metal of the lock as she pushed herself through the small gap. She pulled the door shut behind her and swung around, desperately searching for Jeremy.

The kitchen was empty.

'Jeremy?' Emma called quietly as she stepped towards the back door.

Where is he? Where did they go?

If she could get out of the house she could make a run for it and hide in the rainforest. But fear for Jeremy's safety held her back. Emma turned to face the darkness of the hallway. Slowly walking along the hall, she stepped into the kitchen, stumbling as her foot hit a solid shape on the floor.

This time, she didn't hold back her terrified scream. 'God, no!'

Jeremy was on his back, his head hard up against the metal leg of the old combustion stove. His eyes were closed and a trickle of blood ran down his neck. Gulping down deep breaths, Emma dropped to a crouch and put her hand on his neck, desperately searching for a pulse. A fast, thready beat pulsed against her spread fingers.

She reached for his shoulder to pull him into the recovery position, forcing herself to breath evenly and stay calm. She wondered whether Troy had made a run for it.

'Come on, Jeremy, open your eyes.' A sob tore at her throat. 'Please be all right.' At a glance it looked as though the blood was coming from his ear, indicating severe head trauma. She knew she needed to get help. Fast.

A laugh chilled her blood and she looked up. Troy was standing above her. 'No time to help your doctor boyfriend, sweetheart. It's time to get back in there with your friends.' His cruel hands grabbed her hair and pulled her head back as he dragged her to her feet.

With a superhuman effort she pulled away from him and lunged for the back door. But Troy grabbed her again and shoved her away from the door, jarring her hip against the sink. A shaft of pain ran down her right leg and her knee buckled. She half crouched on the floor, her breath coming in ragged gasps.

'I'm sorry Emma, but I can't let you get away.' Troy was leaning almost casually against the closed door. For a moment, there seemed to be regret in his voice 'There's too much at stake.'

Emma shook her head, unable to believe this was the same man who had shown such concern for the environment, the same man she'd kidded herself she was attracted to.

She glanced down at Jeremy but he hadn't moved. Her determination to get them out of this situation, away from Troy, firmed inside her as hard as steel. If she could get to the phone she could call for help.

Emma straightened her knee and pressed back against the sink, her hands behind her back. The curtain moved behind her fingers and a memory of Wilma hit her.

'I'll do anything you want, Troy. Take the birds, the snakes.' She lifted one hand and waved to the room. 'Although it might be hard to get them now.

'I can do without them. Those palm cockatoos more than make up for a few snakes.'

Bending her knees slightly, she tried to hold back a whimper as pain shot down her leg. Her fingers scrabbled quietly behind her, feeling for the shotgun.

'So shall we go back to the snakes now?' He glanced at his watch before looking back at her with a grin. 'I have a plane to catch.'

Emma grabbed the shotgun and swung it onto her shoulder, hoping, begging, and praying that it was loaded.

The metal pressed cold into her skin and she aimed it at Troy's legs, her finger hovering on the trigger. 'Give me my phone.'

'No.' He laughed and took a step towards her and Emma lifted the gun and aimed the barrel at his chest. 'Are you prepared to risk it, Troy?'

Again the laugh, but this time he stayed where he was. 'What would a doctor know about a shotgun?'

'Oh you'd be surprised. This doctor grew up in the Northern Territory. My sisters and I learned to shoot before we started school.' She clicked her finger against the trigger and he pressed himself against the bench. It was surreal; she should be at the clinic starting her appointments, and here she was acting like a character in a Clint Eastwood movie.

'I'll let you go.' His tone was wheedling but she wasn't having a bar of it.

'Stay right where you are' She clenched her jaw as she spoke, trying to stop her fingers shaking as she took a step towards the telephone beside the fridge.

Her voice must have convinced him she would shoot if he moved. 'Fuck you,' he snarled.

Without taking her eyes from him, she picked up the phone and pressed the dial button before raising it to ear. She kept one hand firmly on the shotgun, aimed at him.

Dread chilled her veins but she kept her expression bland as she dialled.

She waited a few seconds and then spoke as she kept her eyes locked with his. 'George, it's Emma. I'm in trouble. It's Troy who's behind the smuggling and he's got Jeremy and me at Wilma's house.' Her voice shook and she drew a ragged breath. 'Jeremy's hurt. Please send help.' She threw the phone down onto the table

She lifted the shotgun and touched the trigger as Troy took a step towards her.

'I'm not worried, Emma You won't shoot me.

Emma stared him down and pulled the trigger.

Chapter 35

Monday – Daintree rainforest

Jeremy struggled to open his eyes. His head was throbbing and he could taste blood in his mouth. The floor was hard beneath his head and as he tried to turn, a sharp pain stabbed behind his eyes.

He'd come in the door and called out to Emma when he'd seen the car, but something had hit him on the head as soon as he'd come inside. He wasn't sure how long he'd been out to it, but gradually he became aware of voices around him.

'. . . you won't shoot me.'

There was a dull click and a flash of movement above him and then Emma screamed. His blood turned to ice.

'You silly bitch,' a man's voice yelled. 'Come here.'

Jeremy could see Emma struggling with someone but the room spun as he tried to focus. He managed to roll over. He grabbed the leg of the table with one hand and pulled himself up onto his knees, fighting the dizziness.

'No. I won't go in there.' Emma's voice was desperate. The fear in it gave Jeremy the extra strength he needed to pull himself up to his feet. The room tilted as he swayed and grabbed for the back of the chair. He closed one eye and looked across the wide kitchen but it was like looking through the surface of water. Blurred and distorted. He held the door as he stepped into the dark hallway

A man dressed in khaki was holding Emma and pushing her down the hallway towards a closed door. *Troy?*

She struggled, twisting her head and throwing her arms and legs as she screamed.

'No. No, you can't do it!'

Do what? Jeremy opened both eyes and the pain exploded in his head. As he watched, Troy grabbed Emma's braid and pulled her head back. Jeremy raised his finger to his lips as Emma's eyes met his. But it was too late.

'Jeremy!' As she yelled his name, Troy opened the door behind her. Jeremy took a step forward but the floor swung crazily and nausea overtook him. He grabbed for the wall before he fell again.

Emma spun back in one swift move. She moved so quickly Jeremy couldn't keep her in his sight. Troy grunted and bent forward and Emma shoved him through the door. She grabbed the handle, pulling it shut behind her. Jeremy lurched along the hall to her and Emma reached for him as she hung desperately onto the doorknob with her other hand.

'Can you help me hold it shut?' Her eyes were wide and pleading. As he reached for the door, an unearthly scream came from the other side.

'Get way, you fuckers. No.' The last word was drawn out in another agonizing scream and Emma closed her eyes as Jeremy took her in his arms.

***

A deadly silence came from the other side of the door and Emma slowly let go of the doorknob. Jeremy steadied himself with one hand on her shoulder as they made their way down the hall into the kitchen.

She opened the back door, hanging onto him firmly with other hand.

'Where are you going?' Jeremy's voice was weak.

'I have to get to the Land Cruiser and radio for help.' Once they were outside, she looked up at him. His colour was starting to come back and his eyes were open and alert. 'The phone was dead and I tried to bluff him.' Her voice caught again. 'Do you think he's dead?'

Jeremy closed his eyes as he sat on the step and leaned against the door. 'We'll find out soon enough.'

'Stay there.' Emma ran across to the Land Cruiser keeping one eye on the house. She was still terrified that Troy would emerge.

She picked up the two way radio and switched the dial to the emergency channel reserved for the hospital.

'Judy, it's me, Emma. I need help. Can you send the paramedics up to Wilma Randall's on Cooper Creek Road?' She tried to speak slowly. 'There is a head trauma and a snakebite victim. A possible fatality.' Her voice broke and she dragged in a breath to calm herself. Her lips were trembling and she stared across to Jeremy.

'Tell me when you've done that.' She leaned her head on the steering wheel as she waited. Finally Judy came back on. 'Paramedics are on the way.'

She climbed out and sat beside Jeremy at the back door as they waited for the ambulance to arrive. He dozed off a couple of times, but stirred when she spoke.

'Emma. I'm okay. Don't worry. I hit my head on the stove. He pushed me when I came in the back door.' He tried to reassure her but her smile was wan. 'I'm sure it's only a slight concussion.'

'He didn't just push you. He hit you over the head with

a lump of wood.' She held up her hand. 'How many fingers can you see?'

'Five ... or four and a thumb.' He pulled down her hand and clasped it to his chest.

It started to rain again and she walked Jeremy back into the kitchen and laid him on the kitchen floor. She pulled a couple of tea towels from a drawer and wedged them beneath his head. She then grabbed some blankets and towels and took them up the hallway.

'What are you doing?'

'The snakes might get under the door.'

Jeremy shuddered.

'You're not going to be sick again, are you?' She looked around for a bucket or a bowl but he shook his head.

'No, I'm okay. I was just thinking about Troy.'

'Maybe I should go in there and check.'

'What, and risk your life too? I don't think so. He would have killed you if you'd not been so strong. It would be you, lying in there with the snakes.'

Chapter 36

Tuesday-Dalrymple

Emma's assumption had been wrong. There had been no taipans in Wilma's house. Despite her worst fears, Troy had survived the snake bites from the other species Wilma had collected. The venom of the orange-naped snake was weak, enough to make you very ill, but wasn't deadly. He was still unconscious and Emma had told Greg and Jenny about the situation and they locked the door of his hospital room from the outside.

Emma had called Jeff and asked his advice and together they had phoned the Cairns police. Emma had been hesitant; her trust was shot to pieces but she waited by Jeremy's bedside until they arrived. Greg and Jenny had reassured her that Jeremy was fine. His concussion was mild and he would probably be discharged in the morning. Emma sat beside him as he was monitored in the emergency ward and watched his chest rise and fall as she slept. She was still awake when Chris came to the door and beckoned her out.

Two men in suits waited in the corridor. The detectives from Cairns were ready to talk to her. They had acted quickly on the information Jeff had conveyed for her, and there was already a police guard at Troy's bedside.

Sergeant Smith had been detained and had broken down quickly and confessed everything including the fact that Jock Newby provided the drugs to sedate then animals. Newby was at the police station but had denied any involvement. They couldn't locate Craig Anderson; he hadn't been seen since Sunday night. Sergeant Smith had been arrested and they said it was likely he would be charged with attempted murder. They were also liaising with the fire service who had advised that the fire had Emma's house was highly suspicious.

Emma held onto Jeremy as she walked him out of the hospital the next morning.
She stifled a yawn. Between worrying about Jeremy and checking in on Wilma, she'd had a wakeful night. She'd been concerned about how Jeremy would react to being in the emergency ward, but he'd handled it surprising well.

Emma and Jeremy crossed the car park to his car. One of the paramedics had driven it back last night. Yesterday's rain had cleared and washed the sky to a brilliant blue. The laden cane train chugged down the middle of the highway and the sweet smell of the cane drifted across. Squawking birds swooped through the branches of the Poinciana tree and broke the quiet of the morning as they squawked their displeasure at their interrupted feeding. Orange blossoms drifted onto the lush green lawn and Emma took a deep breath of their delicious aroma as she walked around to the passenger side. 'Wait, I'll open the door for you.'

'I'm not an invalid,' Jeremy said with a smile.

'I'm used to calling the shots, remember It's a bad habit of mine you'll have to break.' She grinned back at him. It seemed like days since she'd last smiled. 'Wait till you meet Dru. I'm sure she'll tell you my nickname when we were kids.'

'*You* tell me.' Jeremy settled into the front seat and

pushed her hand away as she reached over to do up his seatbelt. 'Emma!'

Her smile turned into a chuckle. Maybe it was because she knew everything was safe now; maybe it was the brilliant weather; maybe it was knowing that Wilma was well on the way to recovery. She leaned over and kissed Jeremy's unshaven cheek. Maybe it was because the man she loved was sitting beside her and she was taking him home to the place she had agreed to move into.

Yes, she loved him. Almost losing him had been the catalyst she needed to admit the truth to herself. But she hadn't told him yet.

'Go on. You're not getting out of it that easily.'

'All right. She used to call me "Mrs Bossy Britches".'

Jeremy's laugh deepened her contentment.

'Dru and I were a pair. Poor Ellie was the odd one out, and I tried to boss everyone around. I guess I'm still the same.' She started the car and headed towards the shops. First stop was to buy groceries.

'Are you sure you're up to a trip to Port Douglas tomorrow?' She waited as the only set of traffic lights in Dalrymple turned red. She'd called Dru last night.

A stern look was the only response Emma got. She pulled into an empty car park near the door at Woolworths, and was surprised when Jeremy opened his door and followed her.

He waved a finger at her. 'Don't glare at me. I'm fine. There's a couple of things I want to pick up too. I'll meet you at the car.'

By the time she returned to the car with the laden

trolley, Jeremy was leaning on the side of the car, deep in conversation with George, telling him about the arrests.

'Where did you spring from?' she asked as she lifted a bag of groceries from the trolley.

'Doctor Em.' The old man nodded at her tersely, and then turned away without answering.

'I told you to stay out of it. Coulda got yourself killed.'

'Don't *you* start on me, George.' She opened the back door of the four-wheel drive and Jeremy walked around to help her unload the trolley. She bit her tongue as she went to tell him she could do it.

'I had a bad feeling about that Troy bloke all along.' George's wrinkled old face scrunched up in a frown. 'I knew that young copper was bad, but I never picked the old Sarge. He's been here for years.'

'And what about Jock Newby?' Emma handed the last bag of groceries to Jeremy to lift in. 'He's denying it but Troy and the Sergeant both said he was in it. I can't believe it.'

'Probably why he didn't want you and Wilma in the rainforest. Wouldn't be surprised though. Seems like half the town's involved,' George said.

'I'm just glad it's over.'

A smile crossed her face. 'How would you like to come down to Port Douglas with us tomorrow? To visit Mum?'

A broad grin split his lips and his gap-toothed mouth hung open in surprise. 'I'll be in that.'

'Can you meet us in town about eight?'

***

Jeremy managed to sneak his purchase into the house while Emma took a shower. He'd hidden them on the floor under the seat of her car. He smiled, listening to her singing in the shower; he'd teased her about that when they'd been at uni. She couldn't hold a tune.

Afterwards, they sat outside on the porch of the old house. The neglected garden looked more welcoming in the soft afternoon light as the sun dipped behind the mountain peaks. Emma had prepared a salad while Jeremy opened another delivery. He'd managed to set up the portable barbeque without any help.

Emma sat back in the cane lounge that had been left by the previous owners. Her feet were tucked beneath her and she was wearing one of the sarongs she'd bought at the shopping plaza before she'd gone into the grocery store. She'd looped the ends in some fancy arrangement and they flowed around her ankles as she'd walked out onto the porch.

He stood and stretched. His headache had receded to a small niggling ache and he was well on the road to recovery. His meeting with the state manager had gone well although his boss had been taken aback by the excitement in the small town over the weekend. He'd been pleased with Jeremy's report and had requested a list of the resources and the staff he required for the first clinic at Quarantine Bay.

He was going to be busy, but he was looking forward to it.

'Stay there. I've got something for us.' He turned to the door and Emma smiled at him as he headed inside.

'Grab the steaks while you're in there. They've marinated enough.'

He'd managed to hide the bottle of champagne in the back of the fridge behind a few bags of fruit. Now he pulled it out and reached up for the two glasses that he'd bought with it at the bottle shop.

He was just heading back out to Emma when he heard Emma's mobile ringing. Dangling the glasses between his fingers and holding the bottle in the other hand, he walked out to the verandah.

'I'm on my way, Chris. Be there in ten. Not sure about Jeremy. He's not up to it.'

He frowned, not understanding what she meant.

Emma's face was set as she put down the phone. 'There's been a multiple car pileup just south of the ferry crossing. A police car went under a road train. Two confirmed fatalities, and another three critical. They've already called the chopper in from Cairns. I'm needed in emergency.'

'No.' Jeremy shook his head and his gaze was steady as his blue eyes held hers. '*We're* needed in emergency.'

'Oh, Jeremy, are you sure?'

'I am.' His stomach was churning but he would overcome this.

***

It was a night of horror. Craig had been pronounced dead on arrival, and the driver of the car behind the truck had died at the scene. Emma had watched Jeremy closely as they gowned up and joined Chris and Jenny in emergency.

Two of the tourists were quickly assessed as having severe penetrating injuries, and once stabilised were transported to Port Douglas hospital for specialist intervention.

Emma and Jeremy and the medical team in emergency

worked until midnight to stabilise the other woman. Both her legs were broken but the decision had been made to operate here at Dalrymple to relieve the load on the hospital at Port Douglas.

'Three units of whole blood please. As quick as we can. She's lost a lot of blood.' Jeremy's voice was calm. Emma took the cardiac leads and placed them on the women's chest as Judy passed over the IV tray.

'IV set up tray is ready, Doctor Langford.' Judy's voice was calm. 'If you need to intubate, I'll get that ready first.'

Once the surgery began, Emma focused on her role but flicked an occasional glance to Jeremy as he worked.

After a while, she relaxed—as much as she could in theatre—his eyes were clear and focused and his hands steady. Confidence and authority emanated from him.

Craig had been the sole cause of the accident. The truck driver was only slightly injured but dazed and in shock. He described how the police car had waited at the side of the road and pulled out in front of his truck as he had accelerated down the hill. He'd hit the brakes and the truck had jack-knifed, the first trailer rolling over on its side, and the second slewing around and hitting the car coming in the other direction. He kept repeating. 'I couldn't stop in time. He drove straight at me.'

By the time they climbed the stairs to Jeremy's house out, Emma's eyelids were drooping. He unlocked the door and took her into his arms. 'You look exhausted. Why don't you have a shower and go to bed? I'll clean up out here.'

After he'd cleaned up the remains of their uncooked meal, Jeremy sat on the verandah looking out into the inky darkness for a long time. Despite the tragic events of the past few hours, and the loss of human life, the night had filled him with strength. As they'd fought to save lives in the emergency ward, his faith in himself as a medical professional had been reaffirmed. He was able to let his fear go. Now it was time to let the past go.

The champagne and the glasses sat forgotten on the table by the door. Finally he opened the door and went inside. He was too wired for bed, instead he stood for a while watching Emma sleep before he headed to the study. He opened his briefcase and his gaze settled on the small velvet box holding the ring that he'd bought for her all those years ago. He picked it up and flicked the case open. The deep green emerald ring nestled in the white satin and the diamonds glimmered in the light.

He snapped it shut and put it safely deep in his briefcase.

One day.

He put it back, turned the light off and headed for the bedroom.

He lay beside Emma and rubbed gentle circles on her back until he drifted off to sleep beside her.

***

The raucous noise of the cockatoos woke them at dawn. Emma was exhausted and had slept soundly. She wanted to call in at the hospital and check on Wilma before they headed to Port Douglas to visit her family.

'Bacon and eggs?' Jeremy called from the kitchen. 'I don't like the look of this stove. I think something's living in it. I'll fire up the barbeque.'

'Sounds good, thanks.' Emma stepped out of the shower and quickly dried her hair before leaving it loose. She slipped on one of the new dresses she'd picked up in town and a pair of flat strappy sandals, before applying a light touch of makeup. A smile tilted her lips as she applied a touch of lip gloss. George was sure to make some smart comment about her wearing a dress, but she wanted to make an effort for Mum and Dru.

And for Jeremy.

She was so proud of him. Last night as they'd worked side by side in emergency, she'd seen the Jeremy of old. The calm and competent doctor. Not a shred of arrogance, or a hint that a city doctor knew better. None of the hesitation she'd seen in him on Saturday night.

But she sensed there was something on his mind this morning. He was quiet as he turned the eggs on the barbeque. Emma carried the plates and cutlery to the table on the porch, and glanced at the bottle of champagne and the two glasses that he'd put on the table last night. Condensation had left a damp ring on the tablecloth around the bottle. She crossed to the edge of the porch where the gas was still hissing under the barbeque plate, and put her hand on his shoulder. 'Almost done?'

His pale blue eyes were glistening as he turned to her and put his arms around her.

'What's wrong?' She lifted her arms and cupped his face in her hands. 'Are you okay after last night? Or are you nervous about meeting my family?'

Jeremy chuckled. 'Neither. After my family, I'm sure they will be delightful.' He glanced at the bottle and glasses sitting on the table. 'Everything is right now. And it's going to get even better.' He ran his hands gently down Emma's bare arms before he stepped away and pulled down the cover of the barbeque.

She walked across to the table but Jeremy followed her and took her hand before she could sit down.

He looked at the bottle of champagne. 'I was going to have a toast last night, but I guess it'll have to be orange juice instead.'

He picked up his glass of juice and lifted it.

Emma smile and lifted her glass. 'What are we toasting?'

Jeremy smiled. 'To Jem and Em. The couple most likely,' he said.

He held her gaze, his expression full of love. Joy burst through her and warmth unfurled in Emma's chest. Her own eyes filled with tears and she let them run unchecked down her cheeks. Slivers of pink tinted the eastern sky as the sun cleared the treetops to the east. A pair of palm cockatoos flew over squawking, and Emma lifted her eyes as the sun rose over the Daintree.

Another spectacular Daintree sunrise.

'To Jem and Em.' She closed her eyes as his warm lips settled gently on hers.

THE END

Dru's story is next in ***DIAMOND SKY***

344

Available at Annie's store-free postage
https://www.annieseaton.net/store.html

Acknowledgements

The Daintree Rainforest is a unique, fascinating and amazing part of our planet. Visiting this World Heritage site in 2014 raised our awareness of the species and plants that are being threatened by human intervention. I hope by reading this book, readers across Australia—and the world—will appreciate the biodiversity of the Daintree rainforest and help protect this pristine environment.

The writing of Daintree has seen me continue on my writing journey and fulfilling my lifelong dream. Seeing my second book come to print, I have been supported by so many people in my life. I would like to acknowledge them here.

To the many friends I have made in the writing world and who constantly support me on my journey. I often say I have found my 'tribe' and I value the daily contact with like-minded people all over the world. Again, a special mention and thank you to my critique partner, Susanne Bellamy.

And to my wonderful family. To Ian, the love of my life and my partner in research as we travel this magnificent country seeking stories each winter. I could not do this without you.

To our children, Kate and Dane, and their partners, Alex and Elizabeth. Thank you for your love and support.

A special mention for our talented daughter-in-law, Elizabeth Clare Smith for the wonderful map of the Daintree Forest in the front of this book. To our grandchildren, who love having a 'famous' —I can always hope —Nannie Annie who writes stories!

Again, a special mention for my wonderful aunt, Maureen Smith, who not only supports me, but supports so many Australian writers by reading, loving and sharing their stories.

I would also like to acknowledge and thank the Kuku Yalanji people of the Daintree rainforest whose history inspired my references in Daintree.

And to you, the reader: Thank you for choosing this book. I hope when you read, that you love it and talk about it, and that maybe you will want to visit this wonderful part of Australia. I hope you enjoy Ellie, Dru, Dee and Sandra's stories. Drop me a line at annie@annieseation.net

I would love to hear from you.

Reviews on Goodreads are always welcome and much appreciated!

All Annie's books are available in print at Annie's store

eBook links:

https://www.annieseaton.net/books.html

Print Store:

All books are available in print at Annie's store

Free postage

https://annieseatonstore.ecwid.com/

Look for Annie's next series: **THE AUGATHELLA GIRLS**

• **OTHER BOOKS from ANNIE**

Whitsunday Dawn
Undara
Osprey Reef
East of Alice

Porter Sisters Series

Kakadu Sunset
Daintree
Diamond Sky
Hidden Valley
Larapinta
Kakadu Dawn

Pentecost Island Series
Pippa
Eliza
Nell
Tamsin
Evie
Cherry
Odessa
Sienna
Tess
Isla

The Augathella Girls Series
Outback Roads
Outback Sky
Outback Escape
Outback Wind
Outback Dawn
Outback Moonlight

DAINTREE

Outback Dust
Outback Hope
An Augathella Surprise
An Augathella Baby
An Augathella Spring

Sunshine Coast Series
Waiting for Ana
The Trouble with Jack
Healing His Heart
Sunshine Coast Boxed Set

The Richards Brothers Series
The Trouble with Paradise
Marry in Haste
Outback Sunrise
Richards Brothers Boxed Set

Bondi Beach Love Series
Beach House
Beach Music
Beach Walk
Beach Dreams
The House on the Hill

Second Chance Bay Series
Her Outback Playboy
Her Outback Protector
Her Outback Haven
Her Outback Paradise
The McDougalls of Second Chance Bay Boxed Set

Love Across Time Series
Come Back to Me
Follow Me

Annie Seaton

Finding Home
The Threads that Bind
Love Across Time 1-4 Boxed Set

Bindarra Creek
Worth the Wait
Full Circle
Secrets of River Cottage
A Clever Christmas
A Place to Belong

Four Seasons Short and Sweet
Ten Days in Paradise
Follow the Sun

Others
Deadly Secrets
Adventures in Time
Silver Valley Witch
The Emerald Necklace
Christmas with the Boss
Her Christmas Star
An Aussie Christmas Duo (two Christmas novellas)

• **About the Author**

2023: Winner of the long contemporary RUBY award for *Larapinta*

Finalist for the NZ KORU award 2018 and 2020.

Winner ...Best Established Author of the Year 2017 AUSROM

Long listed for the Sisters in Crime Davitt Awards 2016, 2017, 2018, 2019

Finalist in Book of the Year, Long Romance, RWA Ruby Awards 2016 *Kakadu Sunset*

Winner ...Best Established Author of the Year 2015 AUSROM

Winner ...Author of the Year 2014 AUSROM Best Established Author, Ausrom Readers' Choice 2017 Book of the Year

•